Totally Bound Publishing books by Katherine McIntyre

Tribal Spirits
Forged Alliances
Forged Decisions
Forged Contracts
Forged Futures
Forged Redemption

The Whitfield Files
Of Tinkers and Technomancers

I0658899

Tribal Spirits

FORGED CONTRACTS

KATHERINE McINTYRE

Forged Contracts
ISBN # 978-1-913186-22-7
©Copyright Katherine McIntyre 2019
Cover Art by Erin Dameron-Hill ©Copyright April 2019
Interior text design by Claire Siemaszkiewicz
Totally Bound Publishing

FORGED CONTRACTS

Dedication

To those who battle the demons in their head and keep fighting. That's true bravery.

Chapter One

A month had passed since Finn Kelly had left, and with every day that passed, Raven's composure unraveled a little further.

Her grip tightened on the wet rag as she slid it over the chestnut surface of the bar, cleaning the sticky spilled beer and the rings left from the bottles. The dusky afternoon light spilled through the windows of their haven, Beaver Tavern, which had divots in the floorboards and a lingering scent of cedar that reminded her of home. Already, old man Gene had wandered inside and was nursing a pint at his usual spot, and a couple of the younger guys in the pack were arguing back and forth over their burgers.

Everything remained the same as normal, and yet her entire world had grayed around the edges. She'd moored her anchor to the wrong ship and wasted close to a decade distracting herself with the wrong guy. And no matter how much Sierra offered to spar with her and Jer made excuses to swing over to watch a flick or crack stupid jokes, they couldn't stop the way her chest throbbed, or how her skin itched so badly she wanted to tear it off.

Raven wasn't an idiot. She'd always known Finn Kelly wasn't in love with her, but he'd been the closest thing to feeling safe. When he'd driven off in his Challenger with his mate at his side and left the pack behind, he'd shattered that comfort. Now the lengthy shadows set her on edge, and each night when she returned to her empty apartment, her adrenaline spiked with every creak and groan of the old timbers.

So, she'd spent more time behind the bar, picking up as many shifts as she could, if only to drown out the memories she'd locked away ten years ago. Ones that crept closer with each passing day, threatening to drag her under.

Raven dropped the rag underneath the counter and straightened her ponytail, which had begun to slump in the hour she'd been here. She couldn't stop moving if she wanted to, amped up in a constant state of vigilance that wore her wolf to the bone.

The door to Beaver Tavern creaked when it opened again.

Jer stepped inside, his presence commanding her attention the same as always. *Not like anyone could help but get swept up by the sight of him.* The man's looks caused the air to vanish from the room and his sexual magnetism made her whole body flush with a single glance.

He caught her gaze and a heartbreaker smile rose to his lips, enhancing dimples that made her heart speed up every time. His clever eyes danced and his eyebrows tilted with a wicked edge, inspiring lust from just about every girl who crossed his path. He skimmed a hand through his tousled chestnut locks with an effortless grace as he sauntered in her direction. Based on the way her body reacted every time he entered the room, she should've been chasing after Jer all these years.

Except, with Finn, she'd felt safe. She'd been able to mute the turbulence storming within her, even if only for a little while.

Jer was another story.

His presence ripped her wide open and forced her to feel with such a strength she gasped for breath. She couldn't hide or escape from the constant pulse of surrender, surrender, surrender. Raven would never be able to take the risk. For her, the options narrowed down to fight or die, and the fight for her own mind never ended — not after the past she kept secret to this day.

Besides, even though Jer managed to conceal his pain behind so many easy smiles, the hurt ripped into her as if it were her own. He fought his own daily battle — they both did. And with the stormy seas buffeting the two of them around all these years, she could barely believe they hadn't drowned. Anything more than friendship might sentence them both.

"Have you been getting any sleep?" Jer asked, flattening his palms on the surface of the bar. Concern ringed his tone, concern she didn't want to face.

"More than you, stud," she responded with a sharp smile. "Though don't take that as an invitation to go into the tawdry details of your latest conquests. I've heard more than I ever wanted to know from the other pack females."

He shook his head, a half-smile on his face as he took a seat. "Talk is cheap. You know if you ever want to verify for yourself, all you have to do is ask." He said it with smooth perfection, a delivery that would make most girls squeeze their thighs tight. Except Raven had the stupid curse of soaking in emotions like a wet sponge, and his offer wasn't brimming with heat. The wave of hopelessness crashing off him slammed into her.

The guys might tease Jer for his distractions, but most of them egged him on, half in awe of his prowess. Not many people understood how he'd withered away over the years, losing himself in the chase, the same way Raven had thrown herself into Finn. She'd recognized his damage early on, a mirror to her own, and if they ever collided, they'd rip each other open until nothing remained.

Raven grabbed a pint glass from the stack and began filling it with the porter he drank on the regular. She placed the beer in front of him. "Keep on wishing, babe," she purred. "I'm STD free and want to remain that way."

She wielded her tongue like a whip because she valued Jer too much to become another distraction for him, another notch on his bedpost. And after Finn had left their damaged trio, the two of them had fought to stay afloat against the rising tides. He shook his head, the smile clinging to his face even though his eyes didn't reflect it back.

He lifted the pint to his lips and swigged with an unsettling quickness. She hadn't been the only one off as of late, but whatever had changed with Jer, he remained tight-lipped on the subject.

Ever since the East Coast Tribe had left the area, quiet had returned, since the powerful shifter governing force tended to set garden-variety shifters on edge. However, it wasn't the peaceable serenity that arrived with the cool autumn breezes. The pebbling chill in the air promised trouble, no matter how hard she tried to convince herself otherwise.

"How are the new responsibilities?" Raven asked, picking up the rag and continuing to polish the same gleaming spot, over and over.

"Finn left some pretty big shoes to fill as Sierra's beta." Jer placed the glass onto the counter and slumped forward. "She's encouraging as anything, but she holds back around me. Finn knew how to push through that shit—the bastard was so thickheaded he'd ram right through most folks' hesitations. I don't operate his way."

"So, what you're saying is it's an adjustment." Raven couldn't help her wan smile at the sight of him there, fingers raking through his curls, exasperated. That was the Jer she'd first met, a sweeter one who felt more than he'd ever admit. Those glimpses were worth the slight distance she kept between them, how she'd never succumbed to the temptation to slip into his bed. And Spirits above, there had been so, so many times she'd wanted to over the years.

"Give me contracts and arbitrations with pack disagreements any day over this beta nonsense. At least I make bank doing that business, and I'm arguing already presented cases. Beta business means having an opinion of my own and standing behind it, all the shit Finn and Sierra get their rocks off on."

Raven would be lying if every mention of Finn's name didn't make her wince, but she kept her mask in place, same as she'd been doing for years.

The door to Beaver Tavern creaked open. The scent drew her attention at once, and her wolf perked to attention. Not pack.

Not pack, but familiar, in the worst sort of way.

Christian Denzel strode into Beaver Tavern with a smirk on his lips and the devil in his gaze. He hadn't changed in over a decade, with the same sweep of dark hair and even darker eyes against alabaster-pale skin. The moment Raven caught sight of him, the pint glass she was preparing to stack almost slipped from her grasp. Out of the ghosts to appear from her past, only one would be worse than him.

His coyote scent attracted attention as folks looked up from their tables when he walked by. But he didn't pay them any mind. His gaze branded her, and she couldn't tear hers away. Most of the time, she was safe behind the bar at Beaver Tavern, as if it created a barrier between her and the rest of the world. However, right then she was chained there when her wolf lunged in her chest, begging to run, run, run, anywhere but this place.

The squeak of Jer's chair when he faced the intruder snapped her to attention.

"If you're looking to stir up trouble, you stepped into the wrong bar," Jer said, lifting his pint. Even though he gave him a lazy glance, only a fool would trifle with their pack lawyer. He was sharper and smarter than almost any other Red Rock.

"Me? Trouble?" Christian said in mock surprise as he took a seat. His gaze fixed on her with a steadiness that carved right underneath her skin. "I'm here to relay some news, and maybe catch a drink with an old friend."

Raven swallowed hard. *No.* The past lay behind her, one she hadn't brought along when she'd joined the Red Rocks. Her insides chilled colder than the ale in the taps. Jer glanced to her then Christian, his eyebrows furrowing in response. She needed to defuse this situation now, before Christian went running his mouth and ruined everything she'd built there.

"What can I get for you?" she asked, her voice coming out like battery acid. If she'd had liquid silver on hand, she'd dump it straight into a pint glass and force it down his throat. Christian's face was one of the ones she'd buried from memory, and his sleazy tone one that whispered in her mind when she tried to settle for bed. The brand on her hip felt as if it burned from the phantom sensation of past regrets.

A grin rolled to Christian's lips while he leaned forward at the bar. "I'll take a pint, darling. You look like you've been doing well for yourself."

Raven poured a pint of their cheapest ale and shoved it forward, foam sloshing over the edges. Christian's expression never changed, mocking amusement gleaming in his eyes. Unlike the teenager she'd known back then with his flannels and jeans, he now wore a suit, giving him a city-slicker vibe that married so well with his sleazy personality.

"Where do you two know each other from?" Jer asked, glancing between them. Raven tensed, and Christian's laugh scraped against her nerves. The gazes from the other patrons in the bar prickled along her skin, an awareness she couldn't shake no matter how hard she tried.

Before she could make up some lie, Christian interjected. "We ran around in the same circles in our youth, but I haven't seen this one in years. Almost like she's been avoiding us."

Raven's grip tightened on the rag she held, and her claws pricked out. "Maybe because the lot of you were assholes. Drink your beer and get the hell out, Christian." Her words came out low, but they seethed with intent.

He took a sip from his pint before unleashing another grin. This one glittered with the insidious intent she'd expected from the start. "Hey now, I showed up for a reason. Figured the Red Rock Pack should get *some* notice."

"Notice about what?" Jer had been paying attention, but it was clear this commanded his full focus.

"I've been hired to represent the Coalition of Human Rights. As much as they dislike our kind, they needed a shifter on the inside to handle the bigger problem, because what they detest even more are the pack formations and the Tribes themselves. Collections of shifters are a threat to humanity," he recited, as if he'd been practicing the speech in front of the mirror.

"Selling out your own kind?" Raven interjected. "Color me surprised."

"I haven't seen you working around these circles before, and I know most of the other lawyers in the region. Who's your employer?" Jer asked, tapping his fingers along the surface of the bar.

Christian's grin widened. "I work for Hansen Associates in Philadelphia. A bit of a distance from the hick central I grew up in."

"And what does the Coalition want?" Jer asked, his voice the sort of calm promising imminent explosion. "We keep to ourselves, and our relations with the local humans have been nothing but friendly."

"Oh, didn't you hear?" Christian said, with the assured smile they wouldn't have heard whatever filth he prepared to expound. Raven needed to retract her claws, but the instinct thrummed inside. Her wolf was covered in so many scars that she lashed out, begging her to shift and thrash this bastard.

Christian plucked out the folder he'd been carrying and placed it on the bar counter. Raven didn't trust herself to look at it, but Jer's expression darkened the moment he scanned the papers. A low growl thrummed from their new pack beta, and at once, every single Red Rock in the bar turned their way.

She sucked in a shaky breath and glanced down.

'Petition for Sale of Ricketts Glenn State Park.'

The ground slipped from beneath her. "That's our territory." The words rolled out even as the numbness filtered through her veins. Even though Red Rock owned portions outside of the state park that couldn't be touched, when it came to pack demarcations, everyone understood that her pack claimed the rest of it as well.

Christian smirked. "Except, as of late, the state's been behind on payments. The Coalition of Human Rights knows how dangerous these packs congregating can be. Their plan is to buy out the land, and, honestly," he paused to cast a cursory glance around the bar, "if this is all the Red Rock pack is pulling in, I doubt you'll be able to outbid them."

Raven couldn't help herself. Her fist went flying right toward the smarmy bastard's face.

Christian's hand shot up to catch it. Her knuckles thudded against his callused palm. No matter how he might play pretend at being genteel, the man was the sort of dangerous bred from the worst places. The chestnut bar dug into her hips while she strained at the seams to keep from shifting. Jer cast a worried look her way before he snagged the folder from the surface of the counter top.

"Temper, temper, Tigerlily," Christian murmured, igniting the flames inside her all over again. That nickname. She'd last heard it on *those* lips. Raven was going to be sick.

She stepped back a pace, her claws slipping out and fur beginning to prickle along her skin as if she was a kid again who couldn't control her shift.

"What's going on here?" a commanding voice rang out from the door. In the frame stood the woman who'd kept the pack together, the one who would fight intruders tooth and claw to protect their territory. Sierra Kanoska had arrived.

Chapter Two

The moment the door slammed open, a taut thread inside Jeremiah relaxed. The Red Rock alpha had competent on speed dial, and if anyone could send this asshole packing without inciting a massive conflict, it'd be Sierra.

As much as he should be looking over the envelope in his hands, the pack's resident bartender stole his full focus. Rage wasn't a new look on Raven, but the genuine fear gleaming in her eyes had his wolf lunging forward to protect her. Already, dark fur coated her arms and her eyes glowed silver. She was going to turn any second now, and this could get ugly.

Sierra strode up beside him, and her commanding gaze landed first on Christian, then on Raven.

"I'm going to look over this," he said, lifting the packet the intruder had slapped onto the counter. Sierra nodded and folded her arms across her chest when she faced Christian.

"You want to explain what you're doing riling up my bar?" Sierra asked, her voice as sharp as her claws.

"I could use some help. Rae?" Jer asked, slipping behind the bar. Sierra's mouth twitched in approval, the alpha more aware than he ever could be. Jer rested his hand on her arm, and at the touch, Raven let out a shuddering breath. She locked gazes with him, the intensity in those widened eyes enough to knock him to his knees. The last time he'd seen her this rattled was when Finn had fallen for Navi, which remained a tangled source of bitterness and relief.

"Yeah, I could use a breath of air," Raven responded as she glanced at Sierra for approval. Sierra offered her a nod even though she fixed Christian with 'scary eyes'. Jeremiah prayed he never received that sort of look, because he'd watched his alpha in action, and the woman was a vicious fighter.

He led them out of the bar, his heart thrumming so hard it might explode. Rae wasn't the only one close to losing control back there. Every time he tried to grasp at the core of him, it spiraled further and further away. Sweat pricked on his brow. He nodded at his packmates on the way out of Beaver Tavern, clutching the envelope like a lifeline. He didn't question if Raven would follow—based on the caged look she'd given him, she'd been looking for an out from the moment the coyote douche had stepped into their bar.

Jeremiah strode out into the sun, its beams heavy with end of summer desperation. His fingers itched and his claws threatened to break free. He'd gotten a cursory flip-through of the documents in Beaver Tavern, but they were legit. This threat was serious, and if this sleazebag lawyer they'd hired made any headway for the assholes in the CHR, the Red Rock pack could find themselves out of a home. The Coalition's reputation for shifter hatred had been growing every year, as did their meeting attendance.

Raven stepped out beside him and almost collapsed. The air whooshed out of her and she bent forward, her hands on her knees as she stared at the ground. Ragged breaths escaped from her throat, and her long, glossy hair slipped past her shoulders to obscure her expression.

Fuck, that bastard's arrival tore her up something fierce. In one breath he wished Finn was still there, and the next familiar self-loathing coated him like slime. Because he'd never be the one she leaned on, no matter how much he'd yearned for it over the years. He was always the runner-up, always the replacement for his best friend. Jer knew he'd never be anyone's first choice, for beta or for a partner.

Not like I blame any of them. Ever since Joe Ganzorig had vanished and his supply of meds had dried up, Jeremiah's tenuous control had been slipping.

No one wanted to deal with a bipolar head case like him — not for long. Not if they had any other choice.

He leaned forward, placing a hand on Raven's back. He'd never been able to extinguish the attraction to her, no matter how hard he tried. The way she moved with a ballerina's grace, the paint splattering the edges of her clothes from when she shut herself away and worked on canvases for the day. He'd fucking stab himself with silver if it meant a genuine smile from her — one that reached her eyes for once.

"Rae, who is he?" Jeremiah asked, his voice a low scrape. She straightened from her crouch, even though she didn't sever the connection of his hand on her back. Instead, she stepped closer, the dark ale and maple scent of her the same intoxicating blend as always. She'd driven him to distraction, to the point where hooking up with every female in the vicinity had just intensified his longing.

Raven shot a nervous glance at the bar before her gaze settled on him. "If I tell you this, you've got to swear no one else finds out. No one." The implication was clear—she was asking him to keep this information even from Sierra. Despite the heat from the sun, his skin chilled with nerves. Whatever she had to tell him was serious. The lengths he would go to for this woman unsettled him even more.

"Why don't we take a ride?" he murmured, heading toward his bike. What they both needed was to shift and run into the woods, but they couldn't talk like that, and Jer needed answers. He handed over the envelope. "You get to keep this safe, okay?"

Raven offered him a smirk. "However will I handle such a formidable task?"

He shook his head, grinning, while he settled onto his Harley. He found the grips and Raven slipped in behind him, wrapping her arms around his waist as though they belonged there. Maybe this hadn't been a great idea after all. The way her slim form pressed against his back had his livewire libido thrumming. He revved his bike, the engine buzzing beneath him as he kicked the stand down. Raven's grip tightened, her claws pricking out, burrowing past his shirt into skin and betraying the state of her nerves. He relished the bite of them as he set off across the parking lot, clouds of dust billowing in his wake.

The wind tumbled his curls around, and he zoomed faster and faster along the asphalt, the country roads ones he knew by heart. He'd been traveling them his entire life, having grown up amidst the pack with both of his parents still Red Rocks. Unlike Finn and Raven, he'd had the perfect childhood—great upbringing, sweet parents—it wasn't their fault they'd produced damaged offspring.

Soaring down the road on his Harley and running through the forest in his wolf form were the closest he came to feeling as though his feet settled on solid ground. As if he wasn't grasping for fragments that leapt further and further away. The vibration of the engine traveled through him, and Raven's grip didn't falter. For a brief moment, Jeremiah pretended they hadn't raced away from the bomb the intruder had dropped in their own bar. That the Red Rock pack wouldn't have yet another threat looming on their horizon.

It was just the golden sunlight, ink-stain asphalt and the woman he'd always wished was his.

Ahead, the Maple Run river peeked into view, and gravel and dirt collected along the roadside all the way up to the gleaming water, one of the most popular fishing spots in the area. Jer pumped the brakes, his Harley stuttering while he slowed. As fast as they'd set out, the ride had come to an end. His need to know the tempest brewing in Raven's mind kept him from continuing down the road until the hum of his engine and the heat of the sun melted his worries away.

His tires crunched over the gravel, and he kicked his stand out. Raven let go, hopping off the seat before he'd even come to a full stop. She dropped the envelope onto the ground next to the bike. He swiveled around to face her, but she paced back and forth across the stretch of beaten earth and chewed-up gravel.

"Hey," Jer said, trying to grab her attention. She looked at him and forced a shallow breath. "It's just me," he continued. "You know whatever you've got to tell me is no judgment, okay?"

Raven pursed her lips as she ran a hand through her hair, gathering those silken strands as she tugged. "You say that now, but you have no idea, Jer."

"Does Finn know?" Of all the idiot things to leap from his mouth, that would. Because Jeremiah liked to hurt like he liked to breathe—it was an inevitable part of existence.

Raven's lips pursed at the mention of their best friend and her former lover. "Not what I'm about to tell you."

Jeremiah's throat dried. He hungered to know, all while he hated himself for the constant competition in his head. Their eyes met, and the weight of the situation descended, a choking tension making it tough to breathe. Real, genuine fear hid behind Raven's eyes, and he just wanted to reach out and pull her into his arms. Based on the way she hugged herself, the second he tried, he'd get decked.

"I trust you, Jer," was all she said and all she needed to. He would protect her secrets.

Sweat pricked on his palms and his wolf lunged forward, begging to run free. He gritted his teeth, keeping the wild thing restrained as best he could. *Not like I'm doing a great job as of late.*

Raven reached for the waistband of her cargos and tugged to expose more of her porcelain skin. On the side of her hip was a brand, an angry red curve with an arrow through it. Except the area had been mutilated by dozens and dozens of scratches he recognized as claw marks.

"What's that?" Jeremiah asked, his voice cutting through the silence between them. They were stepping into forbidden territory here, and he had the feeling they couldn't turn back from this truth she kept secret.

"It's the Landsliders' mark," she murmured, her fear as fragrant as the crispness in the air. Jer took a pace back, his eyebrows furrowing on instinct. The Landsliders had funneled illegal drugs through the region. They were the ones who'd worked with the defectors from the Silver Spring pack who'd bombed houses filled with innocent shifter families. They had lit up Beaver Tavern.

"You're not one of them." The words trailed from his mouth. "Tell me you're not."

Raven threw her hands out, taking a step toward him. "This was from before I ever joined the Red Rock pack, Jer. I wasn't involved in any of the current mess."

Her words weren't processing—all he could see was the angry mark on her hip and the flames as their tavern burned. Whatever he'd been expecting, it wasn't this.

"Please," she whispered, her voice hoarse. "Please don't look at me like that."

"How could you keep a secret like this, Rae?" He shook his head, the disbelief still flooding through him. Her hand drifted to the scars on her hip, the claw marks, and the plug slipped into the socket for him. The scars were self-inflicted. "Unless it was a dumb thing you did as a kid…and you've been running from it ever since."

A breath escaped her, mixed with a sob of relief. She staggered forward another step, closer to him, and he closed the distance. She sank into his arms as though she belonged there, and the heat of her caused his tangled mind to pulse.

"My folks had died, and I didn't have any family— anywhere I belonged," Raven murmured into his chest. "The Landsliders welcomed me in, and at the time I already stole to survive. A little more didn't seem like a bad thing."

"Why didn't you tell anyone?" he asked, his voice soft, showing him perhaps feeling as lost as she probably did. Her glossy hair brushed across his skin, and he couldn't help the heat rising within him or the way his wolf paced. His wolf had been picking up speed in his chest in the last couple of minutes, and a fever, a deliriousness swept over him. He'd wanted this closeness with Raven for so long it had formed a constant ache.

Yet this secret was one he shouldn't keep from the pack. *Her history with our enemy.*

"I've wanted to," she murmured. "So many times, I came close. But I love this pack, this home, more than anything. The fear of getting thrown out froze me every time."

"You know you need to tell Sierra," he responded, and a hush followed, one that echoed through the clearing.

Raven pulled a pace from him to meet his eyes. Her hand found his, the connection the one thing keeping him grounded. Energy flooded through him, the sort demanding him to move, to run, to shift, but he stayed here with her instead.

"I promise, I will," she swore. "But I'm asking you to keep my secret a little longer."

She stood before him, the loneliness of her path radiating off her. Her lips pressed together, two petals against porcelain skin that always glowed in the sunlight. Her carved eyebrows, soft brown eyes and delicate nose all gave away her Japanese heritage, her face framed by thick, glossy hair he'd imagined against his sheets too many times to count. Jer wanted to drag her to his chest, wrap his arms around her and promise it would all be okay — even if the words were a lie.

Too much.

The sensations grew too much. She was here, Finn was gone and no reason barred Jer from giving in. No reason forced the distance between them any longer.

His heart thumped like a wild creature in his chest and his wolf keened inside him.

He took one step forward, the pull as inevitable as the tides crashing to the shore.

Before he could stop himself, before he could even question what he was doing, he closed the space between them.

Jer leaned down and captured her lips in his.

In the decade he'd known her, they'd never kissed. They'd shared enough lingering looks to bury him and casual touches that he longed to be more, but Finn had been the barrier keeping them from making the mistake of ruining each other's lives.

However, once her petal-soft lips brushed his, a rightness settled in him, a connection he only had with his wolf. Raven melted into the kiss, responding with tongue and teeth as she bit his lower lip. The maple and dark ale scent of her had him reeling, and he inhaled the tension in the air. She moaned against his mouth, the sound traveling straight to his cock. No other woman enthralled him like this.

This kiss was the culmination of waiting too long, of all the pent-up lust and longing. All at once, Jer drowned in the feelings even as the touch between them gave him breath. The thrumming in his veins hadn't died but intensified, and need burned in him to keep going, keep going, keep going.

Raven broke the kiss first.

"Jer, where did that come from?" she asked, concern and a knowing he hated shining in her dark eyes. "Are you on your meds?" This was Raven, the one who'd seen him through too many swings to count over the years, and the one who'd helped him back on the wagon every time he fell off. Of course she'd ask.

"Fuck," he cursed, kicking the ground to send gravel spraying. Raven didn't back away but ignored the pebbles flying by. The heat threatened to combust inside him, and his wolf howled away, charging in his chest over and over again. Was he in a manic swing? He'd been doing so well after Ganzorig had gone missing and he'd gone through the last of his meds.

He'd just kissed Raven.

He ran a hand through his curls. "It's not always about my meds, Rae," he spat. "Maybe I'm tired of denying what's existed between us all along. I'm tired of deluding myself with other women, when the only one I've ever wanted is standing in front of me."

Raven opened her mouth, slipping her tongue out to wet her lips. Shock registered in her eyes, followed by panic. Her shoulders squared, and everything that had been easy and free between them mere moments ago dissolved.

"I've got to go," she said, barely glancing at him before she bolted for the woods.

Jer sank to his knees, the pounding in his chest, his ears and his mind reaching a roar. Raven raced away in the distance, in human form one moment, but the next she'd stripped down and shifted into a wolf. His touch was a poison, infecting everyone around him until he pushed even her away.

Helplessness squeezed him as though he was a wet rag as a harsh breath escaped him.

Some pack beta he was. Jeremiah stared at the strewn gravel, right at home in the chaos. After all the years of dodging around their feelings and all the thousands of ways he'd hoped the kiss would play out—it had never been like this.

He'd fucked up, but why the hell did anyone expect anything better from him? He'd been born a mistake.

Chapter Three

The sunlight seeped into Raven's dark fur while the pads of her feet churned up the mud and stones as she vaulted deeper and deeper into the forest she knew better than herself. Ever since she'd joined the Red Rock pack, Ricketts Glen State Park had offered more than refuge — it had become a living heartbeat.

She should've stayed.

She should've made sure Jer was doing okay after he'd gotten her out of Christian's presence. He'd listened without judging while she'd revealed her vile truth, but the way he'd kissed her had made her heart break.

Out here, the wind whistled through the trees, and she tried to focus on her ragged breaths and the wide trunks she dodged around. *Not like it helps.* The kiss had overridden her circuits. The feel of his hot mouth on hers and the vanilla and leather scent of him had her wolf pawing inside her chest. The thrill of the forbidden raced through her, and no matter how hard she

27

churned the mud or how she soared through the forest, she couldn't run fast enough to escape it.

He'd been in a manic state—she'd caught the gleam in his eyes, how he moved and talked faster than he realized. Yet, as much as she wanted to dismiss the words he said, ones that engraved themselves on her bones, and even though she wanted to pretend their kiss hadn't happened, she couldn't deny the way it made her feel. As though the frost had melted off her and she had awakened in spring for the first time.

Jer had always been dangerous, because he slipped past her pretenses every time. She'd stepped to the chasm to see how far she could fall, and there was no end in sight. When he'd placed his arms around her and their lips had met, it was as if he'd stepped up to pull the girl inside out of hiding, the one who she'd protected since *that* day. Her heart pounded even faster while she dodged another tree trunk and leapt over some brambles. Those memories grayed the fringes of her mind, threatening to numb her from the inside out.

In the distance, the rush of falling water beckoned, a crispness threading through the air. Her fur gleamed in the sun like obsidian and sights and scents intensified in this form. No matter how damaged she'd become over the years, her wolf never abandoned her. Rivulets of water glistened through the trees, one of the dozens of waterfalls crashing through this place. The insane human rights folks couldn't take Ricketts Glen away from them. Christian had stolen her youth—he wouldn't steal her home too.

'Just join, Tigerlily. The Landsliders will keep you safe. You'll have a family.'

He'd known all the right words to manipulate her. Thirteen and dumb, she'd fallen straight into the pit.

Screams snared her attention, the inhuman ones of a mountain lion.

Raven bolted in the direction of the sound. The Red Rocks might be a pack of wolves, but for the past couple of months now since their alpha had mated, they'd allied with the Silver Springs pack, Dax's mountain lions. Quiet reigned for a few blessed seconds before the screams began anew. She didn't question for a moment that they were cries for help.

Raven picked up the scent trail easily — whoever had been racing through the woods had crashed on heavy feet, leaving plenty of snapped twigs, not finessed enough to manage a light trail. Her heart squeezed tight as she sniffed the ground. The mountain lion scent, a musky cat odor, was newer, not as developed.

Oh, hell.

Raven bolted, the wind ruffling her fur. She moved like a strike of lightning. Ahead of her, the waterfall roared, muffling some of the cries, but she operated on gut instinct at this point, the scent as clear and vibrant to her as the blue sky overhead. Where were the cries coming from? Sunlight glinted off the water, shadows deepening amidst piles of crunchy leaves and bony twigs protruding from bushes.

The cry resounded again, driving straight into the heart of her.

Raven didn't bother to look ahead. She followed the sound.

Her feet carried her forward as she sailed over mossy stones, splashed past one of the tributaries from the main waterfall and launched herself around a cluster of bushes.

The sight stopped her still.

Marcy and Rick's little girl, Daria, lay sprawled on the ground in her mountain lion form. Her leg had gotten caught in the maw of a wolf trap — but this wasn't one of the average variety. The sheen of the metal, the way the girl's skin had grown raw and red, fur falling off around the spot — the traps were silver, which caused permanent damage to her kind.

Daria locked gazes with her, those eyes so young and filled with terror. God, Raven knew that look like she knew her own buried heart. She let out a howl in response, a hoarse one filled with the words she'd never speak.

Her brain shut off. Her limbs transitioned as she began to shift, the fur dissipating as her skin reappeared. The muzzle shrank and her bones sank into place while she returned to human form. Her hair brushed her back, and within seconds she crouched on two feet instead of four, her soles sinking into the matted autumn leaves.

Raven didn't hesitate. She bolted toward Daria, and her knees hit the ground with a slap as skeletal leaves crumbled beneath them. The ten-year-old trembled, but her cries ceased the moment Raven stopped in front of her. The kid's body shook, her fur in steady vibration. Bile rose in Raven's throat. She wanted to puke.

Instead, she slammed her palms onto the levers of the trap.

The maw opened with a creak, right as the silver seared her hands. Raven bit on her tongue until it bled, choking back her scream. This was the pain of raw flames, but she held the levers down until Daria tugged her limp leg out from the trap. She let go of the levers, even though the pain radiated across her skin to the point her teeth hurt. Raven's mind screamed, but she remained silent and calm while Daria let out shuddering breaths.

"Sweetheart, I'm going to get you home, okay?" Raven said, leaning forward and gritting her teeth to ignore the pain. Daria nudged her arm with her nose, and even in the brief motion, she could feel the whole-body trembles racking the poor girl. Raven swallowed hard as the coals of a pure rage stoked inside her. She didn't betray an ounce of the anger while she scooped up Daria, helping her onto her back even though her palms screamed at the touch.

Raven settled the weight of her mountain lion friend onto her back and adjusted to get a good grip, even though the brush of the fur against her abraded palms made her vision flash white with pain. Daria trembled from the shock of her wound and her right leg dangled uselessly. Raven couldn't focus on the injury — she set her gaze forward, clenched her teeth and began walking through the woods.

If the Coalition of Human Rights had set these up, they were asking for war. No one hurt their pack and threatened their lands without facing fierce retribution. Raven wouldn't let Christian get away with this.

Even if it meant facing the monsters from her past.

* * * *

By the time Raven reached Beaver Tavern, she swayed on her feet. Between the extra weight on her back, the pain in her hands and the distance she'd crossed through the woods to get there, her mind had evacuated a long time ago. The road might've been the shorter route, but most non-shifters would've freaked at the sight of a naked woman carrying a mountain lion cub along the asphalt. At this point, she was moving on sheer will alone. Daria's breaths had evened, but her leg needed attention, stat. Not for the first time on the walk,

Raven regretted bolting off into the woods. The kiss with Jer and the run-in with Christian felt light years away.

However, if Christian was still lurking at her Tavern with a smarmy grin on his face, she'd find the strength to strangle him with her scorched hands.

The familiar tavern, her second home, was all pale walls framed by rich mahogany lines, a cozy and welcoming place. Even from here, the scent of grilled meat and ale wafted her way, accompanied by the hint of smoke that had lingered ever since the attack a couple of months ago.

She summoned the strength to head around the back. At this point, Kyle would be working the evening shift. Gravel stabbed into the worn soles of her feet, which weren't callused enough to handle the beating she'd put them through. However, her wolf wasn't big enough to tote a mountain lion the right way without damaging Daria's leg further.

The moment the back door came into view with the orange pail wedged in the middle to keep it open, a knot inside her chest unraveled. She staggered up to it, knocking the door open, and made her way into the kitchen, where their latest recruit, Carrie, was working away at the grill. When the redhead caught sight of her, she almost dropped her spatula.

"Grab the others—she needs help," Raven wheezed out as she lowered Daria to the ground. The girl whimpered but remained quiet, her voice probably raw from the time she'd spent calling out earlier.

Carrie didn't hesitate, leaving a burger sizzling on the grill while she raced to the front of house. Raven staggered over to the shelf where they kept the spares, and she threw on a pair of gym shorts and an oversized tee. Most folks around here didn't know the Landslider symbol, but with their recurring appearances and now Christian's involvement, she couldn't take the risk anymore.

Her feet left smudges of dirt stained with blood across the tiled floor, and Raven winced as she continued to move, knowing once she stopped, she'd drop. She made it over to the dishwashing sink, set the water on blast and grabbed rags from the overhead shelf. Exhaustion stretched inside her, a rubber band about to break. Her vision blurred for a moment and her breaths had been coming out ragged for a while now. She crouched beside Daria with the wet rags and began to wipe out the grit from the open wound.

This poor girl had weathered the bombings on her home to now deal with this. *No child should have to go through so much pain so early.* Those experiences didn't help anyone grow — they left permanent scars.

Daria raised her head to look at her with brown eyes soft and filled with trust, the sort that broke Raven's heart. The sort she would *never* betray. She ignored the heat in her eyes while she cleaned Daria's limp leg, sucking in a sharp breath as the girl flinched from the pain.

"I'm sorry this hurts, sweetheart," she murmured, keeping her voice calm. "We'll get you patched up, and you'll be healing in no time. You're being so brave."

Daria leaned forward to nuzzle against Raven's arm, and she swallowed a lump in her throat. She would kill Christian and the entire CHR if they had set those up. As if anyone else could be behind this. *Not like my kind would be planting silver traps in the woods.*

Gene busted on in, followed by Jer's dad, Derek, and the two guys slammed to the ground beside her.

"What happened?" Gene asked, careful fury flickering in his eyes. At once, Derek went for the first aid kit and brought the bundle of bandages and disinfectant their way.

"I went out for a run through Ricketts Glen — she got caught in a wolf trap. Made of silver." Hidden wolf traps were dangerous, and silver ones made the intent quite clear. Raven sucked in a harsh breath, swaying where she crouched. The exhaustion had her barely able to focus, let alone stay upright.

Gene placed a hand on her shoulder, the weight a familiar one. A permanent bachelor, the man didn't have any kids of his own, but he pitched in with raising the cubs like their entire pack did. For orphans like her and Finn, Gene was the first one they'd run to when problems cropped up.

"Rae, you need to go lie down," he insisted. "Did you carry her the entire way from Ricketts Glen?"

Raven thrust out her jaw. "I wasn't about to leave her."

"You did the right thing, but look, you're making a mess in this nice, clean bar." His eyes gleamed with gentle amusement.

Her lips quirked. Of course he'd let her keep her pride. "Like this bar hasn't seen bloodstains before." She rested her palm on his leg, wincing as she tried to push herself up. Gene placed his hand over hers, flipping her palm up to reveal the raw, red skin, fresh as a burn. Raven's concern had been getting Daria out of the trap, but now that she looked at her damaged hands, the reality settled in that she wouldn't be holding a paintbrush right for quite some time.

Gene shook his head. "We're going to take care of those hands before you go anywhere."

"I'm not a kid," she responded, giving him a look. "I can take care of a little wound clean-up myself."

Derek crouched beside them with the wound kit, and he set to work on Daria's leg, splashing disinfectant on the site and finishing the job Raven had started. Apart from some ugly wounds that would take some time to heal, it didn't look like the trap had pierced through bone. The silver marks might leave some scars, but with a shifter's accelerated healing and her young age, she might even be able to dodge most of the aftereffects.

Gene swiped the bottle of disinfectant and splashed it onto a couple of gauze pads. "Give me your hands."

She knew that tone, so she wrinkled her nose and offered them up. As much as she resisted anyone taking care of her, Gene, Finn and Sierra had always pushed past the defenses she threw up. Gratitude warmed her chest every time, even if the words to thank them dried on her lips. At Daria's age, she couldn't have ever imagined being a part of a pack who cared what happened to her.

Jer was a different beast—not only had he done everything in his power to defend her all these years, but he didn't need to push past her defenses. He'd seen into her heart from the beginning. When it came to him, gratitude was too soft an emotion to describe the longing that gripped her by the throat and held her under the water as she begged to surface for air.

Gene splashed the antiseptic on her palms, but exhaustion had sunk in so deeply that she didn't even flinch when another wave of pain seared through her. He cleaned them out and wrapped them up within seconds, a lot faster than she would've managed by her lonesome.

"Guess I owe you a beer for that one," Raven murmured, offering a half-smile.

Gene clapped her on the shoulder. "You owe yourself some rest. Go home. We're going to take care of Daria and call Marcy and Rick."

Raven was going to offer a lazy salute, but her arms didn't want to respond. The fear, the ragged run and the constant throb of pain leeched any remaining energy. "Yes, sir," she murmured, casting a glance to Daria. Already, Derek had wrapped her up and was preparing to lift her and transport the kid somewhere more comfortable.

She'd gotten Daria out of the woods.

Raven rose, throwing every remaining ounce of energy into the movement to keep Gene from offering to drive her home. She made it out through the door by some miracle and dragged her weary body over to her Honda Civic. The car door clicked as she spilled into the driver's seat, unable to even shove the key into the ignition. She leaned back in the seat. Just a light nap, and she'd be good to drive.

As she closed her eyes, all she could see was Daria's frightened eyes. Deep in her gut, Raven knew.

The horrors had just begun.

Chapter Four

Jer hadn't been sitting idle for a couple of minutes before his phone rang with a call from Sierra.

"What's up, boss?" he asked, pacing back and forth across the gravel.

"Meet me at the Red Rock cabin and bring the envelope the smarmy asshole delivered." As always, his alpha was efficient to say the least.

"Well, when you're sweet talking me like that, how can I resist?" he responded, heading to his Harley with the envelope in hand. He needed something to throw himself into or he was liable to explode.

Sierra snorted. "I'm immune to sass, Streaky. Did you forget who I'm mated to?"

"I'll see you in a few," he responded, slipping his phone into his pocket as he settled onto the seat of his Harley. He rolled the envelope up, tucking it into the holster bag attached to his bike. The second he revved the engine, the hum of it resonated with the way he buzzed. Jer peeled onto the road, slamming on the gas as he soared along the lonely path. His head had become a beehive, and Raven's retreating form when she vanished into the woods kept cropping up on repeat.

Fuck.

He careened faster down the highway, redlining as the wind seared his skin, the sun scorched his back and he tore across the pavement like he might take flight.

All too fast, the familiar path to the Red Rock cabin reared into view and he slammed on his brakes. His bike skidded as he slowed, weaving back and forth along the road. With this energy burning through him, he needed to drive his girl another hour or two. He hadn't felt this alive in years. Not since his folks had put him on Ganzorig's blend of meds.

He bit back another curse while he wheeled down the beaten-dirt pathway toward the Red Rock cabin, a building made of beautiful heartwood glowing under the sunlight. Smoke puffed from the stack, in case the three cars in the driveway weren't enough of an indicator that his alpha had called together a meeting. He recognized Dax's truck and Sierra's beat-up junker, but he couldn't place the new addition of the Ford Explorer.

His Harley sputtered as he came to a halt and turned the engine off. He was three strides toward the door before he even took a breath. Jer ran a hand through his curls. Raven was probably right about him being in the middle of a swing, but hell if he could do anything about it. *Not like I can hop to Ganzorig's place and grab more meds.* Ever since the guy had disappeared, so had the source of Jer's sanity.

Jer strolled to the door with the envelope in hand, a little battered around the edges after he'd dragged it from place to place. The moment his hand rested on the doorknob, the heated voices from inside carried his way from the open windows. He licked his lips, trying and failing to bring himself down from the cups-of-coffee jitters that raced through him. *Fuck it.* He'd be gasoline to this lit match.

He threw open the door and marched in.

Once he walked inside, he understood the reason for the clamor with crystal clarity.

Not only had Lucas, a member of the East Coast Tribe, returned, but he'd brought with him the bastard who'd torn the Silver Springs pack apart. The one who'd dragged the Landsliders and their bombs to the pack's doorstep. The man who'd led them to burn Beaver Tavern.

Drew Williams.

A growl ripped from his throat before he could help himself, and his claws slipped out. Jeremiah staggered into the room, his heart racing a thousand miles a minute. Even though the guy stood there now with his head bowed and lips pressed tight, all Jer could see was the man who'd rolled out of his car the morning of the final fight with Dax, wearing aviators and a vicious grin after having set their tavern on fire. After having cost Seamus his life.

He couldn't help it. He tore across the room as though someone had set flame to gunpowder.

Sierra caught sight of him first. "Jer, stop," she shouted, her voice rising to the rafters and cutting through the snick-snick of the overhead fans.

Except he didn't halt. His legs pumped beneath him, mind abandoned.

"Stop." Lucas' voice boomed with the resonance of command.

Before Jer could take another step forward, his limbs froze in response. Lucas was all muscle, a formidable force on his own without the addition of his Tribe abilities. Those imbued at birth with the Great Spirits to govern the rest of the shifters had preternatural powers and could force other shifters to do their bidding by a mere command.

"I told you to step down, Jer," Sierra repeated, her voice tense and low.

A breath rushed out of him as the reality crashed in. He'd ignored his alpha's orders. No matter how much the sight of Drew burned his veins, Sierra's word was law around here and as beta he should've upheld it.

"Don't worry, Jer," Dax called over to him. "We're all miserable that my brother's here." Amusement flickered in Dax's eyes, but only a fool would underestimate the Silver Springs alpha. Jer had watched him battle out at the campgrounds and knew the prowess of the man Sierra had chosen for her mate.

"Sorry, boss." He looked at Sierra, responding at last. She nodded, though the way her gaze lingered a heartbeat had his gut twisting. It wasn't as though his bipolar issues remained a secret amongst the pack, but no one knew he'd been going off his meds for the last month.

"We're good, Jer. We've got a bigger problem on our hands," she said, casting a careful glance at Lucas. The Tribe member nodded at him, and Jer's limbs became his own again. A shiver trickled down his spine at the intensity of the hold, at how any of the Tribe members could bend other shifters to their will. It might be the only way for them to stop pack wars when there was a bunch of growling beasts in full rage mode, but still.

Somehow, Finn had managed to mate with one of those scary fuckers. *More power to him.*

Lucas ran a hand through his short-cropped dark hair and heaved a sigh. "Look, I'm not thrilled to be back in this rinky-dink town either. But with the frequency the Landsliders keep cropping up, we can't afford to keep you guys in dark any longer. You're going to need real help on this one, and Drew's the only one who's been involved. He's going to be far more useful outing his former friends as penance than if we throw him in a cell to rot."

"So we're supposed to trust the guy who broke my pack in two and threatened the lives of children?" Dax's voice simmered.

Lucas shook his head. "No. You're supposed to trust the Tribe."

"How are we supposed to do that when a rogue Tribe member is behind this mess in the first place?" Sierra criticized. Jeremiah took another few steps forward to stand beside her, his eyebrows furrowing at the statement.

Lucas crossed his arms. "That's supposed to be covert information."

Sierra fixed him with a look. "Like I'm not going to do the research on a threat to my home and my pack? You guys have done a great job trying to bury records of Mackey Kendricks, but folks around here have long memories."

"He's more dangerous than you know," Drew murmured, the first thing he'd said since Jeremiah had entered. A chilling awareness rang in his tone, one that made Jer want to flip open the locked box, even though he had an inkling he wouldn't like the truths he uncovered. "You think the Tribe's mind control is terrifying?" Drew's gaze rested on him. "Try blood oaths linking dozens of shifters to their compulsion."

Jer's mouth dried. He'd seen the mark of the blood oath not even an hour ago on Raven's hip. The Landsliders weren't just a direct threat to his home, his family and his pack. Whatever had destroyed her in the past must've had to do with her time in the Landsliders. She'd been trying to hold her shards together for too long, reapplying the glue again and again. And if the Landsliders returned to exact more punishment, there wouldn't be any pieces left to pick up.

"If this area's such a hotbed, then where's the rest of the Tribe?" Dax asked, leaning against the wall while he crossed his arms. His gaze hadn't left his brother even while he talked to Lucas.

"They're chasing down another lead on Mackey—he was sighted up north," Lucas explained. "The moment we heard word of the Coalition making a claim on Ricketts Glen with a former Landslider at the helm, it couldn't be coincidence. So, Drew and I are here to assist."

The sweat on Jeremiah's palms imprinted on the envelope he still clutched tight. There was a fair amount of legalese to go through, so he'd have a lot of sleepless nights ahead of him. Just because he'd taken up the role of pack beta didn't change his case workload in the field, with the Red Rock pack his number one client.

"Just a question, but who's going to work alongside Drew without trying to rip his head off?" His voice somehow came out level, probably because he fixed his gaze on the window rather than the traitor who stood feet away from him.

"You are," Sierra said, placing her hands on her hips.

He groaned, unable to help himself. "You're a sadist."

That drew a smile to her lips. "You knew that before you signed up to be my second in command, Streaky. Why do you think Finn leapt at the first chance out of here?"

He snorted. Sierra might be tough, but he'd never met a person more committed to justice in his life. She didn't give any commands she wouldn't follow herself, and if stepping in line and tolerating Drew Williams was tough for him, it would be a thousand times harder for her with the personal damage that had been done to her mate.

"You won't be working with him alone though—I'm not that much of a bastard," Sierra said, walking over to the kitchenette on the other side of the cabin, where a carafe of coffee lay abandoned. "Pick whoever you work with best, and the two of you will keep him in line."

"Sounds like you've got it under control," Lucas said, his deep, rumbling voice echoing through the cabin. Jer's insides thrummed with an unending symphony of screeching violins he couldn't quiet no matter how he tried. He resisted his bitter laugh—*under control*. He'd never had an ounce of it, even when the meds kept him in line.

"Man, is this what it feels like to be picked last for dodgeball?" Drew drawled. "Better dust off my wounded pride."

Dax met his brother's eyes. "Joke if you like— whatever helps you sleep at night. No one in either of our packs has forgotten what you did or the losses you inflicted. Each one of us bears wounds from those nights."

Drew didn't flinch, but Jeremiah recognized the self-loathing in the ex-Landslider's eyes, the same one that visited him too many nights to count. He couldn't explain it, but the look in Drew's eyes combined with the mention of Mackey earlier had him curious. He hated Drew — that wouldn't change — but he needed to know the whole truth behind the attacks, not just for himself.

Lucas shrugged. "Look, I'm not expecting for the two of you guys to kiss and make up. That's not what this is about. Mackey Kendricks has been stirring trouble along the East Coast for far too long, and every step he takes destabilizes the region a little more. Now the anti-shifter population's riled up, and it's hard to believe he doesn't have a hand in this."

Sierra fixed up a cup of coffee and pulled out four more mugs. "I'm assuming the rest of you assholes want some?"

Jer shook his head. "I'm good for now." With the way his heart raced, a cup of coffee might cause him to combust. A line creased between Sierra's eyebrows, but she didn't say anything. A talk was probably coming later, once the visitors weren't around.

"As if you left any for us," Dax said, slinking over to his mate with feline grace. He leaned around her to grab the cup, pinning her to the kitchenette in response.

Sierra swatted at his shoulder. "Down, boy. We have company." Dax's lips curled into a smug smile as he snagged his coffee, feigning innocence — a laughable trait on him. Jer couldn't help how his heart squeezed at the simple sight. Not the sexual tension — he'd slept with most of the single women in the pack — but the intimacy. One person saw past his hollow smiles and empty charm. The only one he'd ever be willing to take the next step with.

And after his fumble earlier, she probably never wanted to speak to him again.

Every mention of the Landsliders had him thinking of her too, of the monumental confession she'd trusted him with. He glanced at the others. Sierra and Dax stood by the kitchenette together, regarding Drew with caution while Lucas leaned against the opposite wall, an immovable force. He should tell them. Yet he couldn't betray Raven, not after she'd trusted him with a secret even Finn hadn't known. The painful bud of hope begged to unfurl, and for a moment he indulged it. He'd longed for her with a desperation that kept him up, one no amount of midnight jogs or one-night stands could abate.

"What are we going to do about this?" Jer asked, tossing the envelope onto the big oak table none of them bothered to use. He needed to be anywhere but inside his head right now.

"You tell me, Jer," Sierra said, lifting her cup of coffee and taking a long sip. "Have you gotten a chance to look over the paperwork yet? What leg do we have to stand on?"

"This situation needs to be handled with caution," Lucas interjected, his dark gaze scanning over each of them. The man emanated formidable even without the fancy Tribe tats. "Tensions between shifters and humans have been rising. This isn't our first run-in with the CHR, and they seem to be gaining more of a following with every incident."

"Joy," Sierra muttered, leaning against the counter.

Dax's phone went off, the sound drawing everyone's attention. His mouth tightened as he glanced to the screen.

"Hey, Marce, what's up?"

Within seconds, a storm brewed in Dax's eyes. His grip tightened around the cell so hard it was a fraction from breaking, and a low growl vibrated from him. Sierra placed her mug onto the counter. Despite her calm movements, the sharpness in her eyes and the readiness in her stance broadcast her concern. No one needed ozone in the breeze to sense the oncoming gale.

"I'll be there." Dax, by some miracle, kept his voice level. The second he slipped his phone into his pocket, he strode to the door without a word. Sierra loped along with him, telegraphing where he'd go.

"What happened?" she asked as she snagged her keys from the holder on the wall.

Dax paused, his hand resting on the doorknob.

When he turned around, the Arctic look in those usually easy eyes froze Jer's blood.

"Raven found Daria in the woods. The bastards set out silver traps."

Chapter Five

The nap in her car ate through a few hours, and by the time Raven got home and washed up, night had fallen. She was hungry enough to gnaw off her own arm. Raven leaned back into the cozy black chair, one of the couple surrounding her coffee table on the far side of her one-bedroom apartment. Her violet walls glared down at her, everything in her house accented in shades of purple, chrome or black.

That was, apart from the canvas stretched across most of the floor in her living room. An easel with her latest piece propped up in the center, an attempt at the Northern Lights. She'd left her capped paints scattered on the floor, and for the life of her couldn't summon the energy to tidy them. The scorching pain on her palms didn't compare a fraction to the memories bubbling to the surface. Tonight was the sort that drove her to look for a distraction. For years, this type of night had led her to Finn's doorstep, then his bed.

Except he had left. And she was alone.

Raven stared at her delivery menus, the hunger driving her to indecision. The knot in her chest tightened to the point of pain, to the point where every breath became a struggle. This was what she'd been avoiding these past few years.

A knock sounded at her door. Raven's heart surged, and she almost leapt to her feet until her body disagreed with sudden movement. She'd take any distraction right now. Instead, she lugged herself from the comfy embrace of the chair and staggered to the door.

She turned the doorknob with her fingertips and tugged it open.

Her breath hitched. Jer stood in her doorway, his plain white shirt and ripped jeans clinging to his toned, perfect body. His tousled chestnut curls made her fingers itch to run through them, and his wild eyes glowed with appreciation as their gazes met. With him standing in front of her, so close, it was impossible to forget how his lips had pressed against hers. How his touch sparked her dormant body to life again.

He flashed a grin—not the charming one he tossed to any woman walking his way, but the apologetic, real one that made her knees melt. "I heard what happened and thought you might want a friend," he started. The way he buzzed like a livewire confirmed her suspicions that he was in a manic swing. "Or food," he said, lifting cartons in a plastic bag. "Or I could leave this and fuck off. Trust me, I'd understand if you wanted me to go."

Normally, Jer spouted all slick lines, but she'd seen him during his worst swings, and when he was like this, he tended to ramble with honesty he'd regret once he came crashing down. After their kiss earlier, inviting him in was a bad idea. For the longest time, her situation with Finn had formed the wall she needed to keep from indulging in Jer, and vice versa.

Now, not only was the barrier gone, but she'd tasted his lips, and she'd be lying if she said she didn't want more.

His eyes burned with a vulnerability that struck her core, the sort she couldn't deny, even when she tried to frost over. He'd always been her real weakness, no matter how many people believed her heart belonged to Finn. Affection and sex didn't come close to the way she ran fever hot around Jer or how she felt raw and exposed.

Raven reached out and placed her hand in his. "Come on in."

She was so fucked.

Jer stepped inside her apartment, and he might as well have been made of pure electricity. This close, she couldn't help but notice the way his shoulders hunched as though he was prepared for a scrap at a moment's notice. She didn't miss the envelope from earlier that he'd rolled and tucked into his back pocket, the edges frayed. Raven counted her blessings he hadn't worn his glasses, because that would've thrown her remaining self-control right out the window.

"Did you crack into the papers yet?" she asked, closing the door behind him. The click echoed through the room, a reminder she'd invited trouble into her home.

Jer walked over to her chrome round table and placed his bags down. "Who gives a damn about the papers? Gene told me you got hurt?"

He turned to face her and crossed the distance, coming a few steps away before he paused. The heat in his hazel eyes spelled out what he remembered, and her body lit on fire, as if those careful hands were touching her skin and his hot mouth was pressed against hers.

However, once his gaze landed on her blistered palms which she'd unwrapped to let them breathe, and he soaked in the already healing scratches across her bare feet, his eyes darkened.

"What happened out there, Rae?" His voice came out in a low growl. Pure murder dwelt in those eyes.

She ran a hand through her hair on instinct and winced. Her palms.

"Daria was stuck in a silver trap. She needed my help." Her voice scraped and she couldn't dispel the images of Daria lying there helpless or the ghosts of abject terror that whispered through her.

He wrapped his hand around her arm. Raven couldn't help it—she jerked back on reflex. Only after he pulled away did the relief set in and the spark of a thrill at his touch coursed through her veins.

Hurt flashed in his eyes, but he took a step back. "Sorry, sweetheart. Just worried."

Raven lifted an eyebrow, keeping her face composed even though her heart raced a thousand miles a minute. "Save the sweethearts for the conquests you're dragging to bed, stud."

He snorted, a grin that didn't reach his eyes sliding onto his face. They were both liars who'd been playing the same game for far too long. Every time she watched him do that—deflect or offer a fake smile—she couldn't escape the way she'd plastered her own on. She pushed past him to the bags he'd brought, the scent of melted cheese causing her stomach to rumble.

"Fine then, if you're not going to fuck me, at least help me demolish the metric ton of mac and cheese I picked up." He flashed her a real smile this time, and her mouth dried. She wanted him like the first stroke of her brush to a new canvas.

"Red Pelican's?" she asked, her hunger getting the better of her. She peeked into the bag.

"Like I'd get anything else?" His dimples needed to stop — he was already too pretty, and after tasting him for the first time this afternoon, she had an undeniable urge to bite them. "The hostess kept blinking at me when I picked up the order. Poor little human obviously isn't used to shifter appetites." Sensuality curled around the words, and Raven fought the shiver begging to run down her spine.

"Poor thing indeed," Raven muttered, scratching the side of her neck. "No one warned her the big bad wolf was showing up on her doorstep."

"Big bad wolf? I like the sound of it. Want to call me that while I drive deep inside you?" he teased, the normal flirtation not as dangerous as one ounce of vulnerability from him.

"You're incorrigible," she shot back, grabbing dishes from her pantry before popping open the takeout containers and shoveling the glorious contents into bowls. Steam wafted from the golden macaroni dripping with cheese.

"Busting out the fancy words now?" Jer continued with an amused grin. "Don't tease. You know how a big vocabulary turns me on."

Raven pursed her lips to hide her smile as she handed him a bowl and fork. "Yeah, okay. Keep your big vocabulary in your pants," she responded. Raven glanced to the bowl in front of her, holding the steaming contents gingerly to keep her palms from pressing against that heat. "Thank you, Jer. Tonight would've been terrible if you hadn't come over."

She couldn't look up to meet those eyes, because if she did, she'd be sunk.

His fingers wove through hers, his touch so careful, and the way they fit together caused her heart to twist like a rag. When Finn had been there between them, she used to be able to ignore Jer's longing looks and the touches that lingered too long. But now, Finn had ditched town, they'd kissed and she needed him like a missing limb.

"You know there's nowhere else I'd be," he murmured, the hoarseness in his voice the sort of serious she couldn't avoid. Not after what he'd confessed earlier. Right now, he buzzed like he hadn't shifted in days, the way he got when he was in a manic swing.

"What happened with your meds, Jer?" she asked, regretting the words the second they came out. Yet she couldn't help it. Apart from his parents, she and Finn were the only ones to get the full extent of his struggle with bipolar — the rest of the pack might know, but they didn't understand.

He pulled his hand back and strode over to her black recliners, his features dark. That hesitant door that had opened between them slammed shut. Raven let out a half-breath and followed him over, sinking into the other recliner.

"I'm fine, Rae," he insisted, spearing a couple of macaroni before shoving them into his mouth. "When Ganzorig up and disappeared, so did my supply, but I've been managing fine." Before she could hide the disbelief in her furrowed eyebrows, his gaze landed on her. "Don't," he murmured, pain flashing across his face. "Don't look at me with pity."

Her heart squeezed tight. That look, she knew it so well. Raven rested her bowl on her lap and lifted her hands. "Hey, now, I'm the one who deserves pity." She waved her palms around, a smile lingering on her lips. "I'm the dumbass who scorched her hands with silver."

Just as fast, the irritation faded from him, and he sank into the diversion she offered. Jer arched an eyebrow, drawing attention to those lashes, ones Maybelline would kill to get their hands on. "You haven't touched your food at all, and don't pretend you're not hungry. I can hear your stomach grumbling from here."

Before she could make an attempt to eat, he hopped up with his fork and attacked her bowl. In seconds, he lifted a forkful of the glorious food to her mouth, and she couldn't help but succumb. Once the salt of the cheese hit her lips, a low moan escaped her. Jer's hazel eyes flared gold, and she shifted in her seat. The look traveled right between her thighs to a pulse that hadn't abated from the moment he'd stepped inside her house. Her wolf perked to attention inside her.

"Okay, okay, I got the hint. I'll eat," she said, a laugh escaping her even as she squeezed her thighs tight. She snagged a forkful of the mac and cheese, lifting it to her mouth. Jer hadn't moved, his gaze transfixed on her while she slipped it into her mouth, the tines resting on her lips. She couldn't draw her eyes away even if she wanted to, and tension flooded the air between them. Jer like this was unpredictable, and one night together could shatter the friendship she treasured so much. Even now, she didn't know how to retreat from the earlier kiss.

A knock sounded on her door.

Raven's eyebrows furrowed.

"You expecting someone?" Jer asked, placing his half-eaten bowl down on her coffee table.

"Unless New Leaf Chinese started taking telepathic orders, no," she murmured, rising from her seat. She sat her bowl beside Jer's, wariness flooding through her veins as her claws threatened to prick out. The scent she caught was off. Her run from earlier had done little to sate her nerves, with how it had ended — in fact, she'd grown more vigilant than ever.

Each step toward her door caused her heart to hammer louder and louder in her ears. Upon approach, the familiar, loathed scent grew clear, one that had her hands balling into fists. A low growl rose in her throat, one Jer echoed a second later.

"Christian, what are you doing outside my door?" she called out, her fury unrestrained. Unlike earlier at the bar, when she'd had a secret to keep, all three of them were aware of her past with the Landsliders now, even if Jer didn't know the lurid details. Those, she'd do anything to keep him from ever knowing. She didn't want him to look at her with pity either.

Her door creaked as it swung open. The bastard from this morning leaned against her doorframe, his hair slicked back and the same disgusting grin on his lips. Except this time, he carried a bouquet of tiger lilies. Raven's blood chilled to subzero.

"What are you doing with those?" she asked, her words hushed with horror.

"Like an old friend can't drop off some flowers?" he responded, tapping the pink paper cone against his open palm. The lurid blooms mocked her, causing her fingers to numb and her heart to leap into her throat.

"I think she's made it clear she doesn't want flowers from you," Jer growled, striding ahead of her. She reached out, grabbing him by the arm. Like this, he was liable to tear Christian in two.

"They're not from me," Christian said, his gaze meeting hers, pinning her down so she couldn't breathe. Because they both knew who they were from.

Cloves. The choking, gagging scent of cloves.

Her claws pricked out, sinking into Jer's arm, but she couldn't let go.

The wood grain scraping against her back, splinters digging in, ones she'd be tugging out for days to come.

Fuck. Heat pooled in her eyes.

Ragged breaths like puffs of smoke. Scruff that scraped her skin raw.

"Get out, Christian." Her voice wasn't her own. Not her wolf's. Just the beast she'd become.

Christian's eyes crinkled around the edges with his smile, a knowing in his eyes.

Cold sunlight streamed through the window. Voices outside the room echoed over and over again. They'd all heard. They all knew.

"Bye, Tigerlily," he murmured, tapping a finger against the doorframe. "I'm sure I'll be seeing plenty of you soon. Enjoy the flowers."

Jer's neck strained as he lashed forward, bolting out of her grip. The door clicked shut before he could reach Christian. His growl undulated and his fangs had already popped out, self-control becoming a tenuous thing. The hateful bundle of tiger lilies lay on the floor.

Raven staggered forward, placing a hand on Jer's shoulder. Drops of crimson bloomed on his forearm where she'd grabbed him, but he'd said nothing—*not like he ever would*. Numbness prickled up her legs and down her arms. The memories grew impossible to stave off. He turned toward her, his shoulders heaving with unrepentant rage that flickered in his golden eyes. Words stuck in her throat from everything she wanted to tell him.

Yet all she managed to do was sink into his chest, those strong arms wrapping around her.

"I'll fucking murder him the next time he shows his face around here," was all Jer mumbled into her hair. He didn't ask her why. He didn't demand answers she couldn't give. He simply held her tight, as if she might fade away. The way he stretched further and further away himself.

Raven burrowed into his chest, and he rested his chin on top of her head. The leather and vanilla scent of him surrounded her, causing the lingering memories to fade like a bad dream. Here, she was safe. Whether he was manic, depressed or in-between, and no matter if he went to war with his mind on a regular basis, Raven trusted him like no one else.

"Stay here tonight?" she asked, her breath catching with the request. Relying on Jer dragged her to dangerous territory—she'd never wanted another person more in her entire life. Losing Finn might have fractured her, but losing Jer? It would unmake her.

"Like you could get rid of me so easily," he murmured into her hair, not letting her go.

Raven closed her eyes and rested against him, pretending for a couple of moments that this was allowed. That she could have the one man she'd ever loved.

Chapter Six

Jer hadn't slept a full five minutes last night.

He hunched forward in Raven's bathroom, staring at his sunken eyes and mussed curls in the mirror. Suave was not how he felt today — more like he wanted to go jog twenty miles and rope off in the shower after. She hadn't even slept in her bed, because she'd felt bad about not having a comfortable couch for him to sleep on. They'd shifted last night and curled up on the floor close enough to touch. It had been agony.

Jer splashed cold water on his face, though it did little to quash the way his heart raced. He needed to hit the Reset button, even if sleep just meant reprieve from his own mind for a bit. His phone had buzzed first thing this morning with instructions, meaning he couldn't stave off telling Raven what he'd signed them up for. Last night, she'd been so shaken after Christian's appearance that they'd finished eating quickly and hit the sack. Conversation had remained light and superficial, something they'd both perfected through the years.

The envelope containing the petition for Ricketts Glen sat on the table, burning a hole into him. He'd read over the contents at least a dozen times last night, but no solutions had leapt out in the words like he'd hoped. He couldn't piece together any puzzles, not when the CHR assholes were threatening his home and that dick from Raven's past were lurking around. Today would be good. Running through Ricketts Glen always managed to quiet his mind, even when it erupted like Mount Rainier.

He ran his fingers through his hair one more time to tame his curls before stepping out of the bathroom.

"Primp long enough?" Raven called over to him from where she leaned against the wall, arms crossed in front of her. She'd changed into loose olive harem pants and a maroon tank top which highlighted her slim form. With her long hair pulled into a ponytail, she looked fresher than ever, her dark eyes glittering like onyx in the sunlight.

He flashed her a grin as he dropped down into the black chair opposite her. "Sweetheart, you haven't seen primping. Try me when I've got a formal hearing to attend."

Her lopsided grin made his pulse quicken with the way her eyes crinkled as she offered him the slip of genuine emotion few else got from her.

He lifted his phone. "Boss has delivered our marching orders," he started, a prickle traveling down his neck. No way this would go over well. "Happen to remember the asshole responsible for bombing the Silver Springs houses and setting Beaver Tavern on fire?"

"Yes…" Wariness edged her eyes.

Jer ran his thumb across the screen of his phone as he quick-fired out the rest. "So, Drew's back in town and at Lucas' orders, we're to work with him to hunt for some big, bad ex-Tribe member, Mackey Kendricks. I've been ordered to scout with him to find any other silver traps in Ricketts Glenn and may have signed you up to help."

Silence answered him.

Jer glanced to meet her gaze. She gave him a pointed dagger stare that would slice right through any of the biggest, toughest badasses in the pack. Her eyes flashed silver.

"You're telling me we're going to frolic through the forest with the guy responsible for Seamus' death?" she murmured, a low growl humming in the back of her words.

"I'm telling you that I got landed with the task and chose the person I trust the most to keep me from ripping the bastard's throat out." He met her gaze and held it. "Sierra threw down the order, and between the two of us, you've always had the level head."

Raven tugged at the end of her ponytail, looking away first. "If you need my help, you know you've got it."

The light flush on her cheeks had his cock pulsing, because he couldn't control himself for shit right now. *Not like I doubted for a second she'd help me, albeit begrudgingly.* He'd never forgotten who had picked him up when he'd gotten stranded at a girl's place and hadn't wanted his folks to know. Or who'd sat with him during his depressive swings and hadn't talked — just kicked back with a beer as they'd stared into the wilds together. Finn had helped him a lot over the years too, but Raven didn't flinch from his shrapnel words. She didn't try to cheer him up, and sat with him in the silence instead.

"Come on, Jer," she said, brushing her fingertips along his shoulder as she strolled past him. "Might as well get this over with. I don't want any other cubs to get hurt out there."

He reached out and drew her hand to him, flipping it over to look at the palm, which was still red and angry from her injury. "And this time you won't be touching any of the traps bare-handed." He passed her a look, but she pursed her lips.

"I'd have paid any penance of pain to keep that girl from another second in the trap," Raven responded, a steely look in her gaze. Whatever had happened to her in the Landsliders sank deeper than the mark branded on her skin.

She made her way to the door, those hips swinging with the motion, and Jer bit his lip, trying to tame his libido. His wolf surged to the fore every time he was around her, snapping at the tenuous restraints he kept it under. He found plenty of women attractive, and he'd maneuvered his way into most of their beds, but Raven alone inspired an intense longing that sometimes terrified him.

"Who'd you say this ex-Tribe member was?" she asked. Even though she kept her voice light, Jer sensed the tensile thread in it, one pulled pin away from a grenade explosion.

"Mackey Kendricks," Jer responded, loping forward to catch up with her. "Did you know him from your Landslider days?"

Her shoulders tensed a fraction at the mention of his name. "Everyone knew Kendricks," was all she said.

The coldness in her tone implied more than she let on. Raven didn't turn around to look at him, and Jer stayed a pace or two behind on purpose. Something in the way she held herself right then felt so remote that direct contact or anything to bring her to reality might spook her.

"Jer?" she said, the same lightness in her tone, the one that caused goosebumps to rise along his arms.

"Yeah, Rae?" He stepped to the doorframe even though she strode paces ahead toward her car.

"If you see Mackey, don't try to hunt him down. Don't try to fight him. Just run."

* * * *

Jer tapped his foot against the side of the car, alternating between that and dancing his fingertips along the window ledge. Raven had shot him a half-dozen annoyed glances, but she insisted on driving, and even without an ounce of sleep, he still somehow raced along, as though he'd downed a carafe of coffee and not just a cup.

"I could always let you out to run the rest of the way," she murmured, passing him a sidelong glance.

"You want to meet up with Drew by your lonesome?" Jer lifted an eyebrow.

"Are you sure we can't find some ditch to kick him into?" Raven asked, tapping a finger against the steering wheel. They zoomed across the empty roads, crisp autumn breezes filtering in through the open windows. His hair ruffled in the wind, and he slipped his fingers through his curls in a half-hearted attempt to tame them.

"I mean, we could, but then we'd have to face Sierra's wrath." Jer tightened his grip on the door handle, as if he could leap out of the moving car and launch into the mindless action his body commanded of him. "Not to mention Lucas. Those Tribe members are scary motherfuckers."

The wooden sign for Ricketts Glen came into view, and his chest twisted at the sight. If they lost this haven, the Red Rock pack wouldn't simply be losing territory. Each of them would be losing a piece of themselves.

"Yeah, I want nothing to do with the Tribe," Raven responded, her tone cold enough to ice a pond. It wasn't as though Jer needed to make a far leap—after all, Navi had dropped into town, fucked Finn and swept Raven's one true love away when they'd become mates. His stomach hollowed out from the acid pit that always roiled inside him, spurred by a jealousy the years hadn't soothed but intensified. Every knowing look between Raven and Finn had been another slice to his skin, but he hadn't been able to pull himself away, even if he'd wanted to.

"Those aren't the assholes we have to worry about now," Jer muttered while they pulled into one of the main parking lots. Drew was waiting for them, leaning against his Caddy with his arms crossed. With his aviators and a smug grin on his face, the man rolled on pure douchebag. Jer's knuckles itched to slam into something, and they'd found the perfect target.

"Explain again how working with Drew is going to help anyone in the pack?" Raven asked, the incredulous note in her voice one he echoed.

"Apparently the Tribe knows something we don't about Mackey Kendricks. Drew mentioned blood oaths used to force shifters to comply." Jer trailed off. Before he could help himself, his gaze drifted to Raven's hip, the spot where she'd showed him the brand from her past. She'd told him some earlier, but she still held so much back.

Raven caught him staring. "Yeah, Landsliders took blood oaths," she responded, the confirmation in her tone turning his blood cold. Her eyebrows furrowed. "Was Drew one of the current Landsliders?"

"From the sounds of it," Jer said, skimming his fingers on the handle as she pulled to a halt. "Does that mean he might not be responsible for what happened back then?"

Raven's lips pressed so tight they turned white as she switched her engine off. "Compulsion or no, he's the one who stained his hands in blood. He's the one who has to live with the memories of those he hurt."

Jer wasn't sure they were talking about Drew any more.

Before he could ask another question, Raven slipped from the car, the door shutting behind her with a click. Jer didn't hesitate—he hopped out and strode toward Drew. The bastard wore the same cocky smirk on his face, but the aviators might've stayed on for a reason. Jer hadn't forgotten how Drew had flinched the other day over Dax's comment. Eyes couldn't lie the same way as a smile.

Drew offered a lazy wave. "About time you showed. I was about to head in by my lonesome."

"So, we're the clean-up crew?" Jer asked, slipping his hands into his pockets. They'd be shifting, no doubt about it—he could scent out silver in his wolf form far better than he'd scout in this body. "Or does Lucas have some other motive he didn't share?"

Drew's mouth quirked with a half-smile. "You're not as stupid as you look, Taylor."

"The same can't be said of you." Jer strolled up to him. Raven moved with a silent grace beside him, her gaze pointed as she emanated caution.

Drew snorted. "We're here to search for signs of foul play. Not sure what we can do on the legal front to combat their claims on Ricketts Glen—that's your territory, lawyerman. However, we can at least discredit the CHR if we find active proof they set up the traps, or even if they have bigger plans in mind."

"Then what are we doing wasting time jawing off?" Raven responded, as on edge as him, the livewire tension stretching through the air. She didn't hesitate, tugging off her shirt, which placed her stunning breasts on display. A second later, her harem pants hit the ground, and he couldn't help but imagine those long, lithe legs wrapped around his waist. Jer's blood boiled when Drew's attention flickered her way.

"She's not interested in traitors, Williams," Jer shot back while he yanked off his shirt. Raven had already begun to transition and didn't bother making a comment.

Drew flashed him a charming grin as hollow as his own. Within seconds, Drew stripped to nothing, and Jer couldn't help but notice the angry red brand on the man's hip. *Same location. Same Landslider mark as Raven's.* His mind churned a thousand miles too fast for him to ever catch up, so instead, he tugged his pants off, threw them onto the growing heap beside Drew's Caddy and began to shift.

Claws replaced his nails and fur grew across his skin, the prickling sensation sweeping over his body. His bones and muscles adjusted, and Jer surrendered to the shift. He landed on all fours. No longer bare feet, but paws hit the ground, padded and tough. The decay in the air tingled even stronger in this form, as though the sun beat down heavier against his thick fur and the melody of the forest filtered into his ears as if he'd popped on earbuds to hear the music.

Raven trotted ahead of him, her namesake-colored coat streaked with silver, just like her eyes in this form. She pawed back and forth against the ground. The same anxiousness swept through him, filling him with the need to run through the woods. To run and run and forget about everything that crashed down onto their pack as of late. After years of relative peace, their region had become a hotbed for machinations to threaten not only the local packs, but the shifter populace as a whole.

If Mackey Kendricks possessed the abilities of a Tribe member and figured out a way to spread his mind control en masse, it would throw the shifter packs into a panicked frenzy, and the humans had already grown wary. The news would instill the sort of fear that inspired revolutions. The sort that led to innocent blood being spilled.

Jer bolted forward, taking the lead while he plunged into the thick of the forest. Leaves crunched under his paws, twigs snapped and sparrows trilled as they flitted from branch to branch above him. Running through this section, they were able to avoid any of the humans who stuck to the trails—shifters carved their own paths through the woods.

He raced along, hearing the quiet pound of Raven's and Drew's footsteps behind him. He needed this freedom. As he soared over rocks, over the slow trickle of a small creek winding through the dirt, and over the patches of mottled grass and moss, for the first time in days, he caught up with the thundering in his mind.

The scents barraged him, from the tingle of the churned earth and mustiness of stones to the brazen freshness of the blades of grass amid the stench of decaying leaves. He wasn't picking up silver anywhere, and he'd know the smell over anything else. Jer careened as he whipped around a tree, leading them deeper and deeper into the thick woods and farther away from the paths. Threads of chatter from humans who trekked the trails filtered his way, but the deeper into the groves of pine and oak he wandered, the less he heard voices.

Until he came to a section of the woods where he heard nothing at all.

Jer slowed, and Raven leapt to settle next to him, the sleek obsidian of her fur gleaming under the sun. Drew slunk up beside them, the large mountain lion rivaling Dax in size with umber eyes and massive claws.

The ground trembled, pebbles vibrating near his paws.

Jer's ears pricked to alertness as he scanned the clearing. The birds had evacuated and the squirrels had raced off or hidden, all of which meant trouble. Raven nudged him in the side before loping a couple of paces forward. Between the trees in the distance, he spotted the first sign of movement.

Two wolves and a bear burst forward past the thrush of pines, these shifters larger than normal. Their paws thundered while they pushed past the trees, sending dirt and pebbles flying in their wake. Their size wasn't the only thing off. Jer's blood froze.

Those eyes.

They weren't the melding of human and beast. No intelligence remained in the reddened eyes, as if all the blood vessels had burst. Foam collected in their mouths and the frenzy of their movements bled with the promise of violence.

And those crazed beasts binging on bloodlust charged right for them.

Chapter Seven

Those aren't normal shifters.

Raven's senses had pricked to alertness the moment silence had fallen through the woods, and her body stilled. In this form, the forest spoke to her in a way she'd never hear from human ears — and the breeze whispered trouble.

The black bear led the charge, all three of the shifters bigger and more bulging than average, as though they strained at invisible seams. The red gleam in their eyes hinted they weren't operating on normal rage. They were unhinged, foam welling at their mouths while they moved with a chaotic fury.

Raven didn't question Jer's next move. In this state, he'd been buzzing, waiting for something or someone to sink his fangs into. She leapt next to him on all fours as he reared back to prepare for the charge. Innocents wandered these woods, including parents with their kids.

They'd get torn apart.

Drew slunk beside them, poised for action. The man moved with the same deceptive ease as his brother, though he didn't have her fooled. He would snap his enemy's throat at the slightest provocation.

Pebbles and dirt sprayed behind the charging bear while the two wolves pounded just paces behind him. Based on the way Jer tensed and his gaze locked dead center, he'd aim for the big guy. Raven preferred the tactical approach.

She bolted forward, the wind rifling through her fur. Jer might be a skilled fighter, but she moved faster. Her paws sank into the soft earth and her heart pounded at a marching beat. The surrounding blue sky, the sharp blades of grass and the loamy earth all faded away as Raven focused on her target. Worry, fear and stray thoughts disappeared. This was the hunt.

The bear let out a roar that reverberated through the air, those reddened eyes switching focus to her.

Raven didn't pause. She shot forward, one goal in mind.

Closer.

Foam dripped from the bear's mouth. The creature barreled toward her at a terrifying pace.

Feet away.

At the last second, Raven veered to the right. The bear charged past her while she raced straight to the silver wolf. Jer had lagged several paces behind her, but he leapt forward in a flash of russet and was now aligned in the perfect position. He shot off, a loosed arrow to pierce the target—the behemoth of a bear. Distraction was her favorite game to play.

The hot breath of the silver wolf hit her first. It wasn't as though she stopped, even as the space between them vanished. Raven slammed into the wolf, her body hitting the muscled wall with a heavy *thunk*. The shifter stumbled a pace, losing her footing. Her teeth snapped close to Raven's ear, but she tumbled to the stone-laden ground, rolling out of reach.

Jer let out a growl as he launched himself toward the bear. She couldn't let herself get distracted. He might start the fight with the beast alone, but he wouldn't finish it that way. She needed to tackle the peripheral interference.

The silver wolf snapped at her again, seconds after she'd rolled onto all fours, but Raven swerved to the side. Even though the shifter loomed over her, muscles straining against skin pulled too tight in a way that couldn't be natural, the movements were sluggish. These shifters might operate on mindless rage, but they didn't seem to have the same iron discipline as the Red Rocks. Raven's mind whirled, but instinct won out.

Raven whipped around to the side, leading the wolf steps away from where the black bear roared and spewed venom at Jer. The wolf bared its teeth, nothing human remaining in those eyes. She crouched and faced her attacker. Within seconds of stillness, the shifter launched at her.

She'd been waiting.

Raven lunged forward. The silver wolf might be massive, but she was quick. Her fangs sank into the tough muscle of the wolf's flank, and she kept a firm grip while she snapped her head to the side. A roar ripped from the wolf's throat as copper pooled in her mouth. Teeth gnashed, inches away from her ear, but she gripped from the side for a reason. Raven tugged, flesh ripping with the motion before she backed away.

After a gash like that, most shifters would step back, regroup and protect their vulnerable spot. The silver wolf wasn't stopping.

It charged, but this close, she couldn't dodge.

The wolf slammed into her side headfirst. The breath flew from her lungs as an audible thud reverberated through the clearing. She soared through the air before the ground zoomed into view. Raven hit the earth with a thump that shook her bones. Rocks dug into her side and clouds of dirt rose around her, particles clinging to her snout. Raven sucked in a shaky breath while she tried to roll onto all four legs. Pain throbbed through her from the force with which she'd been thrown. Whatever had mutated these shifters into mindless beasts, it made them far stronger than expected.

Jer would be in trouble if she didn't get to him soon.

Drew's growl reverberated through the clearing as the mountain lion clashed with the other wolf in a fury of fangs and fur.

The silver wolf charged, kicking up dirt as it crossed the space between them.

Raven had barely risen, but she ducked her head. Her muscles tensed. Those eyes held no mercy as the shifter raced toward her.

She braced herself. Every inch of her begged to run, run, run, but she knew better. Teeth flashed when the silver wolf lunged for her. *Wait.*

An inch before the wolf's teeth sank into her shoulder, she ducked her head.

The neck was in perfect view.

Raven snapped forward.

Her teeth sank into the thin skin, and she locked her jaw into a vise. Blood squirted onto her fur, but she clamped tighter. The wolf thrashed around, its paws slamming on top of hers and the claws digging in past fur. Even as the slices stung, Raven didn't budge. She kept her grip on the neck, every thrash causing the skin to tear a little more and the blood to flow even faster.

Raven jerked her head to the side, ripping into more of the muscle. The silver wolf stumbled a pace. Blood poured from the gash at a lethal rate. Raven let go of the beast's neck and shook off the crimson that spattered across her fur. The wolf surged forward.

Teeth snapped at her front leg before she could move back. The tips sank in so deep that a roar ripped from her throat. Raven held still—she wouldn't make the same mistake as the silver wolf. Her pulse throbbed as the pain set in, the fangs scraping at bone. Except the blood pouring from the wolf's throat wasn't halting, and the shifter's legs had begun to shake.

Raven gritted her teeth, refusing to move. A second later, the wolf released its grip on her leg as a ragged breath shuddered from its mouth. The legs wobbled again, but this time, those eyes dulled too. The silver wolf crashed to the ground with a shaking force. Raven released the breath she'd been holding while her front leg throbbed from a stomach-squeezing pain.

She tried to pivot her legs back and forth, but the front paw didn't respond as quickly. Her movements would be hampered. The roar of the massive black bear quaked through the forest, bringing dead leaves trickling down from the trees above them. Her injuries didn't matter. Jer needed help.

Drew and the gray wolf he tangled with were locked in a back and forth, tufts of fur floating to the ground and vicious slashes traveling along each other's flanks. Their kind healed faster than humans, but almost every single shifter she'd met carried scars. Drew could handle his fight, and if he couldn't, she didn't give a damn. The traitor wasn't one of their allies, even though the Tribe had commanded them to work together.

The bear thundered forward, pushing Jer farther away and closer to the thick oaks and pines clustered together. Jer was streaming blood in at least five different places from cuts and deep red gouges, which stained his russet coat. Her insides tightened at the sight. The bear hadn't sustained a scratch apart from a couple of matted spots along the expansive inky pelt.

Raven launched forward, her front leg dragging a bit as she shunted her weight onto the uninjured legs. The bear lumbered in Jer's direction, but the stupid, stubborn wolf wouldn't budge. Jer bared his teeth and growled.

She pushed herself harder, racing over the tumbled stones and mossy patches. Each time her front paw pounded against the ground, the pain reverberated up her leg. The bear rushed forward, paces away from Jer. Based on the way the bear led with his right side, the guy would swipe with that limb first. Jer leaned down in a crouch—he was going to dive in and get dirty for the kill, same as she had. Red Rocks didn't shy away from physical confrontation.

The wind ruffled her fur while she surged across the uneven earth between them, hurtling for her target. The bear had left its back open to her, another victim to the mindless rage seeming to claim all three of the compromised shifters. Whatever had turned them into those brutes was a singular sort of terrifying.

Raven leaned on her left paw as she vaulted forward. The bear was so close. She sailed through the air behind the shifter, but he never turned around. He never saw her coming as he closed in on Jer, paws slamming to the earth and vicious teeth snapping. Raven's claws shot out.

She landed with a smack against the bear's backside, sinking the tips of her claws into flesh. The bear reared, paws raised while he prepared to smite Jer. Raven raked down. The bear howled and halted in the middle of his attack, his massive flank heaving. She clung on by her claws as he whipped around.

Jer seized the opportunity. Once the bear's wild eyes roved her way, Jer launched forward on the offensive. He sank his teeth into the bear's side and gripped on tight. Raven redoubled her efforts, digging her claws in as she near climbed up the bear's flank. The beast swiped in her direction, speeding thick claws her way, ones that would gouge deep.

Raven tugged her claws out and let go, dropping to the ground. Speed was her one advantage. The bear slung blows that didn't land, wild swings whizzing overhead as she ducked. Jer sank his fangs in deeper, crimson dripping down his muzzle and melding with the dappled russet tones of his fur. The bear pivoted in his direction, even as he hung on tight with his jaw clenched, not letting go.

No way. She wouldn't let him take more heat in this fight.

Raven lunged forward, raking out with her claws. The bear hadn't even turned around before she dove for the gouges she'd already carved into his flank, the fur matting with blood. The moment her tips sank into flesh, the bear halted mid-swing, Jer forgotten. Blood-red eyes flashed in her direction. Claws descended next.

She yanked back to pull away again, but her claw got stuck.

Panic flooded through her white hot as she tugged and tugged.

The massive arm flew her way. She couldn't dodge.

The blow landed, catching her in the flank, as though someone had smashed her in the side with a semi. The claws sank in deep, and a howl escaped her throat while she thrashed. She yanked her points from the bear's side and staggered back, her breath coming out in ragged gasps.

Jer lunged between them, his muzzle dripping and the many cuts he'd sustained sending a cascade of crimson flecks to the ground.

The bear's blow slammed into him, sending him flying.

A growl ripped from Raven's throat at the sight of Jer sailing through the air and the heavy thump when he hit the ground. She crouched, ignoring the sting of her cuts and the steady throb of pain that rose with every passing second. Her muscles tensed as she reared, ready to spring.

Before Raven could leap, a blur sailed in front of her.

Drew landed on the bear, claws first, and began tearing into him. Those points flashed in a flurry and the bear let out a ground-shaking roar as it whipped back and forth, trying to get the mountain lion off him. She'd never get a better chance than now. Raven bolted forward, diving for the bear's hind leg. Her jaw clamped down and she yanked her head to the side. Jer stumbled ahead, still shaky on his legs while he lunged for the other side.

The bear thrashed, but the movements grew slower with each wild swing. Torn in three different directions, the beast couldn't do much more than respond.

Drew slashed out, and his claws razed the sensitive skin of the bear's neck. Blood spurted across the beaten ground between them, drops splattering on top of the blades of grass. Raven gave a ferocious yank, copper pooling in her mouth as she shoved forward, fangs wrapped around the beast's leg. The bear teetered on unstable feet.

She let out a short yip, and Jer's gaze flashed in understanding.

They sprinted away from the bear, giving a wide berth. Drew followed a second later, moving with a fluid speed neither she or Jer could manage at this point. The bear let out one more ground-shaking roar before it wobbled then fell.

The pebbles quaked when the bear hit the ground, blood leaking in a pool around it.

Raven's heart raced as she stared at the fallen shifters. She took a few tentative steps toward the silver wolf she'd killed. Something had been wrong with them and she needed to figure out what. Raven lowered her muzzle and sniffed. The copper stench of blood flooded her senses, but with her in her wolf form, scent formed a tapestry of individual threads begging to be plucked.

The reddened eyes and the foam dribbling at their mouths made it seem like the beasts had gone rabid. She shoved the throb of pain to the back of her mind as she traveled the length of the body, sniffing for anything unusual. The rich scent of wolf, the earth and the tang of blood all rose to the surface, but beneath that, an off-stench clung to the whole beast—even filtered into the blood.

For it to be in the bloodstream, that meant these shifters either injected or ingested something. Jer padded next to her and nudged the side of her face with his. The motion was simple, sweet affection that splintered her heart. He dipped his muzzle down to follow her lead and sniff the bodies, but when he looked into her eyes, his gaze flashed with concern.

Drew pounded the ground with his front paw and tilted his head in the direction they'd come from. They needed to report this mess at once. This went beyond traps scattered around Ricketts Glenn, and somehow, she had the feeling the Coalition of Human Rights was behind not just the traps but the shifters as well.

And she knew, deep in her marrow, who'd manipulated them.

Chapter Eight

Jer never needed to try hard in the seduction department, but he was pretty certain bleeding all over someone's car didn't top the aphrodisiac charts.

"Here." Raven passed him a towel from her backseat. "You've got so many cuts you're going to start losing blood faster in this form."

"So, you're telling me you'd rather drive with a wolf in your passenger seat?" Jer settled onto the cushion and grimaced as he pressed the dark towel against the seeping gashes he'd earned from tackling the big, bad black bear by his lonesome.

"At least in that form you'd be quiet." She smirked, even though her confident tone didn't disguise the fear shadowing her eyes or how her gaze flicked his way too frequently. Her Honda Civic's engine roared to life. Drew zoomed away in his Cadillac, heading toward the Red Rock cabin they'd met in yesterday. Most of the time, either Sierra or Dax could be found there, and they needed to wash up wounds and regroup. "Are you sure you don't want me to take you to the hospital?" she asked.

Jer lifted a brow at her. "I'm not going to dignify that with an answer. We've got a report to deliver and the pack cabin has seen plenty of bloodstains."

Raven snorted as she raced down the highway. "The worst offender is Sierra. Do you remember before she was alpha and got in the scrap with the big ass wolf from the Yellowrock pack?"

Jer heaved a sigh, one he regretted as pain pulsed through his body like a volt of electricity. "She was covered in so many gashes Lincoln couldn't choose between reaming her out or shipping her straight off to a hospital. Instead, he chose to train her to become the next alpha."

"Let's be honest, Sierra would've become alpha whether Lincoln trained her or not," Raven murmured. "She and Finn had been duking it out from the moment she joined the pack." She lapsed into silence. Talk about the past often did that to her, and based on the lost look in her eyes, her mind had wandered to the missing beta who they used to cause trouble with.

Tall oaks flickered by them, more of Ricketts Glen that could be covered in silver traps they'd done nothing about. Instead, a bigger threat had emerged — as if they needed more problems piled onto their overwhelming heap. Jer gritted his teeth as he settled back, pressing the maroon towel against his wounds. His shirt was already covered in splotches at this point. The cuts throbbed with an intensity that should have brought him to his knees, but somewhere between this morning and the fight, all the restless energy he'd been buzzing on had seeped out of him. It probably had to do with the blood loss.

The Red Rock cabin's winding pathway peeked into view along the edge of the highway, and Raven screeched on the brakes.

She flicked a glance his way. "I'm patching you up the second we get to the cabin."

"I'm fine, Rae," he said, clutching the towel tighter. His head swirled.

She pulled down the unpaved drive, her tires chewing gravel as her eyebrows drew together in one immovable look. "You're being quiet, Jer. Either you're in a depressive spell or you're hurting bad. Don't try to pretend you're sitting there mulling over the mysteries of life." She braked hard before pulling in to park.

Jer licked his lips. Every time he thought she didn't pay attention to him, as if he could scream himself hoarse and she'd never give him the same recognition as Finn, Raven did things like this. She knew him in a way few cared to, and her perseverance through all his swings was some sort of miracle. He made a terrible friend. Not only was he fucking wrong in the head but he ran his mouth when he shouldn't, dove on too many impulses and could piss people off without trying.

He wasn't the kind of guy women fell in love with, just the one they fucked for a good time. When he lied to himself, that could satisfy him. However, it never changed the hollow thump in his chest where his heart used to be.

"I'll be aces, darling," he offered, peeling himself off the seat. Jer winced when he slipped out and caught the darkened stains he'd left in her car. "Sorry about the mess."

"Like I give a fuck," she said, heat in her voice. She stepped beside him, barely paying attention to her own leaking wounds. "We'll go in to talk to Sierra, but don't think for a second I'm buying the bullshit you're trying to spoonfeed me. After we catch her up to speed, I'm driving you to your apartment, and you're going to rest and heal, so help me."

"Yes, ma'am." He tried to swing his hand in a salute and failed as the movement tugged on the gash he'd sprouted along his back. The shifters had been anything but average. Already, Drew's Cadillac was parked in the driveway and the door to the cabin lay propped open. Voices carried from where they approached.

Jer staggered in first, gripping the towel tight. Raven rolled her eyes and brushed past him while she slunk over to the bathroom where they kept a fully stocked medicine cabinet. Sierra sat waiting for them at the round table, and Drew had plunked into the spot across from her.

"Hey, boss," Jer called as he made his way to the empty chair. He spilled into it like mud then leaned forward to brace his forearm on the table. His hand remained on the towel to stave the blood flow from the biggest gash.

"What the hell happened to you, Streaky?" Sierra raised an eyebrow, glancing between him and Drew, who were in two different states of beat-up.

"I made friends with a bear today," he said, cracking a grin. "We had different ideas of what constituted friendship."

Sierra snorted and rose from her seat. "You need to take care of those wounds."

Raven appeared from the bathroom with the familiar white-box medical kit in hand. "On it, Sierra," she called out. "You can take a seat and interrogate these guys. I'll take care of Jer."

Sierra tilted her head in response, an amused grin lingering on her lips. Their alpha had seen more fights than the lot of them combined—half of them she'd picked herself. "So, you're telling me these shifters you guys wrangled with weren't in their right minds?"

"Mackey was using shamans to tweak meth they produced and shipped around the region," Drew started. Sierra caught Jer's eye and nodded.

"That's the off-scent I caught on the bodies," Jer announced. "The same one I smelled at Rossi's lab when we busted it a couple of months ago." Raven crouched beside him, her proximity messing with his head even more than the blood loss.

"Shirt off, Jer," she instructed, armed with antiseptic and gauze.

He flashed her a grin as he shrugged off the now-bloodstained shirt. "Shouldn't be a problem."

Sierra rolled her eyes. "Enough flirting. What would those meds still be doing in circulation with Joe Ganzorig out of town? And why would they be appearing now?"

How the hell was he supposed to pay attention while Raven was placing her hands on him? It might have been to brace him for the pain to follow, but her delicate fingertips had been a large part of his fantasies for a long time.

"Shutting down the meth operation might've closed it locally, but a lot of the drugs had been distributed, and he had ancillary places," Drew said, leaning forward as he pressed his forearms on the table. Even though his blond hair contrasted Dax's dark, both guys possessed strong features made for smirking. Drew might be treating this seriously, but as with his brother, it was hard to take anything he said as a grave matter.

"Going in for the kill," Raven murmured. A second later, all thought vanished. Pain bleached his mind while the antiseptic scorched across the open wounds like fire, and Raven dabbed the gauze across the length of the deep gouges that weren't healing as fast as he'd hoped.

Jer's claws protruded on instinct, digging into the table in front of him. Sierra didn't bat an eye, even though her mouth softened.

"You're missing the main correlation here," Raven said from behind him. She swiped away at the wounds, cleaning them out. "Mackey's right-hand man arrives in town, bringing problems from the Coalition of Human Rights, and silver traps appear in Ricketts Glen, followed by shifters hopped up on altered meth? The CHR might be the pawns in this, but the problem at the core of this is the Landsliders."

Drew cocked an eyebrow at her, and Sierra's laser gaze settled on Raven as well. Jer fought the temptation to nudge her in the side. If she wasn't ready to confess her past yet, she'd screwed herself over, because the slip would place their alpha on high alert.

"We ran into Christian again yesterday, and that got us digging into his past. He used to be a Landslider," Jer said, trying to save the situation. It wasn't as though Sierra bought it, based on the level way she stared at him.

"Let's parse this down into situations we can do something about," Sierra said, flattening her palms on the table. Even though she'd changed the subject, the way she glanced between Jer and Raven hinted she wasn't about to drop it. "Our silver traps and potentially our meth-head shifter problem stem from Christian and the Coalition of Human Rights. Mackey's on a whole different playing field than we're ready to tackle. Which leads us to Christian's proposal."

Jer ran a hand through his hair as Raven finished applying the gauze around the worst of his wounds. The smaller scratches had begun sealing.

The envelope of papers had weighed on his mind ever since Christian had appeared in their bar and smacked it on the countertop. Last night he'd read through the entire thing at least a dozen times, but his synapses had been firing way too fast to settle on any solution. Now, post bear fight, he'd reduced to a crawl, as though every thought sent him trudging through soupy fog.

However, the quiet allowed him some clarity.

"We need to find solid evidence of the Coalition of Human Rights tampering with Ricketts Glenn and some way to tie Christian to the current Landsliders. If we can pin illegal charges on them publicly, there's no way the government will enter into a sale of territory, which will give us the necessary time to figure out a more permanent solution."

Sierra nodded. "Then that's what the three of you are in charge of."

Jer blinked, the room still a little hazy. He wasn't sure if the blood loss was causing it or not, but even after Rae bandaged him up, everything moved a little slower.

Sierra cast a glance to Raven, who stood behind him. He was always aware of her presence, whether she lingered nearby or was pulling pints behind the bar while he worked the pool table with his packmates. "You guys are dismissed for tonight. Take the time to heal up and, Rae, make sure he gets home safe."

Raven's hands settled on his shoulders before he could argue that he was fine. The light perch there reached through the numbness that had descended like a ton of bricks.

"Let's get you home."

* * * *

When Jer blinked, the car had come to a halt. He must've slept through the entire ride without realizing it.

Raven leaned forward, lightly clutching the steering wheel even though they weren't moving. "You awake?" she asked, a grin lingering on her lips.

"Sorry," he murmured, trying to roll his shoulders and wincing when the pain from his still-healing wounds followed. "Guess the fight wiped me out more than I realized."

His apartment lay before them, so close to where Finn had lived. Nobody had moved into Finn's old place yet, and Jer wasn't sure he wanted anyone to. The idea of a stranger living where his best friend used to be for so many years seemed strange. Foreign.

"Hey, Jer?" Raven said, the tentativeness in her voice snapping him to the present. "Thank you. I slipped up with the talk about Christian—my focus wasn't there—and you covered for me, even though it meant lying to Sierra."

He wanted to reach out and wrap his arms around her, but the energy had left him. Instead, he offered a soft smile. "Rae, I keep my promises. You need to tell her sooner rather than later though—Sierra wasn't fooled in the slightest." After pushing the car door open, he forced himself up off the seat. "I'll shift and grab my Harley from your place tomorrow."

Raven's grip remained on the wheel and she didn't look at him. "You got wrecked, and some of those wounds might need to be re-dressed. I should stay with you tonight."

The air left him at the words he'd longed to hear. Except she hid her face for a reason. So he wouldn't see the fear flickering in her eyes. Christian's visit had shaken her last night, and it grew clear that the demons haunting her hadn't left. He didn't mind being her fall guy.

"If you feel like playing nursemaid, who am I to argue?" he responded with a grin, eliciting an annoyed glare from her.

"You're tempting me to turn around and drive on home," she muttered even as she took her keys out of the ignition and joined him outside the car. Jer strode to the door, his limbs taking a second to catch up from the stiffness that had set in while the gashes across his back and chest screamed in silent agony. He scuffed his shoes on the worn mat that said *Get the Fuck Out* and slipped his key into the lock.

"Just a fair warning, I'm going to be shit company tonight," Jer warned as he pushed his front door open. The fight had drained every ounce of energy from him, and even with the woman of his dreams standing at his doorstep, he was two seconds away from curling up on his couch and sleeping for the next week.

"Because you're known for your sparkling personality," Raven responded, reverting to their normal dry repartee. He couldn't help the way his chest ached or how he longed to dig past their light, superficial conversation to the bridge of unsaid words between them.

"When it comes to bringing girls back to my place, I'm on my A game," he said, flicking the light on. He couldn't help the frown creasing between his eyebrows at his stack of unfolded laundry and the dozens of books he'd left scattered on the coffee table, by his burgundy couch and pretty much on every surface but the actual bookshelf. "Maybe I should've brought you in blindfolded. My place is a mess."

The click as Raven shut the door echoed through his apartment, and his stomach squeezed. Any other girl and he'd be working her zipper down three steps in, but they'd never even addressed their kiss the other day, a memory that scorched him.

She skated her fingertips along the gauze lining his shoulders, a light touch that snared his attention at once. Jer turned around to face Raven, who stood right behind him.

"You've seen my place," she murmured. "You don't have to pretend with me."

When their gazes met, the air evacuated the room.

She still rested her fingertips on his shoulder even as he faced her, mere inches away. The touch might as well have been blazing, with the way he noticed it. She'd been ducking her head, turning away and keeping her gaze trained on anything but him ever since they'd kissed. But she looked his way now, and everything else ceased existing.

Whatever impulse had seized him by the throat the other day had long left. He was paralyzed now. Jer traced the shape of her lips, memorized the pulse of her throat and the way several strands of gleaming black hair slipped from her ponytail to stick to her neck.

"You've never had to pretend with me, either," was all he could manage.

That was when she closed the space between them and pressed her lips to his.

Chapter Nine

Raven didn't know what had possessed her.

One moment she was staring into Jer's eyes, watching him retreat the same way she did and the same way they always had around each other when things got too real. The next, she crossed the space between them and kissed him the way she'd dreamed of doing for too many years now.

She perched her fingers on his shoulders and her lips whispered across his, as if the slightest push might cause them to both break. He wrapped his palms around her waist, and she found herself pulled flush against Jer. He was all hard planes and coiled strength, despite his lean frame, and she melted into him. Unlike the impulsive shock of the first kiss from the other day, this was the inexorable collision they'd known would happen from the moment they'd met.

He let out a low growl as he deepened the kiss, slipping his tongue into her mouth. Raven moaned at the sensations ripping through her, like the first splash of color on a monochrome canvas. Her core sparked to life in a way she'd long forgotten while he clutched onto her tightly, as though she might fade away. The scents of vanilla and leather grew so strong around him that she wanted to drown in them. She needed to feel his fingers threaded through her hair and the hard length pressed against her thigh buried inside her.

Their lips met again and again, a hunger tearing through her that had her wolf keening in her chest, desperate to be sated. Her heart had been ripped wide open, making her skin prickle. She wanted to lose herself in the inferno between them or cry from the sheer intensity. He braced her with steady hands even as she swayed on her feet, and she couldn't help but slide her fingertips through his smooth chestnut curls.

Raven had been kissing men for a long time, mostly Finn. The experiences had been pleasant, some even toe-curling, but none of them compared to this. Kissing Jer was the same as stepping in front of a tornado, the buzz of gravitas settling as the winds whipped and the fury seared the sky gold as something approached that had the ability to tear what remained of her to shreds.

He gripped her waist tighter, and she lost herself in the smoky taste of him. This was everything she'd wanted for so long. Everything she didn't deserve. Yet as their lips crashed together again and again, a tensile thread of pure joy stretched tighter and tighter inside her.

Mine.

Raven's eyes shot open, and her grip tensed in Jer's hair. Jer pulled back at the same time she did, her shoulders heaving and ragged breaths filling the space between them. Her wolf howled in her chest and a feeling of rightness settled into her bones, one that made her chest tighten and her mind whirl. *Fuck, fuck, fuck.*

"Well, I didn't think the kiss was that bad," Jer murmured, and she realized she'd cursed out loud. He rested his hands on her waist, and she warred with wanting them there forever and shrugging away to curl into a ball and tear her hair out.

"Did you feel that?" she asked, searching his expression for any sign his wolf might've responded in turn. The word hovered on the tip of her tongue, but she couldn't force it out.

Jer nodded. She rested her fingers in his hair and combed them through his silken curls before placing her palms lightly on his shoulders, her skin still sensitive from the silver burn. Even now, part of her wanted to dive back into the wild abandon of kissing this gorgeous man. She wanted to surrender to the explosive heat between them, the way he made her feel like a crocus unfurling after a lifetime of winter.

"I don't blame you if you want to walk away," he murmured, his dark eyes earnest in a way that broke her heart. "No one signs up for this sort of damage for life."

Words wouldn't suffice. Raven leaned in and brushed her mouth to his in a chaste kiss. The brief contact sent a residual thrill through her, her lips hot and swollen from their collision. She broke the kiss and took a step away from him, desperate for distance lest she be swept away in the tide of emotion his mere touch resurrected. Right now, she needed a level mind even though her attempts at grappling with reason were hopeless.

"Jer, you're not bad news. I am," Raven murmured, tugging on the ends of her long hair. "I've got so much damage in my past, and when I get the nerve to tell Sierra, who knows if I'll even be allowed to stay." Voicing the fears aloud tightened her throat, but she bored holes into the carpet as they left her.

"So, what do we do?" he asked, helplessness clear in his voice. He'd never try and claim her on his own, especially not in the hold of a depressive swing. She hadn't put a pulse on it earlier, but the manic energy around him had faded, and when he wasn't on medication to regulate, a depressive episode would be quick on its heels.

Raven slipped her hand through his and led them past the stacks of books piled in their way until she stood outside his bedroom. Her heart squeezed tight. Part of her wanted to step through the doorway and follow these feelings to their natural progression. She wanted it more than a paintbrush in her hand and more than the first sunny day after weeks of rain.

However, Jer wasn't the only one afraid of dumping their damaged goods on anyone. If they rolled between the sheets now, they might seal the mating bond that had emerged. Meaning, they'd be tied together forever. She couldn't subject someone to picking up all her broken shards for life. She'd been trying for years, and she still might never be a whole person at the end of it.

"Right now, you get some rest," Raven said, squeezing his hand tight. The dark look in his eyes filled with self-loathing was one she understood far too well. She swallowed before continuing. "This isn't me running away, not this time. But I don't even know what my future's going to hold when I tell Sierra about my past. Let me get through the trial first, then I promise—we'll talk for real."

Jer stepped beside her and slipped two fingers underneath her chin to tilt it up. The fierce kiss he left on her lips was a brand, one that radiated through her whole body. Raven curled her fingers into his shirt, and for a single moment she untethered from her past and basked in the hearth-fire glow of the promise between them.

"I'll wait," he murmured against her lips. Raven swallowed, the seduction of his words holding her spellbound. Jer had been waiting so long for her and they both knew it. Her eyes burned with heat and she let out a ragged breath. He stepped into the darkness of his room, but she pulled herself from the doorway. When he looked at her, it made her believe that even with all her broken pieces she might find something real, and the tenuous hope hurt worst of all.

Raven's wolf rammed in her chest as if it remained trapped inside a cage, and maybe it did. Her wolf was one of the real parts of her she'd kept restrained for far too long. Except every time she stepped to the precipice and allowed herself to dream, all she could see was the vibrant orange of tiger lilies crushed underfoot.

* * * *

The next morning, Raven stretched out on Jer's sofa, the stale scent of books and lingering vanilla a comforting way to wake up. However, the moment she sat up, the memories of last night crashed back down on her. Her fingertips flew to her lips on impulse as if she might be able to capture the phantom sensations. Her core thrummed at the memory, and she burned with intense need.

The house remained quiet, even with the trill of sparrows outside the window and the whisper of branches as they drifted in strong winds. Jer must still have been asleep, because there was no hiding his vibrant presence. With the wounds he'd sustained yesterday and the complicated emotions flush between them, she wouldn't go wake him up.

Raven stared at the ceiling. Beneath the layers of loathing and the choking fear, the word *mate* pulsed in her chest like a second heartbeat.

She needed to get moving, now. Raven cast a glance to her phone — good, enough time to swing out before her shift at Beaver Tavern. She headed for the door, but once her boot hit the frame, she paused and glanced back. Everything in this place reminded her of him — the cluttered books like his scattered, brilliant mind, the mismatched bookshelves and a coffee table with a clashing resin veneer. Cozy blankets were piled high on his couch and the chairs swallowed a person whole, just like the man himself.

He deserved the world. He deserved so much more out of a mate than someone broken and battered like her.

Raven squeezed the doorframe tight before her boots clapped against the stairs and she made her way to her Civic.

A quick change into the spares in her backseat had her feeling a little fresher, and within seconds she'd shot a text and hit the road. She needed to make a stop before her shift.

Instead of turning in the normal direction toward Red Rock territory, she made a left onto the road and soared down it. The blue sky was a shock to her system and the sun threatened to pierce through the cold exterior she'd erected. With her windows down, the crisp scent of fall threaded through and the winds batted her hair around. She needed to throw herself into tasks, anything to distract herself from the maelstrom in her mind.

Finn's departure had started it all. He'd been the wall she and Jer had hidden behind for years, even though deep in her heart she'd never been able to quite dispel the way Jer made her feel. Every time he'd laughed and driven off with another girl, a piece of her had died inside. The stark sadness in his gaze had radiated through her whenever she'd flirted with Finn and they'd walked off hand in hand. They'd been hurting each other for years, inflicting more damage than Finn ever could've.

She didn't know how to break the cycle.

Even if they were potential mates.

Before long, she found herself in Silver Spring territory. The trees stretched in thick throngs around here, casting dappled shadows onto the road, and she zoomed toward the neighborhood she'd first seen ablaze. In the bombings, lives had been lost and members of the Silver Springs permanently damaged, and their homes had been ruined in the same way as Beaver Tavern.

Raven pulled down the street which led into a circular drive where the houses of Silver Springs families stood. Several still had construction wrap around the outside from the rebuilding process, but many were already completed, restored to their former glory. Too bad people couldn't be revamped the same way. Broken wood could be repaired more easily than memories.

She parked in front of Marcy and Rick's house, wishing she had stopped at a gas station along the way for flowers, candy, something to give to a kid healing up. Raven tugged at her tee. Presentable, she wasn't, but if she swung home to shower she'd lose the nerve to check in on Daria. *Now or never.*

Raven hopped out of her car, her loose cargos brushing against the gouge in her leg from yesterday that had almost healed. Her palms were another story, still feeling sensitive even after a few days. The sun beat down on her back as she crunched dry leaves underfoot on her approach to the front door.

She rapped her knuckles on the flat surface, trying to ignore the simmering of nerves.

A second later, the door swung wide open and Marcy appeared in the entrance. Her hair had been pulled into a sporty ponytail and she'd donned a pressed button-down and black slacks.

"I'm heading to work, but Rick's working from home in the office to keep an eye on her," Marcy said, smoothing several stray strands of hair. She met Raven's gaze, the worry lines around her eyes all the more evident. "Thank you for rescuing my girl. You're her new hero, you know."

Raven shook her head, her stomach flipping with discomfort. "I'm no one's hero. She's doing better though?"

Marcy jerked a thumb back as she stepped past her, purse thumping against her hip. "Why don't you go check for yourself?" The warmth in Marcy's gaze doused her in cold water. She didn't deserve the admiration in those eyes.

Raven stepped inside the house where the scent of lemon polish filled the foyer. A big wooden banister and steps led to the second floor, and Raven headed there on instinct. If she could somehow avoid Rick and any more gratitude, that'd be peachy. The steps creaked under her boots and the clean lines of fresh wood and neat blue carpeting made her feel even scuzzier.

The muted sound of voices from a TV drifted down the hall, so Raven chose that direction, heading for the bedroom at the far end. The door lay open, offering a peek of the peach walls and tan carpets. Large paintings of frozen landscapes decorated the corridor and she couldn't help but scrutinize how even the floorboards looked polished and new in the wake of the devastation that had rocked this house months ago.

Raven stepped into the doorway and rapped her knuckles against the open door.

Daria glanced up from the swathe of blue blankets she burrowed in. Her injured leg lay propped on a pillow.

"Raven?" Daria said, scooting up from where she'd slumped. She dove for the remote to turn the TV off. "Mom and Dad didn't say you were coming."

"I showed up unplanned," she responded, stepping into the girl's bedroom. "Wanted to swing in and check on my favorite fighter."

Daria's chestnut hair hung in waves, casting a shadow as her head dipped down. The ten-year-old bored holes into the blanket before her. "I'm not a fighter, just bad luck." On any normal day, the girl had the sort of smart mouth that lent itself to mischief, but right now the weight in her eyes belonged to someone far older.

Raven walked over to sit on the opposite end of the bed, moving carefully as her weight shifted the cushion. "Now, what makes you say that?"

Daria stared at her with a sadness in her soft eyes that Raven knew all too well. "Bad things keep happening to us. Bombs, silver traps and even last week I got suspended for fighting back against a human. What was I supposed to do? He cornered me in the bathroom, and I was so scared."

Raven swallowed the lump in her throat as she leaned to place a hand over Daria's. The girl looked at her, lip trembling, and she might as well have punched her in the gut.

"I remember thinking the same thing at your age, that I must be cursed. All that bad luck couldn't follow one person, right?" Raven murmured, keeping her tone gentle. "Truth is, there are some terrible people in the world, and it's our job to keep fighting, even if it's punching out a bully in the bathroom. And once you're all healed up, you'll have beat the jerks who tried to keep you down with a silver trap."

"Is that what you did?" Daria asked, her blue eyes wide with desperate hope. "When you felt like you were cursed?"

Broken. Broken. Broken.

Raven opened her mouth, and the words dried on her lips. Here she was, offering false hope to the kid when she'd been a coward all these years. Hiding, rather than fighting. She didn't want that future for Daria—truth be told, she didn't want that future for herself either.

Raven squeezed Daria's hand tighter while she searched for the right thing to say. When Daria's gaze met hers, steady and shining with the confidence in others that only youth could capture, the words emerged.

"We'll keep fighting, together."

Chapter Ten

Two days had passed since he'd felt the mating bond between him and Raven, and with every fading hour, Jer became surer it was a mistake.

He sat at his kitchen table, staring at the half-finished coffee that did nothing to wake him. He'd slept through almost the entirety of the day after he and Raven had kissed, then yesterday had been a haze of ignoring texts and stumbling out from his bedroom to reheat leftover Chinese he'd given up on after three bites.

He should have been elated after the way Raven had kissed him this time. Hell, he should have been out in Ricketts Glen, hunting down silver traps and pulling his weight as beta. Instead, piece of shit that he was, he had holed himself up inside his house, hiding away from the world and his problems. He sighed and readjusted his glasses that had begun to edge down his nose. It didn't help that even getting up in the morning took a stupid amount of effort. The remainder of his energy went to the slideshow of Jer's past fuck-ups that played on loop.

Raven deserved a mate without damage. Even when he took his meds, he wasn't perfect — he still slipped, and sometimes the effects faded and he and Ganzorig had done some tinkering. She didn't deserve the burden of dealing with his shit for the rest of their lives, even if she was the one person on earth who might understand.

A knock sounded on his door.

Fuck. Sierra had probably showed, wondering why he hadn't responded. Jer chugged the rest of his coffee and slammed the mug onto the table before heading for the door. He had crossed halfway through his living room when the door swung open.

Raven stood in the doorway, the sunlight gliding off her smooth, creamy skin. Her arms were exposed with the heather-gray babydoll tee she wore, and her black jeans had a couple of paint splatters across her thighs and the knees were ripped, but on her it looked perfect.

"Jer, get your ass moving," she called, entering as though she hadn't slipped out the other day without a goodbye. "We've got a CHR meeting to infiltrate."

He paused in mid-stride, his thumbs hooked in the belt loops of his rumpled jeans. "What are you talking about?"

Raven closed the door behind her as she slunk up to him, her proximity the first thing in days that had his senses sparking to life. The dark, sweet scent of her would be his undoing.

"Sierra was ready to march here and launch a full investigation." She fixed him with a look. "I told her I'd haul you out. Ganzorig might've been supplying your meds, but that doesn't mean we can't find another shaman to work with you, Jer. You need to get back on them before Sierra notices much more."

Irritation caused a dull throb at his core. "Like you're coming clean with Sierra about your past with the Landsliders?" he shot back, at once wishing he hadn't.

To his surprise, Raven didn't recoil and just fixed him with a flat stare. "If that's what it takes to get you back on your meds, I will." He opened his mouth, but before he could say anything, she continued. "And no, it's not like I can't stand you without them, Jer. However, I can see you're struggling, and I'd be a shit friend if I didn't help." Her eyes flashed silver, emphasizing her seriousness.

His stomach twisted. Even when he said the wrong thing and tried to push her away, Raven weathered his storms. The one thing that seemed to send her running was the lifechanging potential that rocked through them. Jer crouched to slip on his boots.

"Let me guess, we're teamed up with the shittier Williams brother again." Even standing from the couch took a stupid amount of effort, enough that shame rolled through him.

Raven tipped finger guns in his direction with a grin. "Bingo, charmer. As if that doesn't entice you enough, we've got to blend as humans too."

A smile rose to his lips, the first one he'd entertained in days. "You need to work on your sales pitch, babe. Next you'll tell me we're supposed to go pluck the remainder of the silver traps barehanded." He strode to the door, grabbing his keys from the hook on the wall and his wallet from the end table along the way. Raven knew him well enough to show up rather than asking — she was about the only one who did.

Her lips pursed. She lifted her palms, raised and reddened from the burns she'd received mere days ago. "Already got the head start on that one. Wouldn't recommend it."

"I'll drive, and you can direct me to wherever the hell we're meeting up," he said, waiting by the doorway. "We're taking the Jeep this time, though. If I'm going to bleed all over a car, it better be mine."

"No complaints from me," Raven responded, following him to the door. Inches away, he couldn't help but notice the smudge of bright blue on her cheek.

His thumb brushed over the spot before he could help himself. Her breath caught in her throat and instead of cracking a grin and delivering a witty comeback, Raven licked her lips. God, the motion traveled straight to his cock. Then her doe eyes settled on him, and he might as well have been struck by lightning. They'd unleashed something dangerous between them, something that had grown for so long that once they let it out, those feelings would be too powerful to snuff.

His wolf didn't help at all with the way it preened in his chest, a rightness settling over him like sunlight. The bastard wasn't discouraging this bad idea, even though over the past forty-eight hours he'd thought of six hundred and thirty reasons why Raven deserved someone better than him. They could never be mates, even if the potential scorched like silver.

He let his hand drop, shattering the moment. All he wanted was to kiss her right now, but with the mating bond looming, a glass barrier settled between them.

"We better get going." Raven broke the quiet, tucking a strand of glossy hair behind her ear. A light flush spread across her cheeks, making him want her even more. She darted out of the door, and Jer locked up before following. Time to get his head in the game and act like the pack beta.

* * * *

After a forty-minute drive in the Jeep with Raven, work was the furthest thing from Jer's mind. The sweet maple scent of her reminded him of how she tasted and of the absolute softness of her lips. Even though their conversation flowed like normal, the undercurrent of what had fundamentally changed stretched between them, a taut thread ready to snap.

His head muddled even more, because after he'd spent years sneaking glances at her, Raven was now looking back. Her gaze filled him with stumbling hope, all while the layer of shame was a film on his skin. He wanted her like a clear sky when all he deserved was rain.

"Up ahead." Raven pointed to a building down the road. The community center hardly made a landmark, comprised of drab walls and faded lettering that made it blend in with the surrounding chipped concrete. Already, a slew of cars filled the lot, and an uncomfortable prickle traveled up Jer's spine. They called themselves the Coalition of Human Rights, but the zealots running the organization might as well have launched under a banner of 'All Shifters Must Die.' One well-placed silver bullet from them and his story was told.

The organization had been around for at least thirty years now, but the original intent had been far tamer, simply a way for humans to bring up issues regarding the shifter populace and the different way the Tribe governed. However, in the last five years or so, fear had amplified any concerns into a marching beat, and many of the factions spewed hate speech any chance they could.

"What sort of safeguards do they have in place to weed out our kind?" Jer asked, tapping a beat against his steering wheel.

"Drew said he knew and would handle it." Raven shrugged. "I might not trust the bastard, but he has a remarkable sense of self-preservation."

Jer watched from the car as folks headed toward the glass doors at the entrance, one couple even toting pre-school age kids with them.

His stomach curled in disgust. "They'd subject their kids to that toxic hate?"

"Indoctrination starts early," Raven replied, her tone bitter. The knowing in her gaze had to do with the Landsliders. The more he found out about the organization, the more it seemed like the cult of Mackey Kendricks.

A familiar Cadillac slid into the parking spot beside them. Drew hopped out of his car moments later with aviators on and wearing a rolled-to-the-elbows Oxford shirt as though he was headed to Sunday Mass. Jer slid out, hating his familiarity with the man who had ruined their home and cost so many lives mere months ago. However, as much as he despised Drew, the Landsliders and their leader were the bigger threat, and if taking the devil down meant dancing with a demon, then that was what he'd do.

"Fancy meeting you here," he said, pushing his glasses up as they threatened to drift down.

"Yeah, you know me. Hating on shifters is my day job," Drew said in a wry monotone. He tugged his aviators off, clipping them into his front pocket. "Let's go rah-rah with the rest of them."

"Wait," Raven murmured before casting a pointed glance to check their surroundings. "What's the plan?"

"Follow my lead," Drew said, strolling off in the direction of the entrance before Jer could reach out and grab him. He let out a curse under his breath and quickened his tread to try to catch up with the arrogant bastard.

A few folks stood outside, ripping through their cigarettes before the meeting started. Goosebumps traveled up his arms. He'd been there a decade ago, in front of a community center like this one and trying to stem his nerves with nicotine. His parents had wanted him to try a bipolar support group, but at the end of it, he'd felt raw, angry and even more alone. It probably hadn't been as bad as he'd made it out to be at seventeen, but back then, when he'd taken the podium and started talking, he'd wanted to die.

He had the feeling a Coalition of Human Rights meeting wouldn't be much of a mood changer either. A fierce temptation lodged in him to turn around and sit this one out.

Raven's fingers brushed by his and she gave his hand a light squeeze. "I'm on edge too," she murmured, low enough only he could hear. "We'll get through it." The 'we have to' remained silent. She was all he'd ever needed. His wolf rolled around inside him. Her delicate touch inspired comfort as well as a silent thrill. He couldn't let Rae enter by her lonesome, not when he didn't trust Drew further than he could spit.

"Let's hope Drew's self-preservation instinct is on point," Jer muttered, hooking his thumbs into his pockets while he followed the mountain lion shifter through the swinging glass doors.

Several lines formed across the vestibule between the entrance doors and the internal auditorium. Jer maintained a level mask even though he couldn't help his curiosity. Guaranteed, they tested each person to ensure no shifters stealthed in amongst the crowd. If his palms hadn't been sweating before, they were now.

Raven brushed against him, a seeming accident, but one glance betrayed that she was skating on the same nerves as him. *Fuck it.* Jer slipped his hand into hers, weaving their fingers together the instant they connected. His heart pounded even faster, this time not just from anxiety. This closeness still felt forbidden, as if any moment Finn was going to walk into the room and Raven would bolt straight into his arms.

The man had been her lover and the pack beta.

Jer was Finn's shittier replacement in all facets of his life.

His grasp on Raven's hand went lax, but she gripped him even tighter, as though this meant something more than temporary comfort to her.

Drew didn't acknowledge them once while they continued moving up in the line, closer and closer to where a few big guys stood outside the doors like bouncers, conferring with each individual for a couple of seconds before gesturing them inside. Whatever the CHR did to test for shifters would leave them only seconds to improvise.

Three away.

An older, hunched man held open his palm, and the person at the door dropped something circular into it. Jer squinted. A silver dollar? If he had to guess, they used the old ones made from silver, which meant any shifter's palm would burn. He shot a look at Raven, whose lips formed a thin line as she glanced at her own palms, still healing from a couple of days ago.

And we're supposed to trust Drew Williams, former ally of the Landsliders.

Jer was tempted to run the other way screaming, but instead he continued to trudge ahead as the guards gestured more proven humans into their auditorium, which buzzed with voices. One ahead of Drew. The guard at the door dropped the silver coin into the brunette's palm, and she squeezed before passing it back over.

Drew's turn.

The mountain lion shifter rolled up, cockiness personified while he placed his palm out to catch the coin.

The guard nodded to him and dropped the coin.

Except the coin didn't land on his palm and continued falling toward the ground.

Drew shot down and grabbed the coin before it hit the floor. "Sorry about that," he said as he straightened, his hand in a fist around the silver dollar. Jer's heart stammered in his chest. He waited for the reveal, for the marks silver would scorch into shifter skin.

"Do I pass the test?" Drew said with a grin as he opened his palm, the silver dollar resting in the center.

The guard snagged the silver dollar off Drew's unblemished palm. "Go ahead in," the guy said, tilting his head to the doors. Drew took several paces forward but crossed his arms and waited by the door for them.

Jer's forehead threatened to crease, but he kept his placid mask in place and untangled his hand from Raven's. Somehow, Drew had rigged their system.

Jer stepped up next, placing his palm outward. He didn't bother with the niceties Drew had—he didn't need to schmooze these guys, just pass their stupid test. The guard lifted the silver dollar, and sweat prickled on the back of Jer's neck. If it sizzled, a horde of humans surrounded them who would be searching for their blood. Ones willing to leave out silver traps to maim children.

The coin dropped.

It hit his palm, and he squeezed it tight—no burn. Drew had switched the coin. He stifled his sigh of relief when he opened his palm, which remained unmarked.

"Go on in," the guard gestured, and Jer strolled to where Drew waited, a small smile playing on his lips. Drew kept his other hand carefully tucked away—it didn't take a genius to figure out which one had touched the actual silver.

Raven strode up next and opened her palm. The guard's eyebrows furrowed, and Jer's stomach squeezed tight. She had clear evidence of burns on her palms already.

"What happened there?" the guard asked, a tension straining his voice that had Jer leaning forward, ready to race in her direction.

"Baking accident," Raven replied in her normal droll tone. "Apparently you're not supposed to grab the pan bare-handed."

The guard snorted and lifted the coin. "Better hope you're not a shifter then, because this'll really burn."

"Yeah, ouch," she said as the coin dropped into her palm. She wrapped her fingers around it and squeezed, a wan smile on her face. Raven opened her palm and passed the coin over to the burly guard, who gestured her on past. Raven slunk over to where they waited, and a cord uncurled inside him. She slipped her hand into his again, and this time, he couldn't blame the nerves.

His heart thundered as they faced the doors to an auditorium that was filled to the brim with humans who despised their kind.

"Welcome to the Coalition of Human Rights," Drew murmured as he pushed the double doors open and, together, they entered.

Chapter Eleven

At least fifty people congregated in the community center's auditorium. Fifty people who loathed shifters enough to threaten their lives.

Raven picked a seat in the back.

Jer settled next to her and she rested her palms on her thighs. They buzzed, but not from her burns. She'd held hands with Jer. Even though it was in the middle of a sea of humans who didn't know them and an asshole they had to work with, doing that out in public made it somehow more real. They hadn't talked about the mating bond since a couple of nights ago when it had manifested between them. *Not like I'm ready – not yet.*

She'd never felt something so right in her life, as if a missing puzzle piece had slid into place, one that had hovered right out of her grasp. That terrified her.

Raven had been living with the loathing for so long that the idea of fighting back, of grasping for something better, washed through her like ice water.

Except she'd promised Daria.

Her heart might be racing in the middle of the meeting, but her reflex was always to retreat inward, not slip her hand into Jer's. Yet she kept seeing Daria's searching eyes as the girl prayed her future might be brighter than the hellscape that had descended upon the Red Rock and Silver Springs packs as of late. If facing her fear meant giving Daria even a fraction of the hope she'd never had, Raven would fight.

Because if she were being honest, Jeremiah Taylor was the one man she'd truly wanted.

Jer nudged her in the side with his elbow, a small smile hovering on his lips. "Looks like the grandstanding is about to begin." His dimples deepened, ones she wanted to take a bite out of. The way his eyes gleamed behind those thick-framed glasses didn't help tamp down her attraction either — she'd always had a thing for him in glasses.

"Try to look a little more starry-eyed. Your sarcasm is showing," she murmured, unable to help her own grin. Even though the sheer number of humans surrounding them intimidated her, as long as none of the Coalition members recognized them, they'd passed the test.

"Welcome, all." An older man stood behind the podium, his curls streaked with silver, and oozing charisma. He was the exact sort of charming asshole to work the crowd into a frenzy. "For those of you who don't know me, I'm Greg Statham, the local head of this organization. We're here today to discuss the forward momentum we've made and to show if we unite under a strong front, we too can be powerful."

Yeah, the truly powerful don't skulk through the woods placing traps to maim children. Raven's wolf lunged in her chest, but she didn't betray an ounce of her rage.

"We will not be cowed by the unnatural." Greg's voice rang through the room, echoing to the fluorescent overheads. The crowd watched him in rapt awe, a familiar glaze sliding across their features. She'd seen the same far too many years ago. Mackey Kendricks hadn't begun ensnaring audiences with his Tribe abilities. He'd been able to command their crew through just his resonant baritone.

"The shifters might have their packs, and they might have abilities from the devil himself that allow them to turn into beasts. However, we stand here as humanity's defense. We have the numbers they could never dream of, and in that we shall claim our own power."

Raven swallowed, hard. Drew leaned back in his seat with an amused smirk and his arms crossed, as if the man's words washed over him. Granted, after the terrible things that monster had done, he'd probably heard worse. Jer didn't lunge forward and the blank look on his face didn't budge, but tension poured off him in droves. If he was still in a manic swing, she'd be worried — he tended to leap in on impulse during those. But after needing to pull him out of the house because his response time on texts had slowed to nothing, she knew he'd sunk into the opposite zone.

The man at the podium continued droning on, but Raven forced her attention away. If she kept listening to his drivel or paid attention to the heads in the crowd nodding at every filthy word, her claws would prick out, her eyes would flash and it would be game over. She switched her focus to the gorgeous man beside her.

Jer had gained more scruff after a few days holed up in his apartment, and his curls were the sort of unruly that made her fingers itch to run through them. With those stupidly long lashes, deep dimples and a mouth made for smiling, it was no wonder Red Rock's resident pretty boy had his pick of whatever women he wanted. The thought corroded her insides. She bit her lip and nudged him in the side.

The second his gaze transferred to her, Raven's breath hitched in her throat. His eyes flared to life when he looked her way. Jer made her feel as though she was worth something, which was the exact reason she'd avoided him all these years. Her skin itched at the intensity there, at the absolute, unwavering respect she never deserved even while the hollow in her chest longed for everything he offered.

The maelstrom in his gaze grew more powerful than the entirety of the room.

She licked her lips, unable to help herself. The amount of times she'd imagined him slamming her to the bed and sinking into her was criminal. He had coiled power in a lithe frame that was the polar opposite to Finn's heft, and it had always intrigued her to the point of obsession — to the point she'd masturbated in the shower too many times, alone with her shame.

Jer's mouth quirked, revealing his gorgeous dimples, and he reached over to run his thumb across the pulse point in her wrist, the sort of intimate touch that traveled straight between her thighs.

Lust rolled through in one languorous sweep. *Fuck.* This was the worst time and place.

Things between them had grown far too complex to give in to her impulses, even if she wanted him so badly she ached. After all, if they sealed the deal, the mating bond might snap into place, and he'd be saddled with someone who'd never be whole, no matter how hard she tried.

That doused her flames like nothing else.

Raven kept an ear out for any word of Ricketts Glen or actual plans from Greg Statham, but he continued working the crowd into a frenzy, peppering his words with more anti-shifter hate speech by the second. She tapped her foot against the ground, her ballet flats making a whisper. No one glanced their way, but even still, the weight of their differences slammed into her with every inflammatory word the crowd digested.

The fevered looks on their faces were those of cowards bowing to fear. She knew that intimately, because she'd been doing the same her entire life. Whether aligning with the Landsliders as an orphan looking for somewhere to belong, or relegating herself to someone she could never have for years to avoid confronting her feelings, Raven had sunk to her knees and worshipped at that altar.

"What can you do as individuals?" Greg's voice snapped her to attention. "Remain vigilant. Shifters walk among us every day. Keep silver on you at all times — you never know when one of the beasts will strike." Raven's jaw twitched at the mention of beasts. "Our organization grows stronger by the day, as more of us join the cause. We're working on significant strides to push human interest to the forefront, but we can't do it without you."

She perked to attention. If this was where he discussed sign-ups for sabotage, they could get the necessary evidence and nail the CHR to the cross they'd been constructing.

"Keep attending the meetings, and if we require your help, remember, this is a cause your life and safety depends on," he announced. Raven let a sigh slip. Not quite the easy avenue she'd been hoping for. "We've left out refreshments along the far wall, so please help yourselves to some coffee and donuts. Chat with your neighbors and make some new friends in the Coalition."

With that, he took a step away from the podium, making it clear his speech had ended. Frustration welled inside her. The meeting hadn't been the slam dunk she'd been hoping for, and if this just led to another dead end, she didn't have a clue how to proceed next. The guy in charge might've walked away from the podium, but he hadn't stepped off the stage. Instead, he met eyes with other folks in the audience and crooked his finger. *Curious.*

Chairs started screeching against linoleum. People rose from their seats, some making a mad dash that the meager boxes of coffee and donuts didn't deserve. Drew wandered over to the opposite side of the room, and Raven followed even as she kept watch on the stage. Jer slunk beside her, weaving around people with ease. A couple of bigger guys and a tough-looking chick hopped up on the stage to circle around the leader.

"So, what do you think those folks are plotting?" Jer murmured as they sidled next to Drew.

"I'm betting they're the people we need to be watching out for." Raven leaned against the wall, picking at her nails while she kept sneaking glances at the stage. With each look their way, she memorized more of their features, trying to capture a mental snapshot or at least gauge any indicator of who these folks might be. Jer traced one of the dozens of papers tacked to the wall with his fingertip, scrutinizing the fine print. He continued scouring the surface covered by help-ads and tear-off sheets for everything from contractors to pet sitters.

"I think each one of these folks has the potential for violence," Drew said, keeping his voice low while he scanned the audience. Most of the crowd clustered on the opposite side of the room, tearing the donuts to shreds like the beasts they so claimed to be afraid of.

"That's super helpful," Raven shot back, casting a glance at the overhead fluorescents. They needed to dive in and start talking to people, but she didn't know how to look these individuals in the face after watching the way they'd lapped up the venom Greg Statham spewed.

"Excuse me," Drew said, reaching out past her to an older woman, all grey curls and pastels, who walked by. "We're new to this organization, but after watching Mr. Statham on stage, I've got to admit, it has me fired up." He dripped charm without lifting a pinky finger, his grin melting the stern expression creasing the woman's forehead.

The older woman rested a hand on his arm. "I've been coming here since the beginning. He's always a delight to listen to, and he never fails at inspiring the crowd."

"How do we get more involved?" Drew asked. "I'd love to be out there doing something about this problem." The woman let out a raspy laugh, her eyes crinkling. It was hard to see the warmth when they spoke of actual harm of her kind.

"You keep coming to the meetings, and once in a while, they'll bring in new blood. Statham has a designated crew he works with of people who have proved themselves through the years. We're in good hands with them spearheading this fight."

The crew on stage. Raven bit back a curse. All they needed was a few names, but she had the feeling that if she tried hopping to the platform and striking up small talk, she'd get boxed out and draw suspicion.

Jer stopped pawing at the walls and glanced at the woman. "Is there some sort of ancillary support group we could start? It's hard to deal with the stress on a regular basis when we only have these once-a-month meetings to look forward to." Raven's mouth quirked at watching him lie. He dripped sincerity even though she could feel how he brimmed, as though he was one lit match away from explosion.

A guy around their age strolled by when he stopped in his tread. His stare glided over them, switching back and forth between her and Jer. Dark, wavy hair, thick eyebrows and an open expression—she recognized him, but from where? Even though he wore flannel and jeans today, she'd seen him in all black before, the bartender's uniform. Jarrod's Taproom—Steve worked at a bar in the next town over, one that many of the Red Rocks had patronized over the years.

Not once had she considered the humans on the staff might be choking down this Coalition bullshit.

Raven stepped back a pace. That was the least of their concerns at the moment.

Steve's eyebrows drew together, then clarity dawned in his eyes. He opened his mouth, but Raven had already tugged on Jer's arm. Drew was quick on the uptake, taking several strides forward.

"You're not supposed to be here." Steve's words echoed behind her. They needed to get out of this center five minutes ago.

She walked at a clipped pace, the open doors lying feet away. Steve knew. He knew they were shifters, infiltrating their human safe space. Any moment now, he'd raise the alarm.

The doors loomed, closer and closer.

"Shifters. There are shifters here," Steve said, soft at first. Until he repeated it at a yell.

Fuck.

He might as well have pulled a grenade in the middle of the room. Those words sparked everyone's attention, and in the span of seconds, the weight of their stares switched to them. Fifty people crowded in this place, carrying silver and pushed to the precipice of violence. They were so screwed.

"Run," Drew shouted, taking the initiative. He bolted for the door.

Raven followed, and Jer matched her stride as they raced with speed no human could attempt to compete with. The clicks sounding behind them promised said humans didn't feel the need to keep up. Not when they carried pistols with silver bullets.

One of the guards still stood by the door, and he stepped in the way, a blade glinting in his hand. Guaranteed, that was coated in silver too and would hurt like a bitch. Drew's claws pricked out as he barreled forward, making no attempts at stopping despite the obvious obstruction. Seconds away from collision, Drew slashed out with his claws before the knife could sting.

The man let out a hiss and lunged forward, missing Drew entirely. Jer reached out and shoved, sending the guy stumbling out of the way, but not before the blade swiped against his arm. Jer's jaw clenched but he didn't utter a word. Raven grabbed him by the hand and together, they continued to run toward the entrance.

Shouts that had rippled through the auditorium now rose to a roar. If they waited or hesitated for a second, they wouldn't make it out of this community center alive.

Whistling sounded from behind, but Raven couldn't stop to check. She couldn't dodge, duck or do anything but race to their salvation, the double doors across the vestibule. A flash of silver spat by her, and a second later, her arm seared. The pain caused her teeth to numb, but her legs churned on automatic as she ran. Her life depended on it.

Drew reached the doors first and smacked them open. His footsteps clapped across the pavement, across the empty parking lot that in minutes would be filled with the members from the CHR meeting. Raven choked down fresh air as she burst onto the asphalt, each step reverberating up her shins. *Can't stop. Can't look back.*

Squeaks of shoes, rough, angry shouts and another whistle came from behind them. Raven sent a silent prayer that whoever wielded the pistol couldn't shoot for shit. These fuckers weren't messing around.

Her gaze zeroed in on Jer's Jeep, and they hadn't made it halfway across the parking lot before Jer slipped his keys into his hand. Drew slammed into the side of his Cadillac, fumbling for the door latch.

Jer snagged the door to his Jeep open before landing in the seat and jamming the key into the ignition simultaneously. Raven's breath caught in her throat as she grabbed the handle, her palms so sweaty she lost her grip. All it took was one glance at the entrance of the community center to galvanize her.

All the faces that moments before had been friendly and unassuming were now purple with rage as at least a dozen members of the Coalition poured out of the front doors. Their hatred was the twisted metal of a train wreck, all blistering heat and tangled beams as solid lines mutated into something irrevocably changed.

Jer's engine roared to life while she hopped into the seat, slamming the door behind her. He jammed on the gas pedal and in seconds they were flying across the parking lot, tires squealing across the asphalt. He didn't slow, even as they hit the highway. Even as the angry faces faded behind them and even as they soared far past the range bullets could follow, Raven's pulse pounded in her ears like an army marching to war.

Chapter Twelve

When they returned from the community center, Jer expected to trundle back into his apartment and shut out the world. The adventure today had sucked the energy from him, and he couldn't force himself to care about the end results, though he should. Even if this problem should be his top priority as beta.

Instead, Raven directed them to Beaver Tavern to discuss strategy after the disgusting meeting they'd sat through. She brimmed with energy, her eyes wider than normal and her shoulders braced as if she were prepared to launch into a fight at a moment's notice. Her excitement felt a world away from the slog he drifted through. For the hundredth time today, he couldn't help considering stepping back from his position as beta.

The pack deserved someone better than him.

He pulled into the parking lot of Beaver Tavern, gravel crunching beneath his tires. Amber lights glowed from the window even in the afternoon, enhancing the creamy exterior with its oak accents. If he considered anywhere else home, it was here.

"You sure you want to head to your workplace on your day off?" he asked, tapping the edge of his steering wheel. Truth be told, he was searching for any excuse to get out of this.

Raven shot him a look. "Nice try, champ. If I have to meet with Drew, then you do too." She didn't say more, but the concern gleaming in her eyes said enough. Guilt washed over him—he was a piece of shit for making her worry, and he didn't deserve the concern in the first place. Not like that would stop her. Raven could be a hurricane force when she sank her claws into something.

Jer let out a sigh before he hopped out of his car. "No other way I'd rather spend my afternoon." The sarcasm was a flowing font at this point as he tapped the frame of his glasses.

Raven's lips quirked with her grin. She kept stride with him while they approached the entrance. Drew's Cadillac was already parked in the lot.

Meaning they'd be walking into a minefield.

An eerie hush spread through the bar when he opened the door. Not because the nighttime rush hadn't hit—even at midday, elders lingered around with a beer to chat with each other about pack problems. No, Drew had entered, and the scorch marks that he and the Landsliders had caused on the wall hadn't faded yet.

"Hey, folks," Raven called out, drawing the attention of the three elders by the bar and Candace and Lars who sat at one of the round tables. "I know you're not thrilled about this guy being here." She pointed to Drew, who slipped his hands in his pockets. Even though he affected nonchalance, Jer noticed the slight curl to his shoulders. "But we're working with him. Boss' orders, so get back to your drinks and pay us no mind."

Kyle nodded at Raven from behind the bar, and she lifted three fingers. By the time they'd settled at one of the round tables in the corner of the room, Kyle was carrying three pints of lager over. The glasses clinked as he set them on the table and quick-stepped away, not wanting to be anywhere near his former packmate. Not that Jer could blame him. Drew had been resourceful, but that didn't erase the sins of his past.

"Okay, so who here is tech savvy?" Drew asked, sinking into his seat and snagging a pint.

"Are you thinking of tracking those guys down via social media? All we have is the leader's name," Raven said, sinking into work mode as though she'd never left it.

Jer grabbed a pint and took a sip, foam lingering on his lips. When he licked it away, Raven's glance scorched into him, the heat evident in her gaze. Despite the haze he'd been wandering through, that brought him straight to the present. Lust rolled through him. He wanted her stripped down in his bed, that soft-as-silk skin against his until he lost himself in the sensations.

He needed to stop indulging in fantasies that would never be. Raven might find him temporarily thrilling and might even entertain the idea of them being together, but no one wanted to tether themselves to his mess for the long haul.

Jer lifted his lager and took a longer sip before reaching into his pocket and pulling out the papers he'd snagged.

"No need to go down a social media rabbit hole," he said, spreading the papers across the table between them. "One of Statham's inner circle happens to be a well-known contractor in the area." He'd noticed the guy's picture on one of the pages at the community center and recognized the face as the same man standing on stage. *Bastard even left helpful tear-offs with his phone number.*

Raven scanned over the papers in front of her, running a thumb across them. "Jer, you're a genius. We sat there babbling away to the racist old bitch while you were getting the real work done."

He shrugged, her praise making him uncomfortable. The papers had been smack in front of him on the wall, and he had wanted the excursion over as fast as possible. "Just means we can cut to the quick and stalk him to his next location. Guaranteed, we'll be able to catch him in the act of setting up more traps or whatever else they have planned."

Drew chugged his beer, and the glass hit the table with a thump. "It's a direction, so I'll take it." He snapped the paper with the name and number off the table. "I'll take first shift of trailing this asshole. One of you can take the overnight, then tomorrow morning. We'll keep cycling until we find some proof to nail the Coalition of Human Rights with."

He tipped his fingers in their direction, shoved the paper into his pocket and sauntered off to the door.

"Well, that was the fastest meeting I've ever dealt with," Raven said, taking a swig of her beer.

Jer had already polished off half his pint in the time they'd been talking, so he lifted it to his lips and drank more. He'd spent far too long out, and he and his self-loathing had a date with his apartment and a heavier bottle of liquor.

"Since Drew's ditched, why don't I get you back to your car? I can take the overnight shift, but I'll have to get some shut-eye first." He finished his pint and pushed it over with Drew's empty.

Raven's eyes softened and she traced her fingertip along the rim of her pint. "Yeah, sounds like a plan." Disappointment rang clear in her voice, but for the life of him, he couldn't imagine why. He was trash at conversation when he felt like this, and they still hadn't discussed anything regarding the mating bond. He might not push, but each day they avoided it scraped away at his tenuous self-esteem. Raven began to tug out her wallet, but Jer placed his hand over hers.

"I've got this," he said. "Drew already skipped the bill, and you've covered me for so many beers here."

Raven bit her lip, and damn it if that didn't make him want to claim her gorgeous mouth. Every moment they spent together turned into an agony of longing and restraint. He left the cash out and rose from his seat before he did or said anything stupid. Raven downed the rest of her beer in a gulp before she headed out after him, matching his quickened pace. No one paid them any mind now that Drew had left, but he couldn't help feeling like they were all watching with their own opinions.

Once he emerged outside, the late-afternoon sunlight beamed onto his skin. He hadn't made it five paces past the door before turning to Raven. The predatory look in her eyes stopped him still.

She slunk up to him and wrapped her arms around his neck. His arms prickled with the awareness of the contact between them, of the fact that they stood in front of Beaver Tavern and how this felt like a declaration. Hope cracked him wide open. It was every brilliant book he'd read and every run through Ricketts Glen on a spring morning. It was also silver running across his back, a burning, agonizing pain he'd never been able to divorce from his feelings for Raven.

She pressed her lips to his, and the simple act galvanized him to action like nothing else. He wrapped his hands around her waist, and together they stumbled a few paces. Her back thudded against the cream wall. He hadn't stopped kissing her once, tasting the ale on her lips and surrendering to the first spark of life he'd felt in days. He wove his fingers through her thick hair and fisted it tight, feeling the smooth silk he'd always imagined. He tightened his other hand around her waist, sinking his fingers into her hip.

Raven let out a low moan deep in her throat as their lips met again and again. The sound caused his length to stiffen in a heartbeat, and he was ready to take her right there. He chased the kiss like a rainbow, grasping for the hope, the bliss, all while self-loathing threatened to crash in and suffocate him. Each breath between them heated with desire, and he wanted to keep Raven's arms twined around his neck forever.

Except he'd only ever be a replacement.

Jer stepped away, destroying the splash of color across his monochrome landscape. Raven blinked and dropped her arms off his shoulders in surprise. She tilted her head to the side.

"This mating bond isn't something to play around with, Rae," he said, unable to keep the self-loathing from his voice.

"Who says I'm playing?" she shot back, a fire burning in her gaze.

His chest tightened, the pain throbbing through him so hard he could barely breathe. He'd suffer a thousand wounds compared to the way this sliced. "Just a week ago you ran from my kiss, and ever since the mating bond emerged, we haven't said a single word about it."

She opened her mouth, and God, he wanted her to prove him wrong. He needed the words to pour out of her mouth, that she did want to be mated to him. That she wanted this as badly as he did, even if it was a terrible idea and even if it could never last. But nothing happened. She said nothing.

"I'm never going to be Finn," Jer said. Even as the words came from him, he knew they were the wrong ones.

Her forehead creased, and she slammed a fist against the wall behind her. "Fuck you, Jer. Maybe it didn't occur to you, but I never wanted anyone but you. I'll grab my car on my own." Before he could say anything or even register the impact of her words, she strode off toward the surrounding woods.

A sharp breath escaped his throat, slicing like shards of glass.

He'd fucked it up again. She'd been trying to tell him the one way she could and he'd pushed her away.

Chapter Thirteen

The words had stuck in her mouth.

Everything Raven had wanted to say to Jer and all the feelings and hopes she'd bottled up remained corked. Even when it came to the talk with Sierra she needed to have, the words had fled her. So much for being brave. She gripped her steering wheel tighter as she soared down the highway. Her hair whipped around in the infiltrating cooler breezes, which were all crisp leaves and amber. Heat stung her eyes, but she couldn't go back now, not while her heart raged and venom dripped from her lips.

So, instead, she followed a hunch.

She'd burned a lot of the energy running to Jer's apartment from Beaver Tavern, but her wolf needed to break free anyway. Too long without shifting and a constant strain pulled at her chest, as if she'd burst. The late-afternoon sun cast citrine beams down, sparkling through the large trees that loomed on either side.

Even with the passing hours, she could still feel the ghost of their kiss on her lips, a residual pulse of the thrill that had raced through her. When he'd pushed her against the wall, his hot mouth devouring hers, she'd thought she'd expire on the spot from the intense sensations. And all too fast, it had ended. The hurt flashing in his eyes and the bitterness in his voice when he'd compared himself to Finn lingered even longer.

Raven made a turn down one of the winding roads that led deeper into the woods, large patches of shade falling across the pavement. Raven had shared thousands of kisses with Finn over the years and gone to his bed hundreds of times, and while their chemistry hadn't been explosive, there had been a steady warmth there that they'd both clung to for a long time.

However, the handful of kisses she'd shared with Jer were the most memorable ones of her life.

When she was with him, she wasn't Raven the bartender, the Red Rock pack member or any of the myriad masks she'd worn over the years. With Jer, she found herself, someone she'd forgotten even existed. And that thrilled and terrified her all in the same breath.

All she'd needed to do was tell him.

Instead, she had remained silent and hurt him. Again. Raven pumped on the gas as she hurtled down the winding back roads, ones that featured overgrown trees bowing over with long, spindly branches on either side. Her Civic rolled over larger stones at this point while she traversed up a narrow offshoot, and an errant branch scratched against her hood. It wasn't as if she hadn't accumulated plenty of dents in her day.

Her skin prickled when the house at the end of the path came into view. No cars were parked in the lot, but even approaching this place made her nervous. She hadn't been to Joe Ganzorig's house when he'd lived there as their resident shaman, and after finding out that the bastard did work for the Landsliders? She couldn't pass up the opportunity to see if any lingering evidence might help them in their fight against the CHR. If there happened to be any of Jer's bipolar medicine, she'd snatch that as well.

The house looked abandoned and it had barely been a month.

Faded chalk symbols graced the front door and ivy tangled around the railings of the front porch. Some of the grasses had started fading with the autumn chill, but the heartier plants ran rampant to crowd the house, as if it had emerged from the forest itself. She crept up to the entrance, careful to avoid the soft spots in the wooden steps leading to the door. Raven tested the doorknob — it wasn't locked.

She pushed the door open without a sound and peered through the gap. A musty smell lingered in the air, but the house looked like the total opposite of the woodsy exterior. With cream carpeting, black cabinetry and silver fixtures, this place offered a slice of modern style she wasn't used to. She took one step in then braved another. Silence lingered in the room, bolstering her confidence.

Raven crept into the kitchen and stopped still. Her nose wrinkled and her gaze narrowed at the half-full coffeepot on the counter. That was fresh. She wandered over to the sink where an empty cup, a plate and a couple of used utensils were collected, waiting for a wash.

Sierra had said Ganzorig's house remained empty, uninhabited, but here lay clear signs of someone squatting. Another faint, familiar scent lingered in the house, but she had trouble pinpointing it amidst all the other foreign ones.

She wandered past the kitchen, over to what had once been the shaman's living room. An uncomfortable-looking black couch sprawled out over the cream carpeting against the far wall and several padded chairs were stationed in front of a glass surface coffee table. Folders, papers and a laptop rested on the table and Raven's pulse quickened as she approached. The answer lingered in the back of her mind, the scent she couldn't put her finger on.

One look into the contents of the stacked papers clarified things.

Case documents. Pack bylaws. The history of Ricketts Glen.

Christian was staying here.

Raven backed away several paces from the coffee table, as though her presence might imprint. Granted, her scent already had. A shifter like him would be able to pick out the hint of her in the air. Still, this offered a rare opportunity to dig for dirt against the CHR. She cast a glance out of the window — her car remained the only one in the lot. She gritted her teeth and strode to the stack of papers.

Time to investigate.

* * * *

Night had fallen by the time she rolled up to Beaver Tavern, after an afternoon spent investigating Ganzorig's cabin and cleaning herself up after a crowded couple of days. She hadn't found Jer's meds, but she'd slipped out a couple of papers that looked like leads and sprayed Ganzorig's old air freshener through the house in hopes she could mask her scent.

She had stalking duty tomorrow morning before a full day's shift at the bar. For now, she'd sit on the other side of the counter and down a pint of ale. Ever since Christian had arrived at her doorstep, she didn't feel comfortable spending too much time at home.

She strode to the front door, swinging her lanyard with her keys round and round. Her heart thudded in her ears as she approached, needing Jer to be there, all while praying he wasn't. At this point, he had probably taken over for Drew anyway. As she stepped inside, the familiar murmur of conversation crashed over her, along with the comforting scents of pine and ale. Kyle still manned the taps, busy behind the bar since Beaver Tavern was in full swing at this point.

She tipped her head in a nod to Gene and Derek, who sat together at a round table, hands wrapped around their pints. Doreen and Jace had claimed a table in the back with their daughter Christine as well as Freddie and Van, other pups in the pack. Where once she might've only caught the scent of wolves, of other Red Rocks, now the scent of the mountain lions had become regular with Kyle behind the bar and because more of the Silver Springs pack made this their regular watering hole.

Raven settled at one of the few empty stools along the bar and waited for Kyle to swing her way.

Lana sat beside her, staring into an amber glass of what had to be a Jack and ginger. The woman was poised elegance with her long legs hanging on either side of the stool and her shoulders curved in a slump. After what had happened to her husband Greg, she'd become a regular at Beaver Tavern, haunting the bar stools night after night.

Kyle swung Raven's way at last, bringing her a pint of ale.

"You're a gem," she said, wrapping her hands around the glass as a weight shifted off her shoulders. She and Kyle might not have the years of rapport she'd had with Seamus, but he had fast become a fixture in this bar.

"So, you and Streaky?" he said, the insinuating tone spelling it out.

Because of course he'd piece the puzzle together. "I don't know why everyone insists on calling him that," Raven deflected, taking a quick sip of her ale.

Kyle arched an eyebrow. "Probably because he's already slept with half of the singles in my pack, and we're still new to working together. Didn't think you were interested in being a part of his list."

The embers inside her flared to life.

"Jer's a whole lot more than the pack slut, and I'm sick of hearing about it," Raven snapped at him. "He's the Red Rock beta because not only is he intelligent as hell, he's one of the most dedicated people I've ever met."

Kyle lifted his hands. "I wasn't questioning his character. We all just like to give him shit for his flings."

"You've never been just a fling for him though, have you?" Lana asked, her calm voice tentative as she glanced up from her drink, fixing her gaze on Raven.

Raven's throat dried. She was pinned by the intensity in the woman's green eyes. She spun through a roulette of a thousand and one excuses, but when she opened her mouth, all that came out was, "No."

Kyle ran a hand through his short-trimmed hair. "Well, fuck me, I'm way out of my pay grade here." He tipped two fingers in a lazy salute. "Let me know when you need a fill-up, doll."

Raven forced a grin at him as he stepped away a hint faster than normal.

"Sorry for the intrusion," Lana murmured, lifting her drink and taking a sip. "You can tell me to fuck off for not minding my own business. I don't have a lot going on these days, and I read people way too easily."

Raven shook her head, a tentative grin rising to her own lips. As much as the woman had driven straight to the truth with her, she couldn't help but admire her candor, even if it was a bit unnerving. If she could be honest like that, maybe she wouldn't be in the current mess she was drowning in.

"How'd you piece it together?" she asked, rubbing her thumb against the bits of condensation along the side of the glass.

Lana's mouth twisted in a soft smile, even if her green eyes had carried the weight of grief ever since the bombing when Greg had died. Raven thanked the Great Spirits that Lana hadn't been in the bar earlier while they'd been working with Drew.

"Even when his arm's around another woman or he's chatting up a date here, his gaze is always on you. And your longing looks from the other side of the bar might've been subtler, but like I said, I can't help but pick up on that sort of thing."

Raven swallowed. Her heart squeezed so tight she couldn't breathe. The truth lay brazen in the air, waiting to be grasped and devoured, and even so, she hesitated. The patterns she'd developed over the years had grown comfortable, the pain as much a part of her as the scars on her skin. Now, she stood on the precipice where she might be able to push past the longing that sliced shards into her chest, and she felt crazy for questioning it.

"What are you, part-shaman?" Raven joked, even as the truth settled across her skin, that Jer had shared the same longing and the same pain all these years.

Lana's lips twisted in a knowing smile. "Worse. Massage therapist."

Raven couldn't help the snort that escaped her. She tipped back the lager, enjoying the crisp taste on her tongue, which settled inside her a little like resolve.

"Well, I guess I should thank you," she said. "You managed to find the words I've been searching for."

Lana shrugged while her gaze traced the surface of her drink again. "No need for thanks. It's a reflex of mine. It doesn't do as much good as you'd think."

Raven nodded. She didn't offer to talk about it, because the enormity of the grief in Lana's eyes threatened to swallow her alive. The woman didn't need to give her any warnings, because she was a walking, talking cautionary tale of the devastation falling in love could bring.

As much as the thought terrified her, for the first time it didn't threaten her nearly as much as the idea of never trying, of staying in this painful stasis she'd been trapped in for far too long.

Raven tipped her glass in the direction of Lana's, clinking them together. "I'll drink to that. Hope you don't mind a drinking buddy for tonight."

"I'd like that." Lana's features softened and she took a sip.

Raven did the same. She would break the glass barrier she'd hidden behind for so long and step free.

Tomorrow, she would talk to Jer.

Chapter Fourteen

Even though Jer had caught a few hours of shut-eye, it wasn't enough.

Hell, at this point, a week of straight sleep wouldn't be enough.

Drew had texted him the meet-up location, though, and sheer will alone and a note of urgency in the message was the reason he was flying down the highway at this late hour. He left the windows rolled down, the autumn air bracing as it smacked him in the face, batting his curls around. His chest felt hollowed after the way he'd left things with Rae, but every time he'd picked up his phone to shoot her a text, he'd written it out only to delete it again and again.

She wouldn't want to hear from him, not after he'd flung her old relationship with Finn in her face. Jer pushed harder on the gas, flooring across the asphalt. A canopy of crystalline stars spread out overhead, cold and unforgiving in their clarity. He'd already crossed a couple of towns over, heading into territory more inhabited by humans than shifters. All this time, he'd thought that like stuck with like out of ease and familiarity, not due to genuine fear, but the Coalition meeting had reeked of it.

After he'd witnessed the numbers the anti-shifter cause had collected, the gravity of their situation had crashed in on him. Finding some form of leverage wasn't just about keeping Ricketts Glen anymore. They needed proof to drag the human authorities into this mess, because the Coalition of Human Rights had proved they didn't care about shifter lives. He should be spending every waking hour obsessing over solutions, and yet he could barely force himself to trudge through the day.

Down the highway, the first buildings of a small town rose into view.

Jer pulled in front of the rinky-dink hardware store Drew had specified. The lights were out since this late hour was well after closing time, and a dented metal sign for *Greg's Hardware* graced the front, a log façade that came off a bit hokey. A beat-up red pickup trick sat in the parking lot, alongside an all-too-familiar Caddy. The plan had been to track Larry the contractor without attracting attention, but if Drew had tried to stealth up on the guy here, the mountain lion had missed the mark.

He slipped out of his car, careful to stay quiet. With the chill of autumn that swept through the region, the cicadas no longer trilled at all hours of the night, leaving a resonant hush . His wolf lunged in his chest. He hadn't run on all fours in a couple of days, and the longer between those times, the more a thread tightened within him. Instead of indulging, he crept forward, watching the shadows.

Is this a trap?

Jer slunk around the side of the building, hearing the whistle of the wind through the branches. Shadows stretched from the back, the long, jagged things slicing across the beaten earth and rickety chain-link fence.

He peered around the corner.

"Boo," a voice came from beside him.

Jer's claws were out and speeding toward the intruder right when a familiar scent hit him. He whipped in the direction of the sound to spot the asshole he searched for. His claws stopped an inch from Drew's neck, but the guy hadn't budged, watching him with a lazy smirk on his face.

"Maybe not the best idea," Jer snapped as he retracted his claws and stepped back a pace.

"I was looking for a little thrill," Drew responded, hooking his thumbs into his belt loops. "Watching this asshole make stops and go shopping all day has been so boring I want to stab out my own eyes."

"And where is this asshole now?" The weariness threatened to overwhelm him, not from lack of sleep but the deadening numbness he faced at attempting anything beyond sheer existence.

"Back in his home a mile from here, though the light was left on, so I'm not sure he's asleep," Drew said, rocking back and forth on his heels. "I was debating on just calling you and continuing the shift because it's been a snoozefest, but I need you to check in on him."

Jer cast a glance around, checking their perimeter yet again. His skin prickled with awareness, the predator side of him on the alert. "And what will you be doing?"

"Our good friend Larry met with one of the other inner circle idiots earlier on one of his hardware stops. I broke into the guy's car and stole his contact information while he hung around inside chatting, so we've got two leads to follow." Drew shrugged. "I'm hopped up on coffee and could use the distraction, so I'm willing to keep going if you can trail Larry-boy."

"That's what I planned on doing," Jer said, slipping a hand into his pocket and running a thumb over the case of his phone. "It'll just be watching this guy sleep all night."

Drew didn't say anything at first, a sharpness dwelling in his gaze. But he nodded and offered another of the broad grins he faked as often as Jer. "Yeah, have fun. I shot you a text with his address, so call me if anything happens." With that, the mountain lion shifter slunk away as quietly as he'd arrived.

Jer heaved a sigh and headed toward his Jeep. Alone with his thoughts was the worst place he could be right now, but he didn't have much of a choice. Going home and back to sleep wasn't an option when these assholes had put his pack in danger. He hopped into his car, glancing at the stack of books he'd brought with him, hefty hardbacks of the pack law he needed to sort through. A week ago, he'd have been able to read through the entire book in one night, but every time he stared at the words now, they blurred before his eyes.

Drew had already pulled out of the parking lot, and Jer checked the texted address before following suit. He kept his music on low, a mix of acoustic bluegrass and rockabilly he usually enjoyed. Nothing sparked his synapses as of late, though. He pumped the gas to accelerate, flying down the highway in the direction of Larry's place. The idea of sitting in one spot with minimal distraction while he watched a guy's house was tantamount to torture.

All too fast, side streets cropped up, winding paths of residential which carved into the horde of greenery that dominated this part of the state. Jer turned onto the street and switched his lights off, moving at a crawl as he clung to the side of the road. This small road held at least six houses, but most of them were dark, except for one.

Bingo.

Jer slid closer to the house, stopping in front of the neighbor's, and turned his engine off. From this vantage point, he could pick out the pale front door and a large portion of the sprawling back yard, his enhanced wolf senses a benefit. He'd be able to catch if the guy tried sneaking out.

He settled into his seat and snagged one of the books from the pile, barely able to identify the text, despite the illumination his phone cast over the pages. *Time to watch and wait.*

* * * *

Two hours into surveillance, and Jer's brain had taken him on a lovely tour of all the ways he'd fucked up since Sierra had nominated him pack beta. His skin crawled and his chest ached as though someone had carved out his heart long ago. The only way this night could get better was if Raven showed up to tell him she'd found a new Finn replacement and that he could go die in a ditch.

The damned light beaming from the house flicked off. *Great, now the bastard's going to bed.*

He stretched his legs out and stared harder at the house, as if he could summon the man out of his place by will alone.

The front door swung open. Jer sat up fast, fumbling for his keys. Within seconds, a shadow-swathed figure strode for the sedan in the lot and a moment later, the headlights flicked on. The car peeled out of the driveway, and Jer barely had the time to duck before the sedan zoomed past him.

He jammed the keys into the ignition and followed. Anyone heading out at three in the morning either planned on committing sins and transgressions in the dark, or they were roaming around to stop the wrongdoers. Jer kept his lights off as he traced the guy down the small side road. With how few neighbors he had, headlights would make it too clear he had a tail.

The moment the guy turned onto the highway, Jer gave him some lead time before flicking on his beams and sliding onto the asphalt behind him. After a few minutes on the road with no stops and detours down any side streets, Jer guessed what direction they were heading in, one he'd traveled himself too many times to count. *Ricketts Glen.*

His heart pounded in his chest and sweat was already pricking his palms. He should call Drew to give him the heads-up, but he couldn't afford the distraction. He couldn't afford to lose their one lead.

The familiar wooden sign rose into view within minutes, and, as expected, Larry turned onto the narrow road leading to Ricketts Glen's parking lot. Anger thudded a dull beat in Jer's chest. After the hatred he'd witnessed at the Coalition meeting and after Daria had gotten caught in one of their silver traps, he didn't trust those assholes for a moment on his land.

No matter what the humans tried to claim, this was Red Rock territory. They'd bled here in fights, run through the deep forest as pups and defended this place from intruders of all sorts. Humans just provided a different threat. If they wanted to play with the law, he'd do his damndest to outmaneuver them there as well.

Jer gripped tight to the steering wheel, flipping his lights off before he followed through the entrance. He'd prefer to be stalking this guy in his wolf form, but he needed to be able to take pictures for proof if the asshole tried to set more traps up. By the time he rolled up to the parking lot, the guy's sedan was pulled into a spot, the lights flipped off. Apparently, he'd set out faster than anticipated.

Jer pulled into a spot and turned off his engine. A moment later, he walked across the parking lot toward Larry's sedan. His nose tingled as he caught the scent — not as strong as he'd experience in his wolf form, but shifters still possessed stronger than average senses even on two feet.

He stalked off to the woods, following the faint scent of the human contractor. It didn't take his wolf form to track the guy, since he moved with the finesse of a buffalo stampede. The moment Jer's boots sank into the earth, he caught sight of snapped twigs and footprints carving through the thicker woods, away from the paths visitors traveled. Only shifters or idiots dared to head deeper. The former could find their way out in a heartbeat, while the latter got hopelessly lost in the acres of wild.

The crashing waterfalls buzzed in the distance, but Larry didn't seem to be tromping in that direction. Instead, the footprints took him deeper into the woods. Jer wove around bushes with thorny branches, trying to keep his steps light while he navigated the sea of crunchy, decaying leaves that had fallen. The moon barely infiltrated here, the darkness so thick he could taste it. This was what he'd been wading through day after day.

Ahead, Jer caught the shift of a shadow weaving past the trees at a slow pace. He recognized the height as Larry, but the man wore an overstuffed backpack and moved even slower than the average human.

Larry stopped at a clearing ahead and let his backpack slump to the ground. He pulled something from it and set to work, but Jer hid too far away to get a good shot. Jer crept forward, his hackles rising as he measured each step. Whatever the guy had pulled out from his backpack made his nose itch. It wasn't silver — that, he could identify on the spot, which meant these weren't more traps.

Sweat slicked his palm as he clutched his phone tighter, waiting to get close enough to snap a picture. He edged nearer to a large oak, mere feet away from the clearing where Larry was working. Jer peered out from the edge of the massive trunk, even his own breath sounding too loud in his ears.

Larry hunched over some circular contraption while he dug into the earth with a spade. Jer homed in on the circle, able to distinguish more details from his current vantage point. Unease rolled through him, though he wasn't certain why. He lifted his phone and snapped a couple of shots as fast as he could. Turning back out of view behind the massive tree, Jer checked the pictures he'd taken, playing with the contrast and zooming in on the shot.

Oh, fuck.

He'd seen the Coalition's seriousness firsthand, and he'd witnessed the underhanded lengths the Landsliders would go to, but not this. Never this.

The bastard was setting up landmines.

"Hey, Larry," a voice called out from his right. Two figures approached from the other side of the forest, heading toward the clearing. "We need to be setting these up together. Wouldn't want a wrong step then boom." The laugh that followed from Larry coated Jer with an oily, impenetrable loathing.

They joked.

They set up bombs to harm the innocent shifters and children who raced through these woods, and they *joked*.

The men sauntered closer and closer, their footsteps echoing as they made their way over. Larry called out something to them, and they laughed in turn, tossing out more casual jokes in the wake of the horrors they'd committed. The thread of moonlight filtering through the heavy overhead boughs glinted across the shotguns they bore. Guaranteed, they were packing silver bullets. If he got caught here, not only did they outnumber him, but they wielded the one thing that could destroy him in a single shot.

Jer sank to a crouch. Sweat broke out across his forehead and his heart pounded so loudly it was a miracle the men didn't hear him. He needed to move faster and quieter than any human.

He glanced at the oak tree he was squatting behind. Thick roots sprawled out in either direction, creating divots and holes along the earth. Jer turned his phone on silent before slipping it face down into a small hole beneath one of the massive roots. He couldn't risk losing the pictures, and the Find My Phone app was a lifesaver. Jer then strode several paces forward, pausing at each one to check back. The conversation flowed around the guys, unceasing.

When he'd moved far enough away, he slipped behind another tree and tugged off his boots, then his pants and shirt, moving as quietly and quickly as possible.

A raccoon brushed past him, chittering as it burrowed through more bushes. It didn't bother disguising the sound.

"What was that?" Larry called out. Jer didn't need to look to know they stared in his direction.

He didn't hesitate. The shift overtook him with the effortlessness of a bird taking flight. His claws pricked out and his body began to mutate, hair transitioning to fur that sprouted across his body. He lowered to the ground on all fours and stretched out, his wolf exultant to be freed. In this form, the scents were crisper and the darkness no longer gave him pause. All the details that hadn't been clear in his human eyes grew crystalline.

Boots crunched over fallen leaves, heading this way.

Jer gripped his keys between his teeth before he launched in the direction of the parking lot. Sierra needed to know about this at once.

Chapter Fifteen

By the end of Raven's shift at Beaver Tavern, she was ready to go home and collapse. Sierra had sounded the alarm first thing in the morning, sending most of the pack out to Ricketts Glen to the spot where Jer had caught the Coalition members planting landmines. Everyone had raged, and one dropped match into the tense air would've ignited tempers into fights.

A couple of the pack elders and Jace had had military experience, so they'd been the leads in disarming the landmines those fuckers had placed in the ground. Jer had been holed up for the rest of the day once he'd nabbed his phone and the incriminating photos, and he'd set to the task of constructing their case to shut down the Coalition of Human Rights, therefore nullifying any of their claims. After an intense day of extracting landmines from their own territory, the Red Rock pack had assembled at Beaver Tavern en masse demanding beer, so she'd been beyond busy.

Raven pulled up to her apartment. At this point, she was so tired she didn't plan on even staying up another hour to unwind with a movie but just crash into bed. She spilled out of her car, dragging her unwilling limbs up the steps to her place. Her chest burned with a quiet rage from the morning, but she couldn't say their actions surprised her. After having gone to a Coalition meeting and watched the fear rife in their gazes at the thought that they, a trio of shifters, had infiltrated the human safe space, of course the zealots had resorted to an extreme.

She tugged out her keys and stumbled to her door. Then she froze.

A single tiger lily rested on her doorstep.

Raven had hit the ground on her knees before she grew aware of any conscious movement. Numbness swept through her like novocain. She reached forward and picked up the bloom, not even feeling the stem between her fingers. Instead of the fragrance of lilies she now despised, a worse scent wafted her way. Cloves.

Bile rose in her throat. *No.* No, she couldn't go there.

Her closed door loomed in front of her like a threat. The lock didn't make her safe, not when he roamed out there. Not when Christian remained in town.

A growl ripped from her throat, one that started deep within her. The tiger lily crumpled in her fist as she squeezed, orange petals fluttering to the ground.

Christian must've done this. He has to have. The other option wasn't one she could breach, not now, not ever. She rose on unsteady legs like some newborn fawn, but by the time she reached the bottom of her steps, she'd steadied to a march. Christian would pay for this. He'd been a thorn in her paw ever since he'd arrived in town, shoving her past in her face with no care that she'd spent the past decade running from it.

Someone needed to stop him. She alone knew where he was camped out, so she'd do the honors.

She plunked down in her Honda again, firing her girl to life even though the feeling hadn't returned to her extremities. Her body trembled as though she'd downed sixteen cups of coffee. Within minutes, she'd pulled out of her lot, unable to glance at her apartment in case she was wrong. His presence throbbed in the back of her mind like a tumor, always.

Raven raced across the highway, her car moving at top speed. The sight of the tiger lily on her doorstep had given her a second wind, filling her with so much adrenaline that she choked on it. Her fingertips tapped on the edge of her steering wheel, and she cranked up the heavy guitars and melodic death metal pouring through her speakers. Even the intensity of all the sound, enough that the bass reverberated through the car, couldn't drown the buzzing in her head.

Enough. She was done being terrorized by a ghost of her past. She refused to let Christian keep harassing her and making her afraid to stay in her own home. Raven clutched the raw pulse of anger with all her might, because she teetered on the edge of a cliff, one she might not climb back up this time.

Her Honda tore across the asphalt while she zoomed closer and closer to the turnoff to Ganzorig's house. If Christian was lurking around here and was working with the Coalition, he could cause problems outside of her territory. He might've held a place of power at Mackey's side when she was thirteen, but they'd both grown up. She could fight him now.

She turned onto the narrow side road leading through the deeper woods, to Ganzorig's old home. The skeletal limbs hovered above her car like grasping hands. The crisp air swept in through her open window and she turned down her music, feeling the oppressive hush of the surrounding forest. Her tires crunched on the uneven stones, the heft of her car bouncing up and down as she rattled her way up the path.

Each wisp of wind whispered danger, but Raven gritted her teeth and kept driving forward. She wouldn't be able to sleep in her own home tonight after what he'd done. Out of everyone, Christian knew what that would do to her, yet he continued to taunt and torture her with the memories. Goosebumps prickled across her skin as she crept closer to the house, farther up the winding path and deeper into the woods.

Ganzorig's house stood at the end of the trail, looking entirely different under a night sky. The pale paint streaks on the door almost glowed in the moonlight, and the wild tangle of overgrown plants lent the space a forbidding look, all curling vines and tall grasses. The windows beamed with soft amber light. Christian was home. *Good.* She pulled up in front of the house and clenched her keys like a weapon as she headed for the door.

She stepped onto the front porch step and as it creaked under her boot, she stopped. *What am I doing?* Raven sucked in a shaky breath. A civilized conversation telling him to fuck off. That was why she'd arrived. Because she was tired of not feeling safe in her own apartment.

Before she could take another step forward, the door swung open.

Christian leaned in the frame, a lazy grin gracing his face. His sweep of inky hair and dark eyes melded with the surrounding shadows, and his alabaster skin gave him an almost ghostly hue at this time of night. Fitting. He and the other Landsliders had haunted her ever since she'd left.

"Well now, what did I do to deserve a late-night visit from Raven Takahashi?" he drawled, crossing his arms. The suggestion in his voice made her stomach churn, but it also ignited her anger anew.

"You know why I'm here, Christian," she responded, her voice so acidic it could corrode metal. Her claws had already pricked out at the mere sight of him. The reminders from her past brought her there as though she'd never left. In a way, she hadn't.

"Let's pretend I don't." His dark hair shifted to cover his forehead while he readjusted his stance. "Illuminate me as to why you're marching up to my temporary abode and looking like you're ready to light it on fire. I've done nothing but attempt to strike up conversation with a former friend. As for my job, I can't help if it's a conflict of interest for your pack."

"Is that how you sleep at night?" Raven spat back. Everything inside her coiled tight, one touch, one word away from explosion. "Pretending you're just doing your job? Like your hands aren't washed in blood after years of working for a monster?"

"Now, now," he said, tapping one of his long fingers against his arm. "I don't think you're in any position to sling judgment. I might have stained my hands a few times, but you've done far, far worse with that so-called monster. I, personally, think he's the only one with the right idea."

Rage blanked out her vision, numbing her fingers and toes in the process.

Fuck him. He has no right. No right to say those things to me. Not after...

She'd taken steps toward him before she'd even realized it. Her hand balled into a fist and her claws pierced her palm.

"Leave town," she said, a surprising calm resonant in her tone. "We've got the evidence to bury your case, and if you don't stop poking your nose around in Red Rock business, we're going to bury you too."

"Come on now, Tigerlily. Would you threaten me? I used to be your best friend." Christian watched her with a brisk look in his eyes divorced from humanity. She should've known all those years ago he was a soulless bastard, but she'd been young and stupid. She'd wanted a home and a friend so badly she'd let herself get duped.

Her throat squeezed tight. She hadn't learned the true meaning of friendship until she'd met Finn and Jer. She hadn't found her true family until she'd joined the Red Rock pack. Heat pricked at her eyes as the wave of hopelessness mounted in her, as if the years dissolved before her eyes.

"You're not capable of caring, Christian," Raven responded. "You're so similar to him it makes me sick."

His gaze darkened, and even though she almost missed the movement, his fingers tightened for a second. "I wanted to be him back then, you know? He had everything I ever wanted. Respect, loyalty and you."

Raven shook her head. Her hands bled from the cuts her claws had left, but she couldn't unclench her fists if she tried. The humming in her head increased to the point she couldn't hear anything else. Desire turned Christian's eyes molten, as if she couldn't be more disgusted by him.

"Get the *hell* out of my territory, Christian Denzel," Raven growled, an unrepentant rage ripping from her like wildfire. Her shoulders trembled and her body shook, but whether from anger or terror, she couldn't discern. "You won't be showing up at my bar any more. You won't be showing up at my apartment and leaving tiger lilies. The single one was a sick touch, you bastard."

His forehead creased at the mention. Had she been wrong? Before she could ask him, he took a step toward her until a foot lay between them. The scent of him, the disgusting rank of coyote, made her wolf bare her teeth. She was a second away from shifting and tearing out his throat.

"All those years, I wanted you," he murmured, the sound of his voice a sandpaper scrape across her skin. "But back then, I couldn't touch you. Not while you were his. But now? You're here at my doorstep, and it feels a little bit like fate."

"Go fuck yourself, Christian." Before she could stop herself, she spat in his face.

He blinked at her before reaching up to wipe the liquid from his cheek, the movement as controlled as his expression. "This is an opportunity I won't let go to waste."

The heady lust in his gaze gave his intention away.

Raven's blood turned to ice.

Not again.

Never again.

She tensed, ready to rear back and punch him, when his arm shot out. He wrapped his hand around her biceps with an iron grip, and he tugged her forward. His lips veered down, as though he'd force her into a kiss.

Raven tilted her head at the last moment, using the momentum to ram her skull into his mouth.

"Fuck," he cursed, tightening his grip on her arm, claws coming out and sinking into her skin. The pain pierced through her, white hot, and her head rang, but she gritted her teeth. He wanted her up close and personal? That was what he'd get.

Raven launched her knee up, right into his crotch. The blow landed with enough force to crunch. Shifter or no, everyone had their weak points. As Christian keeled forward, Raven swiped across his face with her claws. He let out a howl loud enough to shake the trees. Red blossomed across his features, blood dripping from the open cuts.

His hold on her arm loosened.

Raven ripped herself free from him and ran. Her boots slammed against the weathered planks of the porch with enough force to reverberate through her shins.

Christian let out another enraged howl. When she glanced back, the fur had begun to sprout across his skin in mid-shift. She needed to get to her car before he transitioned to his coyote form. If it came down to a fight, they'd always been evenly matched in their animal forms, but Raven would die before she let the bastard touch her.

She churned the dirt beneath her. Raven raced toward her car as fast as possible. Her key pressed tight into her bloodied palm as she clutched it hard. Her heart thundered in her chest so loudly it left room for little else. Needed to escape. The situation had set off a mine inside her mind and obliterated any other thought.

Sweat dripped from her forehead, blurring her vision, but she kept her gaze fixed on the car ahead of her. *Closer. Closer.*

Her arms trembled until her entire body shook, but she couldn't let the tremors overtake her now. She needed to get the hell out of there. Christian's growl echoed across the yard, and she didn't need to look back to know he'd shifted. That he would chase after her and wouldn't stop until he'd gotten what he wanted.

Raven slammed against her car, unable to stop her momentum. A second later, she tugged the door open and launched herself inside. Sweat trickled down her face, screwing up her vision, and her arms trembled so hard she couldn't shove the damn key into the ignition. She slammed a finger on the locks.

Christian in his coyote form launched himself off the porch. He was coming for her.

Not again. Not again. Not again.

The words became her marching beat. She forced the key into the ignition and turned it. The engine roared to life, causing the whole car to hum. Christian charged at her, so Raven slammed on the gas, reversing as fast as she could. The tires screeched when she whipped the car around and pumped the pedal again to send her Civic soaring along the narrow path.

At the speed she raced down the unpaved road, her car jumped and jolted all over the place as if electrocuted. Raven didn't slow and she didn't look back.

Stupid. She'd been stupid to go and confront Christian on her own. He had always been dangerous, but the rage had licked up any remaining sense while fear had pushed her to the cliff's edge. Even as she burst through the tree-lined road and onto the highway, her pulse didn't slow. The tremors still seized her body, as if it would never belong to her again.

She couldn't go home.

Her apartment wasn't safe. She wasn't safe. Maybe she was an idiot for even thinking she could be.

However, tonight, she only wanted to be in one place.

Chapter Sixteen

The day had passed in a blur.

Ever since Jer had told Sierra the news early this morning, they'd been working nonstop to fix the landmine problem. He'd managed to get his phone back and retrieved the incriminating photos, but the time for physical action had passed. The next step required a heavy perusal of pack and human law to figure out the best way to proceed with this evidence. However, concentration wasn't possible right now, not with the soul-deep exhaustion claiming him.

He leaned back in his seat and glared at the red numbers on the clock. The hours had passed too quickly, and he'd just wasted time. The Red Rocks relied on him, but again, he'd let them down. Cool autumn breezes swept through his open windows, and the gentle sounds of leaves skittering across the pavement and the occasional car along the highway filtered in.

A screech of tires came from outside, drawing his attention from the paragraph he'd tried to read about a dozen times at that point. He stuck a piece of scrap paper in the page and snapped the book shut. Before he could hop up and investigate the sound, someone knocked on his door.

Jer pushed himself up, a frown creasing between his eyebrows as he headed over. If Sierra was waiting on the other side, he was half-tempted to shut the door in her face, as he'd done nothing but pack business all day long. Right now, he wasn't good company. He stopped for a moment, hoping to hear the creak of footsteps heading the opposite way. Instead, he caught a scent he knew deep in his heart. The knock sounded again, more insistent this time.

He grabbed the handle and yanked the door open.

Raven stood in the entryway. A sheen of sweat spread across her forehead, matting strands of hair to her face, and cuts marred her arms, deep slashes of crimson contrasting with her pale skin. Her tank-top and cargoes were rumpled, her shoulders heaving with shallow, uneven breaths, but none of that stopped him as still as the look in her eyes. She was terrified.

She opened her mouth, but no words came out.

Jer tilted his head, gesturing her inside. She managed to stumble in, and that was when he realized her entire body was shaking.

"Rae?"

What the hell had happened? His wolf rammed in his chest, going berserk to do something, anything, to protect her. However, he didn't have the slightest clue as to where she'd come from or what had happened. She sucked in a shaky breath, but the words weren't arriving for her, not right then.

"Come on in," he said, closing the door behind her. She wasn't the only one terrified. The horror in her eyes had his mind reeling to every worst-case scenario. And he hadn't been there to stop it. The last time they'd talked at Beaver Tavern, he'd pushed her away and hadn't made any effort to reach out since. *Fuck.*

Raven staggered forward another pace, then another one, closing the distance between them. Before she reached him, he circled his arms around her and pulled her tight. Raven sank against his chest, and the shuddering breath that racked her entire body tore him to shreds. He held her there, listening to the cycling of her gasps and soaking in the dark ale of her scent. Every time questions leapt to his lips, they died there. At the end of the day, the why didn't matter when she rested here in his arms. Right then, he would make sure she was safe.

Wetness soaked into his shirt, and he glanced down. Blood dripped from the open cuts along her arms, imprinting on his shirt and trickling to her fingertips.

"Hey," he said, his voice sounding far too loud amidst the surrounding quiet that coated the room. She didn't look up at him, but he could tell from the subtle shift of her body that she was paying attention. "We need to clean your cuts. The last thing you need is for them to get infected while they're healing."

Jer took a step back even though he kept his arm around her shoulder, not wanting to break the connection. He guided her toward his sink, the silence between them growing as oppressive as a loaded gun. Within seconds, warm water poured through the faucet, and he brought her sliced-up arm over to the stream. He took a clean dish towel, added some soap, and with slow, practiced movements, began cleaning the gashes.

Raven didn't say anything or even look at him, her eyes frozen on the scratches along her arm. Strands of her tangled hair were glued to her cheeks, her lips were tight-pressed in silence, and he couldn't help the fear pulsing in his ears and growing louder by the second. He should've been there for her. Once the scratches were cleaned out, he nabbed bandages from the first-aid kit and wrapped her arm. After setting his electric kettle on for tea, he guided her over to his couch.

Raven looked at him with a hopelessness he knew all too well.

She opened her mouth and closed it again.

Jer squeezed her shoulder. "Take a seat. I'll bring you tea, and if you want to talk, we can. If not, you can join me in slumping into the couch and watching the paint peel, because that's about where I'm at right now. I'm great company, I know."

Raven's mouth quirked with the hint of a smile. She sank into his couch before gripping the sides as if she needed to hold on to something to keep from drifting away. Jer swallowed hard and strode over to the kitchen where the electric kettle billowed with steam. He grabbed one mug and hesitated before grabbing a second. He hadn't eaten today, so tea would be a start.

He carried over the piping hot mugs of tea, one in each hand, before settling them onto the coffee table in front of his couch. Then Jer sank into the couch beside her, wrapping an arm around Raven's shoulders to draw her in close.

"This was the one place I felt safe," she murmured, and the words stopped him still.

His heart paused, suspended in painful hope, and an endless second passed before it restarted again. She melded against him perfectly, as if she belonged in his arms, and his wolf quieted when their skin touched. Even though the fear of what had happened thrummed in the back of his mind, a temporary peace existed while she remained by his side.

"Stay here tonight?" he asked. He'd drawn several conclusions—he wasn't an idiot—and he also couldn't bear to let her walk out of the door in this wrecked state. Both wolf and man longed to protect her and care for her, but his wolf never questioned why. She was his mate, simple as that.

Raven's lip trembled, and she sucked in a breath but nodded her response. She drew back from him to grab the mug of tea, wincing as her damaged palms hit the hot surface. Still, she held them there anyway.

Jer leaned back in the couch, sensing she needed the distance right now, even though he ached to wrap his arms around her and pull her tight to his body. As if somehow he could still try to keep her safe. "Want to pick a shitty action movie to watch?" he asked, offering her the remote.

She shook her head. "I've got to get this out or I won't be able to. Finn knew because he needed to know," Raven started.

"I'm listening." Nothing could've torn his attention away now. This—this was the distance between them, the secret of hers Finn had kept that he'd always remained on the outside of. Finn had thrown their closeness in his face before, because Jer didn't know, which meant he couldn't understand the complexity of what went on between him and Raven.

Not like that mattered. In a secret part of him, he had always longed to be the one she turned to in a crisis. She had borne his swings countless times before, and he'd wanted to help so badly that his inability to do so had shredded him to pieces. Yet the years had passed, and he'd remained outside the glass window with her, always.

"But I want you to know. You need to know," she continued, pausing to take a sip of tea. Her gaze didn't veer from the surface of the liquid, as if she could lose herself there. "Back when I ran with the Landsliders, I was raped."

"Oh hell, Rae." Bile rose in Jer's throat, an acid threatening to scorch away his insides. She'd run with the Landsliders before she joined the Red Rock pack. She would've been twelve or thirteen years old. *Spirits above.* He wanted to reach out, to say something, anything, but he caught the way she swallowed, as if summoning courage to continue.

"No Tribe member needed to tell me Mackey Kendricks was dangerous," she murmured, her tone detached and level. "I already learned the lesson."

The monster terrorizing the region is the same one who devastated her all those years ago. The ex-Tribe member who could control shifters with a simple command. *He* had done this to Rae. Rage sparked deep within Jer, a fury that seared his bones and made his wolf howl in his chest. Yet the moment Raven looked at him, the anger muted in the wash of grief rolling off her like the icy waterfalls throughout Ricketts Glen.

"I found another tiger lily on my doorstep tonight, the same kind Mackey used to give me, so I went to confront Christian. He's been camping at Ganzorig's house." She glanced to her bandaged arm. "That's where those came from."

"You can stay here as long as you want," he murmured. Her shoulders braced as though she'd buck back if he tried to hug her, so he reached forward and slipped his hand into hers. Raven curled her fingers around his, digging her nails deep enough to bite.

"Jer, I'm not the person you think I am. I know I've been avoiding the talk about the mating bond between us, but I couldn't force the words out." Her lip trembled and her eyes grew glassy. "How could you want a mate who's broken like me?"

Jer let out a ragged breath, squeezing her hands even tighter. All the hateful words in his head echoed at him, the same thought that had paraded through his mind hundreds of times before. *Fuck it.* He leaned forward and pulled her into his arms to drag her with him back into the crook of the couch. The first tears coursed down her cheeks, hot and wet when they splashed onto his shirt.

He ran his fingers through her hair, smoothing the strands over and over as her shoulders shook and the sobs escaped her. Jer gripped onto her with all his might, as if he could transport back in time and reach the small girl who must've been so terrified.

How could she not see the way her wan smile warmed her features like a hearth fire? Or how her looks always pierced right through the false smile he plastered on his face, day after day? She saw *him*, every single time, when no one else did.

"You're right," he said, "you're not the person I thought you were." She froze, but he never stopped stroking her hair while he continued. "You're far stronger than I ever realized. You think your damage makes you a terrible mate? I'm bipolar, and even when I get back on my meds, I'm still going to go through the ups and downs and fall off the wagon with taking them. My issues are a life sentence, so why the hell would I want to inflict them on anyone else?"

Raven pushed up to look him in the eyes. Even though tears streaked down her cheeks, he caught the familiar stubborn look in her gaze, one that made his heart stutter. He'd seen it every time she'd fought for him when he'd lost the will or hope to fight for himself.

Before she could say anything, he reached up and brushed his thumb across her bottom lip.

"I'm not looking for sympathy here," he said, summoning courage he didn't know he had. "What I'm saying is maybe our puzzle pieces are both dented and damaged enough to fit together perfectly. I knew from the moment I met you that you were the one for me, Rae. Nothing in your past has changed that."

She let out a shuddering breath, digging her hands into the couch on either side of him as she stared into his eyes, inches away from him. Silken strands of her hair draped around him.

"You were the one I wasn't allowed to have," she whispered, her eyes alight with tentative hope. "Finn and I distracted ourselves with each other, but you, Jer, you reached right to the heart of me. If I ever gave in to the feelings I had for you, I knew I'd be lost."

His heart ached so much he thought he might expire on the spot. He'd always believed he wasn't good enough. As though she would never be interested in him the way she longed for Finn. Yet here she lay on top of him, dead serious and telling him the opposite. They'd both been suffering all these years apart.

Raven leaned down to brush her lips against his mouth, the hesitant sweep sparking his synapses to life.

"I'm done running, Jer," she murmured. "I want to be yours."

He captured her lips in his, galvanized by her admission. Despite the tenderness in their kiss, an undercurrent of hunger bloomed beneath it, promising an inevitable collision. Those words were everything he needed to hear from the woman he wanted to spend the rest of his life with, yet hollowness lingered inside him, ready to drag him under. And he knew why—because ever since his med supply had disappeared, he'd been running from his own problems too. *Pretending I could be normal.*

He pulled himself back.

"And I want to be mated to you more than anything," he said, "but I've also been waiting a damn long time for this. I already fucked up our first kiss, and I don't want to ruin this by chasing the wrong time too."

Raven trailed her fingers along his cheek and down around his chin, wonder gleaming in her eyes. "You didn't fuck up anything. It was with you, so it was perfect."

His throat tightened. God, she was everything he'd ever wanted. He still couldn't believe the words that had left her lips, that she lay wrapped in his arms and wanting him. He would fight his demons every damn day if it meant grasping this sunlit warmth for as long as he could.

"Next thing you'll be telling me is that Gene's not an alcoholic either," Jer murmured, deflecting.

Raven snorted. "We both know that's not true." She slid up from him and onto her knees before reaching forward to grab his hand. "Let's go to bed then. It's been a long-as-hell night, and you're going to need your rest, because tomorrow, you're mine."

The desire in her gaze shot straight to his cock and his libido hated him for shutting the door right as it opened. Jer slipped off the couch and stood before leaning down to scoop up Raven from the cushion. She let out a surprised noise that made Jer want to capture her mouth all over again, and she pressed her lithe body against him in pure temptation. She twined her arms around his neck and hung on tight.

He pulled her close to his chest before he crossed the room in quick strides, making a beeline for his bedroom. Once he entered the room, he headed straight for his bed and lowered her onto the sheets. Raven kicked her boots off and they hit the ground with a thump. Amber light from the lamp on his bedstand filtered through the room, the gentle rays barely fighting the shadows.

When he crashed onto the bed beside her, the weight of the past couple of hours, the past days — hell, the past month — came slamming down on him. His mind spun, and he caught how her eyes glistened. Even if she'd been ready and raring to take a spin in the sheets, too much had been scraped raw tonight for both of them.

"Come here," he said. He still had a bloodstained shirt on and she wore her rumpled clothes that smelled like ale from a shift at Beaver Tavern, but he couldn't have been happier as she settled down beside him. He tugged her to his chest and wrapped his arms around her, bringing her body flush against him. The heat emanating from her and the way they fit together was so perfect it sliced him to ribbons. He had wanted this for so long it couldn't be real.

He clung to her with all his might, as if he could somehow convince her she'd be safe, that she was a brilliant, beautiful spark of life he couldn't survive without. Within minutes, her breaths turned even as she succumbed to sleep. Relief ached inside him, a similar pulse to the longing he'd felt for years, as though he was staring at the stars above, overwhelmed by all that existed out there.

Jer rubbed his thumb along her arm in lazy, slow strokes. He lay there in this sanctified moment between them, afraid to close his eyes and find it had all faded to dust. It was a long time before he fell asleep.

Chapter Seventeen

Raven had woken from the best sleep she'd gotten in ages to find herself wrapped in Jer's arms the same way she'd passed out. His vanilla and leather scent made her want to tug his arms tighter around her to bask in it. Her wolf sprawled out, languorous and at ease in his presence. Even though she wanted to lie in bed with him for the next century, she needed to do something she couldn't put off any longer. If she did, she might never summon the courage again. She wrote him a note that she left on his kitchen counter near the coffeemaker and headed out.

The wind smacked her hair around as she raced along the highway in her Civic. Raven hadn't been surprised Sierra had responded to her message to talk, but she had been shocked at how fast her alpha had scheduled the meet-up. Sierra was balancing a lot of problems right now with the Coalition, the Landsliders and the petition for Ricketts Glen, so Raven had figured they'd talk tonight, tomorrow or anything but the 'meet at the pack cabin in an hour' she'd gotten.

Crisp leaves drifted across the highway, batted around by the breeze. The closer she got to the cabin, the more Raven's stomach churned. If she got banished from the Red Rock pack, what would happen between her and Jer? The idea of Sierra casting her out of their territory and family made her throat tighten to the point that each breath grew painful. She needed to do this, but the admission terrified her. This pack was the first truly good family she'd ever belonged to.

Raven couldn't imagine a future without going for runs through the woods with Sierra and Kyle or sitting down for a pint with Gene on a random Thursday. Birthdays, mating ceremonies and new births in the pack where they all celebrated together—they'd all fade away. She would vault back to where she had been at twelve, looking in on cozy families from the other side of the glass. If she got kicked out, she couldn't stay in her apartment or even the area. God, she was going to be sick.

Raven blared her music to try to drown out her thoughts while she charged there at top speed. All too soon, the familiar turnoff for their pack cabin reared into view. Her palms sweated, so slick she slipped on the steering wheel.

Part of her wanted to turn around and call the talk off. It had taken every ounce of her resolve last night to tell Jer about her past. The temptation to return to the numb way she'd operated for years surged like the tide. However, she'd made Daria a promise. And if she wanted to move forward with Jer to complete the mating bond, she needed to do this.

She rolled to the cabin and parked. The lights were already on inside, glowing from the windows, and Sierra's car sat parked in the driveway. Raven ran a hand through her hair, strands sticking to her sweaty palms. *Judgment time.*

As Raven approached the front door, memories followed her with every step toward this place where they'd held meetings, parties or even chats over coffee with other pack members. She and Sierra weren't as close as Raven was with Finn and Jer—Sierra's focus and no-bullshit attitude could be intimidating. But they'd grown up together. Raven didn't ever have to doubt Sierra's affection—at least, not until now.

She turned the knob and entered the cabin. The overhead fans let out a low *snick-snick-snick* and silence settled into the hollows of the main room, clinging to the shadows. Sierra wasn't in the kitchenette even though a fresh pot of coffee had been brewed. Raven followed the scent of her alpha through the house to where the back door leading out to the deck remained propped open.

Raven's feet carried her forward even as her mind resisted every step. Birds whistled outside and fat sunbeams poured in through the windows while dust motes floated about the house like fairy lights. She slipped through the door and stepped out to the deck, which had boards and rails stained a cherry red, matching the multi-hued autumn leaves.

Sierra leaned against the rail, staring out at the forest with a porcelain mug of coffee in hand. Her alpha didn't turn around or offer a greeting, but Raven didn't doubt for a second that Sierra had known the moment Raven had pulled into the driveway.

"What's going on with the Coalition?" Raven forced the conversation out, not knowing how to broach the words stuck in her throat. Sierra still hadn't turned to look at her. Goosebumps prickled up Raven's arms as the fear threatened to swallow her whole.

"We sent them a message," Sierra said before taking a sip of her coffee. Her gaze remained distant, as if her mind wandered a thousand miles away. "The next time they try anything in Ricketts Glen, we're calling the authorities and we've got the evidence to get them locked away. Otherwise, we'll see them in court."

"I'm sure that riled them up," Raven murmured, leaning against the railing. "Too many zealots in one room with that bunch. Christian's camping at Ganzorig's old place too, in case you were looking for the lawyer who stirred up this mess."

"Thanks for the heads-up. Now, let's brush all that distracting talk aside and get to the real problem at hand," Sierra said, turning to face her. Raven gulped at the intensity in her laser stare. "Going to share why we called this powwow? I'll hazard a guess it has to do with the Landsliders?"

Raven opened her mouth, closed it then opened it again. Her eyebrows furrowed on instinct. The wave of cold washed over her, but she clutched the railing for support. "How did you know?"

Sierra arched an eyebrow, the grim look on her face terrifying. Usually Raven could read her alpha, but like this, she had no idea what was coming next, whether the following words would spell her salvation or demise.

"Educated guess," she said in a monotone. "Christian didn't disguise your past association, and I've been told he used to be involved in the Landsliders. Now, here's where you fill in the blanks."

Raven's palms sweated while she gripped the railing tight, looking out into the backyard where the trees loomed. She couldn't bear the force of Sierra's gaze, not right now.

"My mom died when I was little," she started, staring into the wood grain. "Then my father crashed out while drunk when I was twelve. I didn't have anywhere to go, at least not until my friend Christian told me about this group he'd joined with. He said it was like a family."

She could feel the weight of her sodden hoodie the day she'd stood on out on the porch of her empty house with Christian, his eyes gleaming while he told her about the Landsliders. The briefest glimmer of hope had flickered inside her chest.

"Biggest mistake of my life," she forced herself to continue, even though the shakes threatened to descend. "The Landsliders churn you up and spit you out unless you're worshipping the cult of Mackey Kendricks. I stayed long enough for them to do some permanent damage, about a year or so, and got dragged into trouble that probably would've sentenced me given time. However, I ran away, and that's when Gene found me. He pulled me into the Red Rock pack, and I discovered what family could be."

Silence settled between them. Raven should have been begging, and apologies reached her lips but never came out. They all felt like excuses, and her alpha hated those. The phantom burn of the brand on her hip resurrected again, enough that she was desperate to scratch at it. The longer Sierra went without saying a word, the more Raven's mind screamed in agony as she cycled through a thousand and one scenarios.

"You should've told me," Sierra said, her tone as harsh as Raven had feared. Her stomach bottomed out. *This is it.* This was where Sierra excised her from the one place Raven called home. "When the Landsliders emerged again, your history became necessary information to the pack. Information I needed to know."

Raven nodded, swallowing back bile. "I understand. If you could give me a couple of days, I'll have my things packed up," she started, her eyes stinging with unshed tears.

Sierra's eyebrows furrowed. "Now why would you be doing that?"

"Because I was a part of the Landsliders," Raven forced out. A stray tear slipped down her cheek, and she hated herself for the weakness. The weakness back then in joining with the Landsliders in the first place, the weakness when Mackey… *Hell, just everything.*

Sierra shook her head, the hard look in her eyes unchanging. She hiked up one of her pantlegs to expose her thigh. "See these?" She pointed to raised scars along the tan expanse of skin — long, jagged ones. "My brother used to torture me when we were kids — this became a game for him. He left marks I can *never* erase." The sight of them sucked the air from Raven, a vacuum where her lungs existed. She'd known Sierra for so long but would've never expected that sort of trauma from their unflinching leader.

Sierra let down her pant leg and closed the distance between them, lifting her chin as she looked her square in the eye. "After hearing that, do you think I'm unfit to lead this pack?"

Raven's head tilted on reflex as she blinked a couple of times. "Of course not, Sierra. You're the strongest person I ever met." She clenched and unclenched her fists at the sight of those ugly scars. "If anything, the marks make you a survivor."

Sierra stepped even closer between them, reaching out to nudge Raven's chin up with her finger. "Then why would I believe anything less of you?"

"But you said…" Raven started and stopped when the puzzle pieces slid into place.

"I said you should've told me," Sierra confirmed. Her eyes shone with a resolve that socked Raven in the gut. "This is my pack to run, and I need to know these things. However, you've been a loyal part of the Red Rock pack for years. The Landsliders are in your past— that's all I ever needed to know. You've proven your character to me, so your history doesn't change that."

Raven sucked in a shuddering breath, keeping her chin up and not wavering from meeting Sierra's gaze, even as heat pricked her eyes. "You're not half-bad, Kanoska," she murmured, a half-smile rising to her lips.

Sierra's eyes crinkled with amusement and a full grin spread on her face. "That's more like the Raven I know. Besides, Beaver Tavern would collapse without you— seriously, no one else knows how to make the place run as well."

"Hey, good bartenders are hard to find." She leaned forward along the railing, looking out into woods filled with tall pines and majestic oaks that reached out to try and touch the sky. Her chest ached with relief and a warmth so strong she thought she'd stepped into a bonfire. In that moment, she felt as though she might burst, as though her heart strained at the seams.

"Besides," Sierra said with a wink. "I think Streaky would start a riot if you ever left the pack, and it's hard enough reining my beta in on a regular day. Curious how his random hookups have completely dried up." Her pointed glance got the message across even if the quirk to her lips hadn't.

"He's a handful, for sure," Raven murmured, meeting Sierra's gaze. "Thanks, boss."

Sierra's hand settled onto her shoulder, a solid weight filled with the promise her alpha enacted every day. Whatever problems came their way, the pack would face them together. After living so long in fear with her voice trapped within, beating at the walls with endless screams, her truth had been freed.

With it out in the world, Raven was no longer bound, and freedom flooded through her veins like the crisp autumn breeze. Not only could she stay—for the first time in so, so long, Raven would take steps toward the future she dreamed of.

* * * *

Her shift at Beaver Tavern dragged, and she hadn't heard from Jer all day. She would've thought after the raw way they'd left things last night, he'd swing by, or even text, but her phone didn't utter a peep. After the stress from yesterday and the talk this morning, Raven felt as though she'd emerged from a car wreck, exhaustion stretching like taffy inside her chest.

Raven pulled up to his apartment, anticipation mounting inside her. Ever since last night, when she'd bared her scars and he'd accepted them all, she'd been waiting for the chance to finish what they'd started. She'd curved against him last night, all that hard muscle becoming sheer temptation. She'd memorized those long, elegant fingers which had wrapped around her, the tousled curls as though he was always ready to slip between the sheets, and sensuous lips, most of the time twisted in a smirk.

She wanted those lips over every inch of her body.

Raven hopped out of her car. The Jeep lay in the driveway, but his Harley was missing. Her eyebrows drew together while she took careful steps forward. Where would he have gone on the Harley? The lights to his apartment were out, but she approached anyway. The steps creaked as she trudged up them. Maybe she should turn around and go home. The thought settled into her stomach like a stone.

She didn't feel safe there. She wouldn't feel safe until the moment she staggered into Jer's arms.

Her chest tightened as she reached for the knob. It wasn't locked, but that was nothing new. Whether he was home or not, deep in the throes of a swing or skating on normal, Jer constantly forgot to lock up after himself. The thought warmed her chest, closely followed by the familiar lance of yearning she'd been carrying for far too long. *Enough.* Maybe he was waiting inside.

She opened the door and stepped in, greeted by the familiar scent she wanted to spend every morning waking up to. She flicked the lights on. Everything seemed to be the same as when she'd left earlier. A rumpled blanket was still splayed out across his couch, with stacks of papers all over his coffee table, along with hefty volumes about pack law piled beside the legs. Raven tiptoed around to each room in his place, hope draining out a little more with every one she found empty.

He wasn't there.

She sagged into his couch and dragged the blanket to her chest, clutching it tightly. She should head home. Where was he? Her stomach squeezed as her fingertips found the scars at her hip, a totem to summon the ugly thoughts. Maybe he'd changed his mind about becoming mates. Confronting her demons had felt freeing in the moment, but right now the blackness wrapped oily tendrils around her and her breaths grew more and more shallow.

Voicing the ugly truth out loud didn't make her any less broken.

She'd been ruined long ago, and the fool notions of having a mate and a future were just those. Raven gripped the blanket tighter, curling into the crook of the couch. Even if he hated her and wanted nothing to do with her, she couldn't pull herself away. Jer might not be there, but she could feel the imprint of his presence. The pen splayed across scratch paper with too many notes, and the empty coffee mug sitting by the foot of his couch. She adored how his mind ticked, where he'd hit strokes of brilliance and work for hours on something. In the same breath the man laughed loud and easily, and he charmed and flirted his way through the pack.

However, everyone saw those. Only she had gotten to see the pain in his eyes, the vulnerable hesitation in his voice and the beautiful way he splintered and reformed himself every day.

God, this hurts. If he hadn't wanted to be with her, she wished he would've told her she was trash in the first place and walked off. Not let her believe they might stand a chance at something real. A thousand and one reasons flashed through her mind of why he might've gone — to get more information and his phone had died, out for a run and didn't bring his phone with him — any myriad number of things. None of them latched on like the reminder that no one wanted damaged goods.

She should leave. She needed to leave. And yet she couldn't pull herself away from the couch or away from his place. Tears heated her eyes, but Raven didn't bother fighting them, letting the hot, miserable things slip down her cheeks.

Wetness splashed onto the blanket she clutched to burrow into the couch, surrounded by his scent. Loathing skittered across her skin, the exact sort she'd been trying to avoid. She was an idiot for believing even for an instant that anyone could love someone damaged like her. If he walked away from this, she'd be broken beyond repair.

They would talk when he came back. *If* he came back.

Tonight was going to be hell.

Chapter Eighteen

By the time Jer had raced along the road for an hour, his phone had died and he still had another hour out to go. On his Harley, the sun pounded against his back, the wind whipped against his skin and for a brief moment he could pretend it seeped through the numbness permeating him. He'd been through this rodeo long enough to know a depressive swing had him in a stranglehold. *Not like the knowledge does me any good.*

Raven had left by the time he'd woken up, and he'd set to work at once, making the necessary call. After he'd had the phone conversation, he'd locked in on the task, but even then he'd had to summon every ounce of resolve to force himself out of the door and onto the road. He'd forgotten his keys twice while walking out of the door.

The asphalt stretched out from here to eternity, littered with more traffic than normal. He wouldn't get to Allentown until dinnertime, which meant he was stuck in the swell of rush-hour traffic. His wolf growled within him and he fought the temptation to stow his Harley by the side of the road and race the whole way there on all fours. He wasn't in the mood to deal with anyone right then, let alone a stranger, but after the talk with Raven last night, he knew what he needed to do.

He flew along the highway, hitting more congested areas than he was used to in his home out amid the wilderness. High rises crowned the horizon as he neared Allentown, which was filled with the bustle of humans, traffic and smog. Shifters tended to stick to the wide-open spaces, though some tried to tough it amidst all that concrete. He'd never thought of himself as a country boy, but he'd never be able to survive in cities like this. His wolf would go crazier than he already was.

The scents of burned rubber lingered in the air around here and broken glass splintered across the edges of the road, glittering in the golden light of late afternoon. Jer tightened his grip while he weaved from one lane to the other, diving into openings to get anywhere faster than the turtle's pace they were moving at. A crumpled fast food bag drifted across the highway, slipping under tires to get churned out again.

He'd looked up the route a while back and thanked everything holy that Ava Patel didn't live in Allentown but on the outskirts. Once the turnoff to the highway popped into view, he took it, exiting the stream of slow-moving cars and trucks. The air split with honks and the screech of tires.

After a scenic detour down some winding back roads, farther away from the traffic and clustered buildings in Allentown, Jer found himself slowing in front of an isolated home along a suburban street. This one existed at the end of a well-spaced-out neighborhood, and he didn't question for a heartbeat who it belonged to. The bountiful garden out front and trailing into the backyard, and the chimes and carved stones carefully lining the pathway to the front door gave her away.

Shamans always left a mark on their abodes.

Jer pulled his Harley into the driveway, the engine thrumming beneath him and the rumble echoing along this quiet street. He shut his girl off before heading for the front door. Each step forward had him doubting this plan in the first place. All the time he'd spent building a rapport with Ganzorig, and the guy had turned out to be a shithead who worked for the enemy of the Tribe. *Great judge of character I am.*

He reached the door and lifted his fist, ready to knock. It froze there despite the mental nudge forward. He should be at home, working on the case for the pack against the Coalition, not wasting time on personal things. Before he could turn around, the door opened.

A short woman who couldn't have been much older than him stepped into view. While Ganzorig had defied his expectations of shamans, she flipped them. Her dark hair was pulled into a ponytail and her narrow nose wrinkled as she peered at him through thick black-rimmed glasses. She wore a pair of loose jeans and a shirt that said *Have you tried turning it off and on again?* across the front.

"You're Jeremiah Taylor, right?" she asked, extending a hand to shake. "I could hear your beast growling from a mile down the road. I'm Ava."

He moved automatically, clapping his hand to hers then a second later finding himself ushered inside the house.

"Thanks for responding to me so fast," he said, flashing her a grin. Even when the depressive swings hit, he'd mastered his mask to keep the questions at bay.

Ava shot him a level look. "Put those dimples away. I already agreed to help you out here, so throwing extra charm at me isn't going to speed up the process."

Jer's eyebrows drew together. She acted nothing like the other shamans he'd met. She led them into a living room that might as well have been a junkyard with the five different consoles set up in different corners of the room. Wires traveled from each one, big bundles wrapped in zip ties, and the screens cast their glares onto her white walls.

"So, have you worked with any cases like mine before?" he asked, slipping his hands into his pockets while he dodged around a couple of egg carton crates filled with machine parts.

Ava snorted, stepping past a console elevated on a flexible stand in front of her couch. She took a seat there and gestured around the room until her forehead wrinkled. "Huh, I guess I'm not super equipped to deal with visitors. Clear the junk off the chair and take a seat." She pointed to a ripped-up black armchair with a stack of books squat in the center.

Jer picked up the stack and moved them before settling into the seat.

"Shame about Ganzorig," Ava continued, as if she hadn't heard his question. "There aren't many of us period, let alone in this region. Our elders are livid he'd been using his magic for drug trafficking. Persona non grata, that one."

Jer opened his mouth, ready to ask his question again, when Ava swiveled to face him before she adjusted to a cross-legged position.

"I've worked on *dozens* of cases like yours before," Ava said, fixing him with a stare. "Did Ganzorig really have you coming in person to pick up medication? What a savant." She leaned forward to her keyboard and began typing, the glare bouncing off her glasses. "Look, I've got you in my system now, Jeremiah Taylor. I've got the information you sent from your old medication under Ganzorig too. We're working a binding element onto the medication to make sure that A, it doesn't fuck with your beast, and B, your different physiology doesn't disrupt the effects."

Jer ran a hand through his curls. Holy hell, this woman was a whirlwind. However, from here to the doorway, she'd already given him far more information than Ganzorig. Her blunt and brusque attitude offered some comfort, given the fact that most didn't know how to handle a bipolar human, let alone a shifter with the illness.

"The gist of what I'm getting is you'll be able to mail my medication?" Jer asked. That would be a game changer for him. He'd recalled a couple of slips in the past because he'd missed the window of getting out to Ganzorig's in time, and the errant rock had just tumbled into an avalanche from there.

"On an automated, regular schedule. Y'know, like a normal person in the twenty-first century. Good riddance to that fuckwad if he couldn't even handle the basics of our job." The exasperation in her tone drew a grin to his face while she typed away. "I've got a storage of pills below and pulled your type and dosage.

The elders keep me well-stocked because I get the work done and keep the revenue flowing."

"Well, damn," he drawled, leaning back into the seat. "I wish I'd come to you sooner."

Ava glared at him, pushing her glasses up on her nose. "Are you trying to flirt with me, or are you naturally this charming? Because I'll give you the heads-up now, I'm so not interested in guys."

Jer let out a laugh in surprise, unable to help himself. "No, I'm not trying to flirt with you," he said. "I'm just used to swaying people in my favor on instinct. Lawyer by day, pack beta by night." If most people witnessed the ugly stain of the personality he kept inside, they'd run screaming in a heartbeat. He'd had a lifetime to perfect his mask.

Ava blinked. "Spirits help the woman you're actually trying to flirt with." She tugged forward a little orange bottle of pills. The sight of them punched him in the gut, all while relief coursed through his veins. Ava clicked the bottle open and spilled the contents onto her palm. She dipped her finger into a bowl sitting on the console, staining the tip in a blue substance.

"All right, charmer. Sit back and watch some magic," she said, closing her eyes as she sank into the seat. All of a sudden, the energy in the room shifted, growing heavier as if a rain storm loomed on the horizon. Ganzorig had always done this in a private room or before he ever arrived, not out in the open. Jer leaned forward to watch, digging his elbows into his thighs while Ava's breaths settled to a cyclical rhythm.

She began to mumble incantations so low he couldn't discern the words, but the more she chanted, the tenser the air in the room grew. A hazy glow ringed the pills in her hand, and the computer screen in front of her flickered. Wind sliced through the room, even though there weren't open windows for it to flow from. Her chants became louder as the glow intensified with the words, the ebb and flow of something intrinsic calling to him.

The air seemed to frizz—that was the only word for it—when all of a sudden the lights flickered too.

Ava let out one final chant and lapsed to silence. In the wake of her quiet, all the tension sucked out of the room like a vacuum. His skin prickled at the frayed feeling in the air from the residue of the spell she'd performed.

"Didn't realize you could whip that up so fast," Jer said, breaking the quiet.

Ava opened one eye. "Fast, yes. Easily, no. I'm going to be taking an hour or two nap before dinner now."

Jer scratched his nape. "I'm sorry. I didn't realize it took so much out of you."

Ava shrugged, slipping onto her feet. She grabbed the tube and popped the pills into it before snapping the lid back into place. "It's part of the job description. I wouldn't have taken you on if I couldn't handle it." She walked over to him and pressed the pills into his palm. "PayPal me the funds. You'll get faster service if you pay in advance, FYI."

Jer grabbed the pills, staring at the bottle. Ava stood in front of him, not moving away. Her eyebrows drew together and she passed him an irritated look.

"Are you waiting for me to perform a dance or something? I need my nap, stat. That's your cue to take the cute little bike you drive and haul on out of here."

Jer didn't hide his grin. "You're sort of standing in my way."

Ava opened her mouth and closed it before she strode over to her couch. "Right, that would help. Good meeting you, Jeremiah Taylor. If your pack needs a shaman, shoot me a text. I won't respond to any phone calls."

He surged up from the seat and took several steps forward before turning toward the couch to offer his thanks. Ava curled up there, and either she'd fallen asleep, or she was faking it so he would get the hell out. He slipped the pills into his pocket as he sauntered over to the front door. When he stepped outside, he couldn't help glancing back at one of the oddest interactions he had in the past years. If Ava could get him his medication at regular intervals, he didn't care about her weirdness — in his mind, she was a lifesaver.

Jer settled onto his Harley. Night had fallen while he'd been inside there, and he couldn't help but feel as if the time must've distorted with the use of her magic. It wasn't as though that was possible — at least, not from what he knew. Before he went for the ignition, he pulled out the meds. He'd been taking these for so long he could stomach them dry. The sound of the lid popping rang through him like a warning bell. His stomach flopped when he looked at the pills in his hand, circular discolored things. Fuck, he was such a failure.

Guilt flipped his stomach and he couldn't move his hand to pop those suckers into his mouth. These would offer relief. He knew they would. But the loathing curled in his stomach, a pit he could never rid himself of. If he weren't a headcase, he wouldn't have to rely on these. In taking them, he swallowed a life sentence, the knowledge he'd never escape this illness, no matter how hard he tried.

Taking them also meant choosing Raven. Choosing the hope for a life between the two of them as mates.

He'd choose her every time.

Jer swallowed the pills and popped the cap back on. *Not like I feel any different — it'll be at least a week before anything noticeable changes.* But he had taken the first steps, and he'd try his damn best to stay on track. He slipped the pills into his pocket and revved his Harley. Within seconds, he'd veered onto the road and was racing down the small suburban street, heading back in the direction of home.

Time to claim my mate.

Chapter Nineteen

Raven woke up with a start.

The growl of a motorcycle sounded outside.

She blinked the sleep out of her eyes and winced as she sat up from the hunch she'd curled into. She'd fallen asleep on his couch with the knit blue blanket tugged up to her chin. Even as adrenaline surged through her body like lit sparklers, her stomach dropped to subterranean depths. This was the confrontation she feared the worst, even as the person she wanted to see most approached.

Raven ran a hand through her thick hair, trying to smooth the strays while she attempted to stand. Her legs told her to fuck right off, so she remained seated on his couch. She sucked in a shaky breath as the doorknob rattled—Jer didn't even bother with keys. Then it swung open.

He stepped into his apartment, his leather jacket slung over his shoulder and the gray tee he wore displaying his toned chest too perfectly. His chestnut curls were windswept from driving his bike and the shadows sharpened the defined arch of his nose and his angular chin.

His gaze landed on her, and Raven's breath caught in her throat.

The intensity in those eyes was a crack of lightning across a night sky. She couldn't look away, even if she wanted to.

"I saw your car in the driveway, and I hoped…" He trailed off as he crossed the room toward her. "My phone died. I wanted to text you, but yeah, zapped. And my tire sprung a leak on the way home and the whole trip ended up taking way longer than necessary."

He rambled, closing the space between them, yet his eyes never left her. "But you're here." He didn't loom but dropped to his knees in front of her and reached out to tug her hands into his. "You're here, and that's all that matters to me."

Raven's mind whirled like a spinning roulette wheel.

His hands on hers and his firm touch was short-circuiting her brain. And his scent — the leather from his jacket grew stronger than ever.

"Where were you?" she asked, barely daring to hope. Her heart stretched paper-thin, as if any blow would tear it in two. He looked at her as though he saw the moon in her eyes and, God, it made her ache.

"Day one of being medicated again," he said, reaching into his pocket to pull out a bottle of pills before popping them back. "I'm in this for real, Rae."

Raven's mouth opened, but the words didn't come out. Her eyes stung and her heart transported out of her body, as if it kneeled on the floor before her making the promises she'd always dreamed of.

"I…thought you'd changed your mind." The words sounded thick and clumsy when they hit the air, and she cringed. Her skin prickled at how she'd exposed herself, like a turtle outside its shell.

Jer's jaw dropped and his lashes lowered. "Oh shit. I should've left a note." His voice came out in a rough scrape and he squeezed her hands. "God, I'm a fucking asshole."

Her heart clenched tight. He had returned, and he wanted this as much as she did. In the end, that was all she cared about. The pressure inside her chest unwound, but as the relief evacuated, the sight of him kneeling before her, all hard lines and the sort of gorgeous that made her ache, caused desire to take its place.

Raven leaned forward and tipped his chin up so their eyes met. She closed the space between them and pressed her lips to his. His hot mouth met hers, the taste of him like coffee, like coming home.

He snaked his hands around her waist and, at once, she found herself lifted from the couch as he rose to his feet. A low growl vibrated in his throat as he claimed her mouth. Her lips couldn't leave his, and she sucked in a quick gasp of air before diving in for more. As he slid his hands around to lift her, she twined her legs around his hips. She dug her heels into that perfect ass of his while he strode forward with her in his arms.

Fire burned in her chest, the sort to consume her, but after years of standing out in the cold, Raven welcomed the blaze.

The feel of his strong arms around her and the way he carried her as though she weighed nothing sent a silent thrill through her. She couldn't stop kissing him, nor did she want to as their lips met again and again.

The way he bit down on her lower lip and his low growl reverberated through her body had her core thrumming. Within seconds, they'd entered his bedroom, and he fumbled with the overhead light, pulling away from her for a brief second.

Raven grinned so hard it hurt as she clung to him with her arms twined around his neck. Her throat tightened at the overwhelming emotions crashing into her right now, ones she'd pent up for far too long. He carried her over to the bed and slammed her down on it. A laugh flew from her. His palms pressed into the mattress on either side. Raven leaned up to brush another kiss to his lips. He lowered himself on top of her, their bodies pressing together.

Jer pulled back for a moment, hesitation in his eyes. "I don't want to fuck this up, Rae," he said. "We've barely scratched the surface of everything we need to talk about, and I don't want to do anything to hurt you."

Heat stung her eyes. He couldn't be more perfect. Jer didn't need to elaborate for her to understand his concern. Raven twined her arms around his neck and didn't look away when their eyes met.

"My triggers are weird things, though fucking on the floor is out of the question," she said, her voice surprisingly steady. "But, babe, we've talked enough. I've been wanting you for too many years to count, and I'm done waiting. Even if we denied it for years, we both knew this was meant to be."

Raven played with the collar of his shirt, tugging at the fabric with her finger. Pinned beneath him, she couldn't feel safer even as her heart raced as though she flew across the freeway.

He offered her a lopsided grin, the sort that, combined with those dimples, made her squeeze her thighs together. The concern in his eyes turned molten, the look one that set her veins on fire. He trailed his finger between her collarbones, the light touch making her shudder. She wanted him so badly that each breath became painful.

"So?" she asked, her own vulnerabilities washing over her skin.

"Enough talking. Enough waiting," he said with a wicked grin that lit his whole face. She'd burn the whole world down for a genuine smile from him. Jer lifted the hem of her tank top and leaned down to brush his lips against her skin, right by her hips. Her breath hitched. She'd wanted him for so long her core ached for him already. When he bit down a moment later, she let out a low moan, the sensation rushing through her entire body.

He continued to work her tank top up, moving at a slow, agonizing pace while he kissed her stomach, her hips, before he sucked and bit the sensitive skin. With a snap, her bra loosened and he slid both that and her tank top up and over. The fabric hit the ground and her bare back settled on the rumpled sheets of his bed, the scent of him growing so strong she wanted to rub herself in it.

Her wolf was at attention the entire time, present with her. She'd been patient, her girl, and when she met Jer's eyes, they flashed with the gold of his wolf.

He licked the sensitive tip of her nipple, causing her to buck forward. He didn't hesitate, continuing to tease her until her entire body screamed for him. She needed him inside her, now. Raven reached to pull his shirt up and over. He shrugged out of it, and she couldn't help but admire the lean muscle and smooth skin she wanted to sink her teeth into. Raven licked her lips on instinct, and as their eyes met, his flared with lust.

He grabbed her shorts and, within seconds, they were unbuttoned and on the floor too. She should feel exposed lying naked on the bed in front of Jer. She'd always felt a thread of discomfort with her partners, needing the control to keep pieces of herself out of the equation. But with him? She was ready to let go. Raven had never trusted anyone more in her life.

"You're fucking gorgeous," he murmured, trailing his hot stare the length of her body. He spread her legs apart and sank between them, and Raven let out a ragged pant at the sight. Nothing was sexier than how he lowered to her pussy, at least, not until he leaned forward and put his clever tongue to use. Unlike the way he'd teased her, this first lick wasn't tentative or exploratory. He licked her as though he knew every inch of her body.

Raven tilted her hips forward as gasps flew from her throat, her mouth drying at the pleasure that shocked her all the way to her toes. He thrummed his tongue against her clit to the point that moans tore from her throat unbidden. Her fingers dug into the sheets and she gripped tight. He continued to lick and suck at her dripping pussy, unrelenting in his attack. Her thighs trembled from the sensations rocking through her.

She couldn't look away, mesmerized from how he devoured her whole, even as her vision shuttered to white, and her elbows dug into the mattress. *Close.* She was so close that her core tightened to the point of pain. His gaze flickered up from between her legs, and their eyes met. The simmering look from him combined with the way he sucked at her clit pushed her over the edge.

Raven's entire body trembled as euphoria rolled through her like a tide crashing to shore. She tilted her head back, sweat beading along her forehead while she leaned into the mattress. Ragged gasps wrung from her throat, and she panted like she was in heat. Jer slunk up the length of her body, and even the jeans he wore couldn't hide his impressive bulge. As he slid up, the fabric brushed against her sensitized skin and she let out a moan.

Even though she was still coming down from the first orgasm he'd wrung from her, based on the wicked way his eyes danced, it wouldn't be the last. Except he hadn't gotten rid of his goddamn pants. Instead, he pressed lazy kisses on her hips, up her stomach, and between her breasts until she went out of her mind.

"Are you planning on fondling or fucking me?" Raven couldn't help herself, her eyebrow lifting, even as he grinned. The confidence in his stare seared right through her, but she felt it in every deft stroke of his tongue bringing her right to orgasm.

He smirked, pressing over the top of her, his hardness making her insides pulse with need.

"Maybe I want to hear you beg for it," he murmured into her ear, the hot whisper traveling straight to her core.

Raven shot him a glare even as she bit down on her lip, unable to deny how turned on she was right then.

Jer simply returned to teasing her nipples, the languorous way he toyed with her driving her to the point of insanity.

"Fine, damn it," she cursed out. "Please, fuck me now, before I lose my mind."

His dimple deepened with his grin and she groaned out loud.

The snick of his belt caused her stomach to tighten with anticipation, and a second later, he shucked his pants and boxers to the ground. He climbed back over her, even the sight of his length making her mouth water, all before he slid against her again. The way he brushed his heated length along her soaked folds made her delirious. Her nipples brushed against the hard muscles of his chest, the sensation pushing her into overload.

"That didn't sound very sincere," he murmured against her mouth before he claimed it. He drove his tongue in deep with a kiss so possessive her core clenched tight.

When he pulled back, a mere inch separated them, but she stared straight into his eyes.

"Please," she whispered, unable to help how her chest squeezed. Here and now, this was real. They'd both hidden behind masks for too many years and deluded themselves into thinking they'd be fine frozen in suspension. However, here with him, life gripped her tight by the chest, like the birdsong that rippled through the chilled air on an early morning and the churn of paws into the earth on a run through the woods.

Jer pressed his mouth to hers, and she sank into the kiss as if her life depended on it. He gripped her hip tight, and a moment later, he brushed the end of his length against her opening. She spread her legs wider as he nudged himself in. Jer went in slow, inch by agonizing inch. Her breaths quickened, pushing her so close to the completion she needed. He slid in with ease because she had grown so fucking wet for him. She needed him to fill her.

As he buried himself to the hilt inside her, Raven's entire body shuddered. She dug her nails into his shoulders, and she met his lips again and again. For a flash of a moment, they froze in perfect stillness in the wake of the connection they'd both waited so long for. But then Jer began to rock his hips, and every thought vanished from her mind.

She moved with him, the sensation of him filling her to completion almost more than she could bear. His wolf flashed in his eyes and he moved faster, each thrust sending a delicious thrill through her body. She bucked against him, needing the skin-to-skin connection like she needed the sun. His mouth met hers again and again, and she drank in the taste of him and the sting of copper from the scrape of their swollen lips.

Jer slammed into her with increasing ferocity, setting a pace she could lose herself in, one that made her head swirl and her forget that anything else existed but this moment here between them. Sweat beaded on her forehead and every time he thrust deep into her, she let out a ragged breath. Her core pulsed and her mind flashed white. Her clit smacked against his skin with the fierce pace he moved, the delicious sting making her pant.

Raven's hips thrust to greet him like the sun's inevitable crash toward the horizon every night. Jer surged with coiled strength, biceps flexing with each movement and those powerful thighs tensing as he drove into her with a fury she surrendered to. His thick eyebrows furrowed with concentration, his eyes blazed with heat and the freckles scattered across his face glowed even brighter in the sheen of sweat slicked across his body. He caught her staring and the grin that spread across his face — it was blinding.

Jer dipped down and brushed his lips across hers right as he thrust deep inside her.

The tenderness in the motion was her undoing.

The orgasm ripped through her, erasing all coherent thought. Her breath left her in gasps and sweat broke out across her skin. She trembled in the wake of the bliss rolling through her. Jer continued to thrust into her as she shuddered from the sensations overtaking her body, until his thighs tensed. Heat flooded inside her, and his cock pulsed with his orgasm. He sank over her, crushing her with his mouth and body. She loved every damn second of it.

Raven wound her arms around his neck as he kissed her long and deep. Their sweat-slicked bodies pressed together in a tangle of heat, the scent of sex lingering in the air. Resolve settled in her, an unfamiliar weight. She'd spent most of her life behind glass, slamming at the panes, yet separate from everything else.

This was the connection she'd dreamed of, the warmth of a hearth and as all-encompassing as the velvet night sky. The flickers of the intensity around Jer over the years paled in comparison to the bond between them, but here and now, Raven accepted it.

Jer pulled back for a second, his long lashes fluttering as he blinked. "I think that's the first real thing I've felt all week," he murmured. She opened her mouth. For so long, words had stuck in her throat from so many things she'd wanted to divulge and so much she wanted to tell him. Raven had always silenced herself. Except, here, with him, her words no longer hid in the shadows. She knew exactly what to say.

A soft smile reached her lips. "That's because you're mine. My mate."

Chapter Twenty

They hadn't crashed out until the early hours of the morning, but Jer somehow managed to wake up before noon. He leaned up to look over at the gorgeous woman who slept beside him, at peace. Raven's mouth was open and she snored lightly. His chest squeezed tight at the sound and seeing the way her shoulders slumped forward in complete abandon. He loved the fact that she snored.

He stroked the soft strands of her hair splayed across his pillow, remembering the moans from last night, the sting of skin against skin when they'd collided again and again. He'd woken with a semi, stiffening by the second at the mere thought of it. Raven's body curved against his perfectly, and he couldn't help slipping a hand around to stroke the smooth skin of her stomach and the dip of her hips. Fuck, he was hard again.

He'd better get up before he woke her out of deep sleep — and right now, she looked far too peaceful to disturb. He tugged himself out of bed but felt as though he was dragging along a massive boulder in the process, every movement growing more sluggish. It'd be at least a week before the meds kicked in — he knew that, but the fact that he popped those hateful little circles into his mouth and they weren't working with a snap didn't do anything to dispel his reluctance to take them.

Jer strode across his room, trudging past the piles of unwashed clothing beginning to overtake the space. When had it gotten that bad? Just a couple of weeks ago everything had been under control and his apartment in some semblance of order. However, when he stepped into the main room and headed for the kitchen, the stacks of books, tipped-over boots and mail splayed across the floor threatened to overwhelm him.

He tried to focus on the coffeemaker. *One thing at a time.* Even that seemed like too much of a task and the stack of papers on his coffee table with his case against the Coalition of Human Rights loomed like a deadline. He should've had them done days ago, like the beta the pack deserved. Instead, he'd been self-involved, wasting a day getting his meds. The one thing he didn't regret was every moment with Raven. When the mating bond had clicked into place last night, it was as though he'd been walking down a tangled path for years only for the destination to finally rise into view.

The coffeemaker started hissing, tar-colored liquid collecting at the bottom, and he leaned against his counter. Soft rustling came from his bedroom, and the next moment Raven stepped out, her rumpled camisole barely clinging to her shoulders and her pants almost hanging off her hips. She ran a hand through her hair, smoothing the ink-stain strands. When her gaze landed on him, he forgot to breathe.

Raven's doe eyes crinkled with warmth as a soft smile curled her lips, and Jer fell for her all over again. Her delicate features contrasted with the resilient woman she'd become, one who had glued her own pieces back together after shattering again and again. He sucked in a sharp breath, barely daring to believe what had happened. Now that the light of day filtered in through his blinds, last night felt like something he'd simply imagined.

At least, until Raven crossed the space between them to press against him. His hands circled her slim waist and he drew her in closer, basking in her scent.

"I'll be honest," he murmured into her hair. "I'm still not convinced this isn't a dream."

Raven reached for his side and pinched, hard.

"Hey," he protested, but didn't let go of her. He was pretty incapable of it at this point.

"There you go. Not a dream." The grin on her face when she glanced at him made his heart twist. He'd seen her smirk so often along with the dry delivery of some sarcastic line, and always, always the longing would follow. His chest would throb with how badly he wanted her and how he wished she would at him even though her attention had always homed in on Finn.

For the first time, he understood. All those years, she had suffered the same.

And with her here in his arms, the longing tugged in his chest, a reflex from years of wanting. Yet instead of the hollowness descending, a warmth filled him that suffused the gray landscape he'd been walking through with a hint of color.

"Looks like you'll have to retire the old nickname," Raven continued, looking up at him, her palms pressed against his chest. "Because I don't share."

His eyebrows furrowed. "What, Streaky? Not like you ever called me that anyway." She pressed her lips tight together and her nails bit into his bare chest. The realization melted inside him like drops of honey into tea. "I should've pieced that together long ago. You know, I hated watching you with Finn just as much."

She let out a low huff. "I know. I was terrified of how I felt around you, Jer. Exposed, real. I had too much ugliness inside to let it out."

His chest tightened and he slipped his finger under her chin to lift her face. "Maybe all those broken pieces make you perfect for me. I was born defective, Rae, and there's no cure for bipolar. This is a struggle I'm going to have my entire life, meds or no."

Yet his breath snared in his throat when their eyes met. No fear existed in her gaze and she looked at him with an unflinching stare. Despite the struggle, she'd chosen him as her mate. Those were the words too precious for him to speak out loud, ones he kept safe inside his heart. He'd never met anyone braver.

"Good thing you're too pretty to stay mad at," Raven responded with a grin. She brushed her thumb across his lower lip, and a growl rumbled in his chest. He tightened his grip on her waist. He was two seconds from carrying her across the room to have his way with her again.

A knock sounded on the door.

"Who the hell is knocking on my door this time of day?" Jer muttered, running a hand through his curls.

Raven snorted. "You mean lunchtime? Because I'm pretty sure it's lunchtime. Might want to throw a shirt on, stud." She trailed her fingers down his chest before she snapped them away and headed for the door.

Jer couldn't help his grin as he stalked over to his bedroom and snagged a wrinkled shirt from the floor. He threw it on and followed Raven toward the door. The knock sounded again by the time she'd reached it, more insistent this time.

"I've got it," he said, stepping beside her to grab the handle. He tugged it open.

Dax stood in the doorway, except the normal amusement in his eyes had vanished. Jer's temperature plummeted.

Before Jer could say anything or even welcome him in, the alpha of the Silver Springs pack strode inside, bringing his thunderclouds with him. Jer closed the door behind him as Dax walked straight into the kitchen. He stopped for a moment then paced forward.

"What happened?" Jer asked, fear gluing to his skin. Raven stepped beside him to weave her fingers through his. The simple gesture planted his feet on the floor again. Dax's eyes flashed even bluer for a moment and he stared at the two of them, his gaze dropping to their entwined hands before the mountain lion looked him square in the eye.

"Sierra's missing."

The words dropped into the room like a bomb. Jer squeezed Raven's hand tighter and he sucked in a sharp breath. Dax hadn't stopped pacing, back and forth, back and forth, his agitation clear.

"How long has she been missing for?" Raven asked. "I just saw her yesterday morning."

"She didn't come home last night," Dax said. "She said she'd be home, and she didn't show."

"Fuck," slipped from Jer's lips. Unlike his forgetful ass, he could set his watch to Sierra's appearance. If she said she'd be somewhere, she would show early or on the dot. "Do you think it was the Coalition?"

"Who else could it be?" Dax threw his hands out, claws pricking to the surface. With the growl in his voice, he brimmed, on the edge. *Not like I blame him.* His heart raced faster than a bullet train at the idea of Sierra in the hands of those fanatics.

Raven's nails turned to claws as well. The tips sank into his skin with how tightly she gripped his hand. The sting kept him grounded, even as his world dropped from under him. Loathing crept in, tendrils wrapping around his arms and his throat until they latched. If he hadn't been such a fuck-up beta, he might've been able to stop this from happening.

"Sierra mentioned sending a challenge to the Coalition," Raven murmured. "Do you think this was in response?"

"I'll kill every last bastard who touched her." Dax's voice simmered even as his eyes flashed with rage. "We've been holding back because they're human, but they went too far. They took my mate."

"Christian has to be behind this," Raven spoke. The name struck a match inside Jer in a flare of fury. He hadn't forgotten the way she'd shown up at his door the other night after facing off against the monster at Ganzorig's old place. The man had caused problems for their pack from the moment he'd first shown at Beaver Tavern.

"The former Landslider?" Dax asked, his voice growing as sharp as his fangs. "Do you think Mackey got involved?" If Dax didn't get a handle on his temper, he might shift into a mountain lion right in Jer's kitchen.

Even though self-loathing scraped across his skin like sandpaper, Jer strode up to Dax and placed a hand on the man's shoulder. A growl escaped Dax, and a second later a fist flew for Jer's face.

Dax stopped an inch away.

Jer didn't bat an eye. "I'm guessing you've checked all her usual spots."

"Everywhere," Dax said, his shoulders heaving. A real panic flared in his eyes—not that Jer could fault him—but something was off about it. Sierra was strong, one of the strongest shifters he'd met, including the Tribe. Even though fear flowed through his veins like ice water, he believed in her ability to survive, at least long enough for them to find her.

"What's going on?" he asked, his voice coming out sharper than intended.

Dax's eyes met his, and his distress grew to that of a wild animal. Whatever happened had gone deep enough to send his lion into a frenzy.

"Damn it, Jer, she's pregnant," Dax whispered, his voice hollow with horror. "It was too early to announce to the pack, but the Coalition assholes took her, her and our child."

Jer's hand didn't leave Dax's shoulder, but he sagged as if he'd been punched in the gut. Sierra was pregnant. That dragged him right out of the mire of self-loathing he'd been drowning in. He was the pack beta, which meant with Sierra missing, he needed to summon the Red Rock pack.

"Raven and I will check a couple of the other pack spots, just in case," he said. "Then we'll meet at Beaver

Tavern, the entire pack. I need you to rally Silver Springs."

Dax looked him square in the eye, and his entire body, which had been buzzing, moving unceasingly, went still. Even though Jer was a headcase, a shitty beta and a thousand other flawed things, he cared about his pack more than anything on this earth. And he'd fight his own demons and the ones the Coalition bred to defend the people he loved.

Jer met Dax's gaze with every ounce of strength he could muster.

"We're going to get our alpha back."

Chapter Twenty-One

Raven thought Christian's return had upended her world, but that had been nothing compared to her alpha going missing.

She clutched tight to Jer while he tore across the asphalt, his Harley rumbling beneath them. He raced faster and faster as though he was trying to speed off the face of the earth itself. Her stomach squeezed for the thousandth time since Dax had burst into Jer's apartment with the terrible news. The pit had grown with every passing hour Sierra remained missing. Heat pricked Raven's eyes even as the cold wind iced her cheeks.

The sun began to set, crimson streaks flaring across the horizon. Tonight, they looked like blood.

The Coalition had resorted to silver traps, planting bombs and now they'd kidnapped. Their behavior had gone from militant to full-blown terrorism, and Christian was the one tugging the strings. Bile rose in her throat. She knew far too well who had directed Christian throughout the years.

Beaver Tavern emerged farther down the road, and the lights in the windows shone like a warning. Raven leaned into Jer's back, pressing against his beaten leather jacket and soaking in the heat and scent of him. Last night felt like another lifetime, even though something irrevocable had altered between them. *Nothing like a kidnapping to kill the afterglow.*

She tightened her grip around him. They'd been holding on to each other from the moment Dax had broken the news, whether through a quick touch, locking fingers or leaning in for sheer closeness. Both of their wolves were freaking out with their alpha in danger and it took everything inside her to keep from breaking into tears. God, just the other day she and Sierra had stood overlooking the forest, sharing scars. If the Coalition had done something to her, if they'd hurt her…

Raven's world turned gray with fear while Jer veered into Beaver Tavern's parking lot. She was afraid of what the Coalition would do, but the truth of what the Landsliders were capable of deadened her veins. She'd experienced that hell firsthand.

She'd never seen more cars packed into the parking lot of Beaver Tavern, almost covering the gravel entirely. She and Jer had started the phone chain as soon as Dax had left to go tell his own pack, and the sight of all those cars was proof that when danger descended on their packs, they knew how to rally. Gravel flew while Jer pulled his Harley into a slim spot. She slipped off first, and only a few seconds passed before Jer's fingers wove through hers. The connection bolstered her right then, keeping her standing even as her knees trembled.

"Ready to do this, beta?" she asked, giving him a sidelong glance.

A faint smile clung to his lips as he distanced himself, the mask settling into place. "Better late than never." Even as he transformed before her eyes into the man everyone else saw, he gave her fingers a light squeeze with the grasp of vulnerability he reserved for her alone.

Gene and Jer's dad, Derek, stood with a couple of the guys from the Silver Springs pack, grabbing a smoke outside the bar. Upon approach, she and Jer garnered looks, most of the focus zeroing in on their intertwined hands.

Jer glanced at Raven, but she didn't have a clue how to announce it to the rest of the pack either.

"Thank the Spirits," Gene let out in a gasp, slapping a hand to his thigh. "Pay up, Taylor. I placed that bet years ago." His gaze met Raven's, and she couldn't help her giddy grin. Of course Gene would've noticed. He'd always been watching out for her.

Jer arched an eyebrow at Derek. "Really, Dad? Your faith is astounding."

Derek slipped a twenty into Gene's palm before he flicked his cigarette to the ground. "I'd hoped you two would make a go of it, but I was never sure it would happen. We all knew she was the only woman you'd ever settle down for."

Heat bloomed on Raven's cheeks and warmth stirred deep inside her.

Gene glanced between the two of them like his sharp eyes seized on something. "Did the two of you…"

Raven nodded, and a grin burst on Jer's face like sunlight amidst the dark.

"Yeah, we're mated," he said, and his father let out a loud whoop. Rick punched Derek in the arm.

"Hey, we'll celebrate later," Rick said, casting a pointed glance to the tavern behind them.

Jer took the cue at once. "Finish your sewing circle gossip and snuff out the cigarettes." He tilted his head toward the entrance. "We've got pack matters to discuss." All the warmth that had emerged at their announcement vanished in the autumn chill of the reality they faced. Their alpha was in danger.

He strode inside to where so many familiar faces crowded around the tables. She'd never seen the place so packed, and Raven had worked at the tavern for a decade now. Kyle had been on shift tonight, but he'd slipped out from the counter to join Ally and Lana at a table with some of the others from Silver Spring.

Dax still paced by the bar, which made for the perfect vantage point to address the group. Some of the parents had stayed home with their littles, but every family had sent a representative to the point where close to thirty shifters were crammed into their little old bar, which now strained at the seams. Growls lit the air and myriad scents overwhelmed. Raven followed Gene and the others to a round table with others from the Red Rock pack, nearest to the bar. Jer walked with her the entire time, but when they reached the seats, he tugged on her hand.

She offered him a grin, even though her stomach twisted in knots. "Go get 'em, stud."

Raven found a seat, watching as Jer sauntered to the bar and took his place beside Dax. She couldn't help the lump in her throat—every other time they'd looked up there, Sierra and Finn had stood together, leading the pack. However, the times had changed. Finn had found his mate, and Sierra hers, which had brought Dax and his pack crashing into their lives. And Raven had accepted her own at long last.

Sierra trusted the position to Jer. No matter how much self-loathing he dosed himself with on a daily basis — she'd heard the bitterness in his tone and seen it reflected in his eyes — Raven believed in Sierra's decision. Jer wasn't just one of the brightest minds among the Red Rocks but a selfless soul who would put every member of the pack before himself. He cared for this family of theirs to the same depth she did. No one ever needed to question his devotion.

He leaned in to whisper to Dax before clapping a hand on the man's shoulder. *God, he must be terrified.* If her nerves buzzed with fear for Sierra, it was a drop in the pond to the avalanche of fear Dax must feel with his mate and future child in jeopardy. The mere thought of it made her sick.

"Red Rock and Silver Springs," Jer called out. His voice echoed clear throughout the room and the moment he spoke, the murmurs of conversation silenced. Raven rested her palms on her pants, her hands grown so slick she hoped they didn't imprint. "Some of you may have already heard, but Dax and I are here to tell you now. Your alpha is missing."

If the room had quieted before, a cemetery hush descended in the wake of this news.

"We believe she's been abducted by the Coalition of Human Rights," Jer started. Growls filled the air, which heated near ten degrees. Necks craned forwards, eyes flashed and a whole mess of shifters came close to changing forms on the spot. Jer lifted his hands. "I know you're pissed," he called out, "but I need you to stay with me right now. Time is of the essence here."

Even though growls rumbled through the tavern, a lot of them quieted in the wake of Jer's words. Raven's heart twisted with both terror for Sierra and pride at how Jer had stepped up to the plate, the combination making her want to hurl. She swallowed hard but her focus never abandoned her mate.

"Dax and I will lead groups to sweep through the area," Jer said, his gaze traveling the room. "If anyone has any inkling of where they might be, come talk to us. Before the hour's up, we'll be dividing into groups and heading out. Sierra has worked tirelessly for us for years, never complaining and always providing an example of strength to aspire to. She deserves the same from us. We won't rest until we bring our alpha back."

Raven dug her nails into the wood of the table. She didn't think they'd be stupid enough to bring Sierra to the community center, and with the denizens of the Coalition spread through a large breadth of the area, who knew where they might be hiding her? The enormity of the task caused her head to spin.

If Christian was behind this…he wouldn't take her to Ganzorig's cabin.

However, one place remained isolated to this day. One she'd been avoiding for the past decade, even though every time she drove past it, her talons dug deep into her skin.

As Jer fell silent, chatter filtered through the room again. The air buzzed as if someone had dropped a live grenade, and all of it descended on her at once. Before she could get up from her seat, the door to Beaver Tavern swung open again.

As Lucas and Drew entered, the tension in the room exploded. At once, pack members shot up from their seats, baring their fangs. Growls ripped through the air, and three of the Silver Springs pack began to shift into their mountain lion forms on the spot.

Oh, fuck. The rest of the pack hadn't realized Drew was back in town.

Raven shot up from her seat right as Dax crossed the room toward his brother.

"Pack, stand *down*. We called them here," Dax shouted, his hands thrust out in an attempt to soothe the crowd. "Lucas is keeping Drew in line, and he's going to help us with our Landslider problem."

"Look at the sort of welcome you're inspiring," Lucas drawled, hooking his thumbs through the belt loops of his jeans. The big guy sauntered in first. Drew appeared unaffected, his face a picture of blasé, but the way he rolled his shoulders back tipped her off. She'd noticed it a few times now, whenever one of them sniped at him.

Dax's words might've kept the packs from lunging forward, but teeth were still bared and gazes flashed as their beasts surged to the fore. Raven pushed away from the table and approached Jer. With Dax addressing the crowd now, the attention had moved off her mate, and she needed to speak to him one on one. Sierra and Jer might've understood and forgiven her past affiliation with the Landsliders, but after Drew's less-than-friendly reception, she wasn't about to drop that knowledge to the general public.

Jer's eyes settled on her at once, and he didn't wait for her to come to him, already striding in her direction. He slipped his hands around her waist and drew her in for a kiss. Relief crashed through her. Even with the fear that gripped her by the throat, the thrill of kissing him in public, in front of the pack, settled something deep inside. His shoulders were tense, but once she rested her palms on them, he relaxed.

He pulled away first, and Raven slid her hands to his chest. A couple of the pack noticed at this point, and Lana offered a less-than-subtle thumbs-up from where she sat with the other Silver Springs members. Raven rolled her eyes even though her lips quirked, threatening a smile.

"Jer," she said, the urgency in her voice drawing his gaze at once. "If Christian's behind the kidnapping, then there's one more spot you're going to want to consider."

"Does it have to do with your shared history?" he asked, his eyebrows furrowing.

She nodded. "The old Landsliders hideout. It hasn't been in use for over a decade, but the abandoned house leads to an underground area perfect for assembling an army, or, hell, a kidnapping."

"I'll make it our number-one priority," he reassured, a confidence in his tone she didn't feel. His unwavering faith made her gut clench. They had been idiots for avoiding their feelings for so long.

Dax's pacing caught her eye and she sucked in a sharp breath. *Maybe that's why.* Even now, he marched back and forth across the planks of Beaver Tavern. His mate and future child were missing. She couldn't even begin to imagine the panic, but one look at Jer and the thought of him in danger made the loss of her parents and her years of loneliness pale in comparison.

They needed to bring Sierra back. She had to be safe. Whole. Raven couldn't permit the alternative.

Jer's eyes met hers. "I know," was all he said, but the serious press of his lips conveyed everything.

Sierra had become the unwavering pillar of strength the Red Rock pack relied on. Without their alpha, the pack would become broken like Raven.

Dax strode over to them with Lucas and Drew following close behind. Where Drew went, Red Rocks and Silver Springs bared their teeth and growled, but they didn't dare lunge with a member of the Tribe by his side.

"We need to head out," Dax said, turning to her and Jer. "We're going to check the community center first."

Before she could say anything, the squeal of sirens split the air, coming from right outside the bar. Everyone stopped mid-conversation to look at the windows where the red, white and blues flashed, enough to constitute a squad of cars. Raven withheld her groan. She didn't have to guess who'd called law enforcement.

"Both of you, take a team out through the back and shift," Jer addressed Dax and Lucas. "I'll handle the cops."

The Silver Springs alpha shot to action like a loosed arrow, a symmetry of muscles and barely controlled rage. His pack members caught sight of him and were rising from their seats in response. Lucas slunk through the crowd to collect his pick of the shifters to join him and Drew. A single look from the formidable Tribe member summoned them.

Raven slipped her hand through Jer's as together they marched to the front of the tavern. Already, tires screeched out front and gravel crunched under boots.

Red Rocks and Silver Springs alike slunk behind the bar which led through the kitchens to the exit leading out to the woods. Dax tipped his fingers in their direction before slinking behind the groups they'd rallied last.

The pounding against gravel grew louder as more cops poured from their cars onto the crowded parking lot. Raven clenched her jaw.

Time to hold the line.

Chapter Twenty-Two

Every minute the cops remained at the bar sawed at Jer's composure further.

"We haven't found anything so far, but we need to do a sweep through the front yard and a little farther to make sure no humans are being held hostage here." The officer crossed his arms as he scanned the bar. His tone rang with mild disbelief, which was entirely justified, because the anonymous tip that had been called on them was some bullshit.

The cops had marched in, pistols aimed, and he didn't even question if they carried silver bullets. However, they'd come to a quick halt upon storming in on a room of about ten shifters sitting at the tables before offering a how-ya-do.

"Absolutely," Jer said, pulling his politeness out of his ass. He offered a hand to shake, which the officer clapped against his own palm. "Whatever we can do to help. There's been some tension with the local

Coalition, and we don't want any more trouble than they're already causing us."

The officer nodded and headed out through the front door where the other cops had congregated. Jer beelined for the kitchen, needing to get out of the pack's sight before he had a breakdown. His heart slammed and a fury burned, liable to explode at a moment's notice.

He hunched against the chrome kitchen sink in the back section of the tavern, his foot tap-tap-tapping on the ground.

His insides buzzed, adrenaline coursing through his veins as though he'd pounded a case of energy drinks. Somehow, he'd made it through the conversation with the cops and hadn't punched anyone in the face. *Pats on the back, there.* He'd shown them the pictures of the bombs the Coalition had planted and filled them in on the current problem of their alpha being missing — most likely kidnapped.

Some of the squad had set out at once, their sirens blaring while they'd soared off down the highway. However, the couple of the cops lingering out front would probably be there for a bit still. Which left him waiting. Waiting for them to clear out, and waiting for Dax to call, text or whatever to tell them where they were at. If they'd found Sierra yet. Even though Jer had brought up the old Landslider hideout, Dax had insisted on checking the Coalition's main meeting place first.

He paced back and forth along the scuffed tile in the kitchen. On any normal day, the back of house was bustling. Given their current emergency, Beaver Tavern was anything but open to the public.

Raven had been passing out a few pints of ale to those waiting with them, her bartender's instinct kicking in, which left him here in the back, pretending he wasn't three seconds away from a breakdown when his people needed him the most. Really, they needed their alpha, but in her absence, he called the shots, and he was pretty sure he was fucking it up every step of the way.

Jer ran a hand through his hair, the thump, thump, thump of his footsteps echoing through the enclosed kitchen. He checked his phone for the fiftieth time. *No response.*

The door swung open and Raven stepped into the kitchen.

He stopped mid-pace as their eyes met. She'd pulled her hair into a loose ponytail, putting the gorgeous slope of her neck on display. Her lips were pressed tight and her eyes reflected the defeat he felt deep in his bones. At least, until she stepped closer.

Raven slipped her hand through his and tugged. Jer couldn't do anything else but follow, the pull between them as inexorable as the tide to shore. Together, they slipped out through the exit and into the crisp autumn night. The scent of bonfires wafted through the air from farther away and the murmurs of the cops drifted from out front. But back here, they faced a forest filled with looming oaks and pines and a sky studded with silver.

"You're buzzing. Like, manic buzzing," she murmured. Her hand never left his as they stared out into the quiet woods before them. "Now that we're mated, my wolf's picking up on it stronger than ever."

"Sorry," he muttered, scrubbing his palm across his face. The guilt tugged him even further down. Now she was stuck dealing with the swings for the rest of her life too. "The meds take at least a week or two to really kick in."

Raven's fingers traced his chin, drawing his attention to her. She shook her head. "No apologies. I just figured we could both use a distraction."

When his gaze met hers, molten desire lit her eyes and his libido slammed in like a heart attack.

"You're so damn perfect," he murmured, closing the distance between them. Dried leaves crunched underfoot. He moved one step closer, then another, until her back pressed against the wall. Her hot breath mingled with his as he crowded her, the insistent pulse in his chest growing so loud he could lose himself in it. Yearning filled him, but not the years of it that had stretched between them to the point he'd almost lost all hope.

No, this was the intense need to bury himself inside his mate, a reassurance that she was here, that they were safe and they might get through this madness.

Jer threaded his fingers through her hair, gripping her nape before he claimed her lips. The kiss between them was as incendiary as a bomb, and Jer sank into the blaze. Her mouth met his, hungry and seeking. She gripped his shoulders, digging her nails into his traps as he slammed her against the wall. She smelled like earth and maple, and he wanted to bury himself inside her.

"Come on, babe," she murmured against his mouth between kisses. "Let loose."

The pounding in his chest reached a crescendo, pushing him to the brink. She knew it and she was offering to ride this out with him. Jer sucked in a sharp gasp, falling for her all over again, as though he'd died and been reborn.

He let out a low growl, one that vibrated between them. Raven's lips curved into a smile against his mouth and the switch inside him flipped. One minute, he was kissing her with tongues, teeth and desperation, and the next, he was snapping open the button of her jeans, pulling her zipper down with a snick echoing in the quiet air. She snagged his belt, yanked it off him and a second later, she dove back in with those nimble fingers.

Jer grabbed her hands, lifting them over her head to pin her against the wall. The way she looked at him, dark eyes gleaming with lust and the tip of her tongue tracing her lips, had his cock aching for her. He was as stiff as a rock and as he stepped in to press himself to her, he brushed his length straight between her legs.

"Fuck me," she growled, bucking her hips against him.

"Manners, sweetheart," he murmured against her mouth, grinding against her. She let out a low, guttural moan that traveled straight south. Raven leaned in to nip at his neck, even as he kept her pinned against the wall. She teased him, pressing her lips along his earlobe, the side of his neck and the pulse at his throat, each kiss making him want to drive into her even more.

Instead, he yanked down her pants and slipped his fingers inside her barely there panties. He had just brushed her folds when he let out a low groan. She was absolutely soaked. He circled the tips of his fingers around and around until she thrust her hips toward him, and that was when he struck. Jer drove his fingers inside her with one hand while he kept the other wrapped around her wrists, pinning her to the wall.

Raven opened her mouth in a scream he muffled with his. He jammed his tongue down her throat while he finger-fucked her against the wall. Her hips bucked with his movements, and she kissed him back as hard, melting to his touch. Like this, he was feral, all the energy pouring out of him as if it was endless, as if it wouldn't vanish the moment he hit another swing. Like this, he was alive, electric.

She wrapped her thighs around his hips as she met his fingers again and again, her breaths coming out in pants between their fevered kisses. She sank her nails into his hand even while he kept her pinned, and she rode his fingers like she couldn't get enough. Raven opened her mouth, and he covered it again with his own, kissing her deep.

She let out a muffled cry. Her thighs tightened and her core clenched around his fingers. Sweat beaded her skin and she sagged against him a moment later, still pinned to the wall.

Jer tugged his fingers out of her, dripping wet with her juices. He was so turned on it hurt, and his balls tightened at the sight of her panting with that subtle flush across her cheeks. He licked his fingers, watching her as she stared at him spellbound.

"Please, fuck me," she murmured against his mouth.

"Good girl," he responded, dragging her pants farther. She shimmied them down her thighs before kicking them off, her underwear following. His gaze traveled to her bare pussy, those long legs then up to the stark strands of her hair plastered to her neck and forehead. Raven always had a breathtaking beauty about her, but seeing her undone reminded him of witnessing the ocean at midnight for the first time. He was in awe.

He lowered the hand keeping her pinned and unsnapped the button of his jeans, drawing his length out. "Wrap your arms around my neck," he instructed as he settled his palms around her hips. He dug his thumbs into the hollow of the bone and gripped her tight as he took one step forward, until she was sandwiched between him and the wall. He brushed his cock against her wetness, and a shudder rolled through him.

Raven leaned up to bite his lower lip, enough to sting, and enough to taste copper. He sucked in a shaky breath, his head dizzying with desire. Need pounded into him with a steady drive he was helpless to deny. He grabbed her thighs and within seconds she twined those gorgeous long legs around his waist. A second later, he nudged into her drenched opening and thrust in deep.

When he sank all the way in, he sagged from the relief shuddering through his veins. She dug her nails into his nape as he rocked her against the wall, slowly at first. Her honeyed heat was the sort he could lose himself in, and even as she clung tight to him, their mouths met again and again. With other girls, he'd been warming himself by the fire. With Raven, he stepped into the flames.

He began to pick up pace, their hips colliding and their skin letting out a hearty smack every time they crashed. With the nighttime hush and the careful autumn breeze drying the sweat on his forehead, he grew separate from everything and became part of it all in the same breath. Here with Raven under the stars, he could forget the pain, the fear and even his own fragmented mind for a few blessed moments.

She rocked against him while he drove into her again and again, her back scraping against the rough brick of the wall. Raven's breaths hitched and sweat beaded along her gorgeous skin, the color of pale sand on a moonlit beach. Even now, she remained present with him, and every time their eyes met, her gaze penetrated deep enough to reach past the self-loathing and his bucket of crazy to the core of him that he'd forgotten.

"Hey, stay with me," she said, a seriousness in her tone that snapped him to attention.

He leaned down to kiss her swollen lips, drinking in the sweet taste of her. "Always," he whispered against her mouth before he closed his over it again to capture her breath.

He slammed into her, the sting of skin smacking against skin keeping him in the moment and the salt of the sweat along her neck as he nipped and sucked. Raven bit down on her lip so hard it bled, and she tried to smother her cries every time he thrust in. He gripped tight to her hips, rocking into her with an increasing speed as he got closer and closer.

Like this, he could erase his fragmented past.

Like this, he could become whole for a few blessed moments.

Drops of sweat beaded along his forehead, and his breaths caught in his throat — ragged, desperate things. The strain inside him, that thrum of energy, coiled so tight he could explode. He poured every ounce of himself into this, until his surroundings blurred and all that existed were the two of them and the way he thrust into her heat.

She sank her teeth into his neck, the sweet sting making his balls tighten, and as he thrust in again, he careened closer. Her breaths were already faster, more frantic, and based on the glazed look in her eyes, she was matching his pace.

He grabbed her hips even tighter and slammed into her hard enough that their chests crashed together and the wall held them both up. She let out a gasp into his mouth. The delicate, raw sound undid him.

White blinded him as he sank deep. His cock pulsed, and he spilled inside her with his lips still pressed against hers. The bliss bleached his mind clean of any other thoughts, anything else but these waves he rode. Jer let out a shuddering breath. Raven's thighs trembled where they were still wrapped around his hips, and his legs shook in the wake of their shared orgasm. She gripped onto him even as he pressed her against the wall.

For several minutes they stood there with her thighs wrapped around him while he was buried deep in her. They both sagged, their breaths echoing in the quiet autumn air.

"Well, that was one hell of a distraction," Raven murmured. She slipped her legs down from his waist to settle her feet on the ground. The wry tone matched her twinkling eyes, and his chest twisted tight.

"I fucking love you." The words leapt from him. He could have kicked himself. There he went, barreling right on in at the worst times.

Raven blinked, but at least this time, she didn't run off into the woods.

Jer ran a hand through his hair, shame infiltrating like poison on their quiet moment. "Sorry, Rae. Ignore that."

She sucked in a sharp breath. "I don't want to." Raven placed a hand over her chest as she met his eyes. "I want to memorize the way your lips looked when you said those words and keep it in my mind forever." Her gaze drifted to the ground. She opened her mouth and shut it again. Raven balled her hand into a fist on her chest. "I want to say it back, Jer. I really do."

He shook his head and slipped his finger under her chin to lift her gaze. "Take your time. You know I'd wait for you forever." It wasn't as if he needed to hear the words yet. Raven always showed her love rather than speaking it out loud. After the mating bond had clicked into place, he seemed to sense more and to understand how the words stuck in her mouth every time she needed to be vulnerable.

"Damn you and those dimples," was all she said, but he caught the way her eyes glowed with the soft intensity of the moon. She leaned up and brushed her lips against his, and he savored the lingering kiss even after she pulled away to grab her pants from the ground where they'd fallen. He hiked his jeans back up and buttoned them, tackling the belt and smoothing his shirt after. Raven had her clothes on and straightened by the time he finished.

He let out a sigh and ran his hands through his curls. "I guess we've got to go see what the cops are up to."

Raven nodded, the gravity returning to her features.

Jer hadn't gotten three steps toward the door before his phone buzzed. He tugged it out so fast it almost flew from his hands. Dax had texted.

Sierra's not at the Coalition facilities. Still missing.

His gaze met Raven's, and her mouth formed a thin line.

"She's at the old Landsliders hideout," she murmured. "I can't explain the feeling in my gut, but I know it." Fear flickered in her eyes so fast he almost missed it. This wasn't just fear for their missing leader, either. It was the dread of the past that had left the scars she carried to this day, ones that had been torn wide open when Christian had rolled into town.

Jer slipped his hand into hers and they headed for the door. "We'll do this, together."

Chapter Twenty-Three

Even though Raven had made the suggestion to check the old Landslider hideout, no amount of preparation in the world could ready her to return to that place. On her darkest days, the memories of the splintered floorboards crept in, along with the drip, drip, drip of old plumbing that had never been fixed. She still remembered the shouts from the others in the crew and how the mingle of voices was at first familiar and over time had grown as distant as the sea.

Her hair batted around from the fierce breezes as she gripped tight to Jer. They sped along the highway at top speed, a parade of headlights trailing behind them as the remainder of the pack followed them to their destination. They'd be meeting Dax and the others there, but time was of the essence. The couple of cops had cleared out before he and Raven had even returned inside, so Jer had made the announcement and everyone had followed.

Her chest burned with the way they'd collided and the look in his eyes when he'd dropped the *L* bomb. Like a slack-jawed idiot, she'd been unable to say it back. She felt it. Every time she looked at him, she ripped wide open with the same overwhelming awe as the sky full of distant stars. She'd never felt more helpless or alive before, and the words lingered on her lips.

Yet she swallowed them back. Years of silence didn't just fade, and right now, her emotions churned fiercer than a summer storm while the wounds from her past bled and bled. Raven clutched Jer tight. The heat and scent of him were the only things keeping her tethered to the present right then. The lone headlight of Jer's Harley carved a path across the dark asphalt, which stretched out like an oil slick at this time of night.

The route they were taking was one she'd traveled many, many times, but it had been years since this had been her destination.

As they passed lone ranches along the road, deep stretches of woods that beckoned with endless darkness, and the road signs she knew by heart, the pit in her stomach deepened.

Up there. It lies just ahead.

The three-story house loomed with broken windows gaping and holes stretching wide in the sagging roof. The wooden planks along the exterior were weathered, splintered and in dire need of repair, but no one had bothered with the place since the Landsliders had evacuated. The phantom breeze of clove drifted by like it always did, and her skin itched. Mackey's presence coated this place in an oil slick.

As they neared the building, Jer's headlight glinted off the exterior of not one, but at least four cars.

Bingo.

Raven tugged on Jer's sleeve, but he'd already taken the cue, driving on by the building. If they stood any chance at getting Sierra back unharmed, stealth would be their only option. He continued down the road for about a mile until they reached an old gas station that hadn't been operating for years. His Harley screeched to a halt, but Raven didn't move at first, feeling as though the ground was still traveling beneath her. She sucked in a shaky breath, summoning some thread of composure as she got up from the motorcycle.

One by one, the other cars pulled into the empty lot, a parade of headlights flashing across the damaged old building and making the shadows even sharper.

"How are you doing?" Jer asked under his breath before everyone started piling out of their cars.

"I'm here," she said. "And if Christian is waiting there, I'll be the one to deal with him." Even if the thought numbed her teeth. She swallowed, hard. The other night remained fresh in her mind, from the desire that had glowed in Christian's eyes to the disgusting words that had dripped from his mouth. Terror seized her body at remembering the first time. She gave Jer a sidelong glance, half-expecting an argument.

Instead, he slipped his hand into hers and squeezed. Out of all the things he could have said or done, the gesture of confidence bolstered her like nothing else.

"Good," he said. "The bastard deserves what's coming to him." His eyes hardened as he stared out to the road with a determination in his gaze that she hadn't seen in a long time. Tonight, he'd transformed into the leader she'd always known he could be. He might think he was a fuck-up, but the man could persevere in the hardest of times. He'd been doing it his entire life against his own mind.

Doors slammed as pack members got out of their vehicles. Kyle loped over first, followed closely by Gene. While most of the others roved out with Dax and Lucas, Jer rallied the remaining ten to his side, and they headed in their direction, brimming with tension. All of them were loaded guns ready to fire.

Raven's wolf paced inside her, a restless, wild thing. She unlaced their fingers, needing to stand alone even as they gathered together. Even so, she stayed by his side for this. The more of the pack that gathered around them, the more the air buzzed with tension, with everyone's beasts on edge. Their alpha was missing. Sierra had been kidnapped by the enemy, and only Dax, Jer and Raven knew she was pregnant.

"Pack." Jer addressed them, crossing his arms over his chest. Everyone turned to face him and Raven's heart pounded even faster at the command in his voice. The abandoned house waited for them through these woods, along with a Pandora's box of memories she'd locked away.

"We're heading into the old lair of the Landsliders, which means we may not just be facing humans armed with silver, but other shifters as well. Raven, Drew and I faced off against shifters who'd taken the drugs the Landsliders have been dealing, and they're berserkers, mindless in their rage. Berserkers are stronger than the average shifter, so don't underestimate them. The goal is to head in and, if they have our alpha, to get her back. If the humans flee, let them. At the end of the day, I value your lives more than theirs."

"What if those berserkers attack?" Kyle piped up.

"Then either fight, or run," Jer responded with a cool detachment in his tone. Raven bared her teeth at the memory of the shifters they'd run into at Ricketts Glen, lost to a drug-induced madness. "They won't stop attacking until they die."

"Are we shifting now?" Mandy asked, pacing back and forth on the concrete beneath them at the abandoned spot.

Jer shook his head. "This is the Coalition. If they see animals, they'll shoot on sight." He turned toward the woods. "We need to be quick and quiet if we stand a chance at sneaking up on whoever's at the abandoned house. Follow my lead." With that, Jer took off in the direction of the tall pines stretched between the gas station and the old Landsliders hideout.

Raven followed close behind, keeping stride with ease. Her palms itched and her nails begged to turn into claws. She teetered on the edge of shifting, her beast nearing the surface at being near this place. The shadows fell over them the moment they entered the forest, while all ten of their pack moved with the graceful stride of their kind. Barely a twig snapped under their careful footsteps and the chilly autumn air made her nose twitch from the rich scent of pine sap threading through the area.

She focused on one step after another, avoiding the dry branches, the skeletal leaves and pale needles forming a carpet along the ground. Her heart pounded in her ears while they carved their way past the skinny trunks of too many pine trees. The glow of the moonlight across the hoods of the cars stood out from the opposite end of the forest, which grew closer and closer with every step. She matched pace with Jer, who strode ahead, unflinching.

The distance was nothing to shifters who cut their teeth on racing through state parks, and even in their human forms, they moved on swift and silent feet. All too soon, they neared the fringe of the forest separating them from the house. All too fast, the ghosts of her past resurrected and threatened to bury her alive.

Raven balled her hands into fists, but the single touch from Jer as he squeezed her shoulder gave her the grounding she needed.

The air ached with silence ahead, as if even the animals knew what horrors had occurred in this place. Kyle stuck close behind them, as did Gene. Occasionally, she would glance back to see the flash of silver or copper in their eyes. Everyone was on edge there, their beasts veering close to breaking free. Jer slowed. They reached the edge of the trees, but Raven took another couple of steps, needing to keep moving.

No shadows slid ahead of them and the house glowered in perfect stillness. Most of the time they hadn't bothered with guards on the outside, not here. The downstairs was a basement that led to secret tunnels and chambers, so most of the house appeared normal to the onlooker. Raven rested her fingertips against the trunk of the tree, scraping them across the brittle surface of the bark.

"There's a side entrance we used to use." Raven trailed off, her gaze landing on the crooked door near the back of the house, where a few broken steps tapered down. "It leads to the basement, which was where we conducted our real business."

"You think they'll have her in the basement?" Jer asked, squinting as he scanned the area ahead of them.

"If she's here, that's the place they'd keep her," Raven whispered.

He nodded and, after another careful glance, took the first steps out past the border of trees. She followed close behind, feeling uneasy at the familiar scent of the earth and smoke there. The stretch of field out back held the char marks of the bonfires they'd built. However, only the Landsliders knew they weren't for enjoyment but design. If she lingered a little too long, the phantom scent of charred flesh still made bile rise in her throat.

As they crept across the sprawl of lawn covered by sedans, Raven's nape prickled. The vacuous windows glared on them as if someone watched from the shadows.

As long as it wasn't *him*. Raven could face anyone but Mackey Kendricks.

She trekked behind Jer, ducking around the cars and sticking to the shadows as the two of them made their way across the lawn. The other pack members moved as quietly, creeping with the silent predatory nature of their wolves and mountain lions. Her breath caught in her throat, and she barely dared to exhale while they tiptoed over patches of flaccid grass. The sheer quiet stretching through the space unsettled her to the core.

There should have been the drift of voices, the chirp of crickets and the rustle of squirrels. Instead, silence reigned and her heart thundered all the louder in her ears.

She crept up to the steps, which had splintered and sunk. The door near hung off the hinges and the screen front was gnarled and torn off the frame. However, her gaze settled on the knob, which contained a couple of shiny spots — oil from hands turning it and areas that hadn't dulled from disuse like the rest. The cars out front gave the clear tipoff, but the use of the side entrance solidified in her mind that the Landsliders were the puppet masters here.

Jer glanced at her as his hand settled on the knob. She nodded and he gave it a careful tug. The door squeaked as he opened it, and she winced at how the sound echoed amidst the quiet. She hoped no one was waiting for them by the basement steps.

He slunk in first, but she followed close behind. The air tasted like dust there, the sort of stale belonging to attics and cemeteries. The kitchen stretched out to the right of them, moonlight cascading across the cracked porcelain of the sink and the mottled surface of the chrome countertops. To the left lay the living room, where the familiar couches had always contained at least four of their pack lounging about. Now, rotting frames were all that remained, the cushions mere wisps of fabric.

And the basement door loomed ahead of them, large and red with the big iron handle, the way she remembered. Out of everything, the door seemed to be the one part of the house that hadn't dilapidated or faded from the passing years.

Before she could reach for the handle, a creak came from the front of the house. It was the unmistakable opening and closing of the door.

One set of footsteps pounded along the floorboards, the owner making no attempts to disguise the sound.

"Oh my, grandmother, what big teeth you have." Christian's voice sounded from the other room, and Raven's entire body tensed. The sound lit her match, and she needed somewhere to direct the flames. "You know," he continued, his lazy drawl echoing throughout this floor of the house. "Wolves happen to reek. The lot of you smell like wet dog."

Raven placed a hand on Jer's shoulder and their eyes met. Worry shone clear in his gaze.

"This is my fight," she said, reassuring him even as the ground felt as if it was falling out from under her. "Lead the pack to get our alpha back. I'll handle this asshole." Christian's footsteps grew louder and louder as he entered the living room.

"Come find us after you tear his throat out," Jer growled, his eyes flashing gold.

His faith in her was the one push she needed.

For a single moment, their eyes met. The world could be burning around them and she wouldn't see anyone but the broken, brave and loyal man she'd claimed for her mate. Jer had marked her from the day they'd met. She only wished it hadn't taken them this long to figure it out.

Then Jer broke away to tug the door open.

Raven headed the other way, toward the living room where the Landsliders had once congregated on too many nights to count. She stepped into the quiet room filled with broken furniture and memories.

Christian stood at the other end. The shadows sharpened his features, those eyes growing as black as ink, and his smile was undeniably cruel. The man might have his throng of admirers, but no amount of charm could bleach the callousness from his expression. The second he caught sight of her, he crossed his arms. "Well now, I hoped you'd be among the bunch, Tigerlily."

That name. This place. Raven was two steps away from hurling her guts out, the pressure behind her skull bursting free.

"This ends here." She bared her fangs at him, already forming as the shift overtook her.

This time, Raven wasn't running. Even if only one of them made it out of here alive.

Chapter Twenty-Four

Every step away from Raven sank those claws a little deeper into Jer's chest.

He crept down the steps, taking comfort in the whisper of the pack behind him as they headed for the basement. If Sierra wasn't there, he didn't know what he'd do. He'd bet his pack's future on this outcome, but the landing remained as dark as Ricketts Glen at midnight.

The closer he got to the bottom, the more he strained for any sort of sound from above, or below.

She remained up there, facing off against Christian by her lonesome. His wolf howled in his chest, commanding him to go back up and protect her, but he continued forward. He trusted her. Some instinct told him this was a battle she needed to fight on her own, one that meant far more than taking down the asshole who'd brought all this trouble on them.

The low murmur of voices pricked his ears.

Jer paused at the final steps and listened. The sound was muffled. He peered past the landing into the obsidian dark stretching throughout the room. Only a single rectangular slit at the top of the room let spare rays of moonlight drift to the floor. Still, the sounds came from somewhere. He glanced back to catch Gene's eyes flashing silver and his nose wrinkling as he sniffed.

Staleness lingered in the thick air, but beneath that, he caught the trail of too many scents to identify. Jer swallowed and took the first step past the landing into the basement. Gray blobs took up most of the room, which were too difficult to identify with the consuming shadows. The moonlight from the window cast a panel to the ground, threads glinting off a doorknob on the other side of the room. This couldn't be the entire basement, since it didn't even span a full room in the house.

A hum came from behind him, but when he glanced back, Mandy looked down at her feet, baring her teeth from her slip of a growl. He met her gaze and jerked his head 'no.' *Not like I'm faring much better.* His claws pricked out, and he was one breath away from shifting.

A crash came from above, the sound flooding his veins with ice.

Raven was up there.

The knob on the opposite side of the room rattled. It looked as though they weren't the only ones who'd heard the sound.

Jer hunched, his neck tightening and fangs forming. His entire being buzzed. A second later, the door flung open.

Two figures marched in, followed by another. The humans strode with a cocky confidence that melted from their faces the moment they caught sight of the pack standing before them. Jer didn't think. He just *moved*.

One moment he stood with his pack and the next he barreled toward the trio at full speed with his claws extended. His heart slammed, but he was operating on wolf instinct alone. All the agitation churning through him found a target in the three unfortunate fools who'd strolled through the door.

The closest guy opened his mouth to shout, but Jer slung his fist toward him. Before a squeak could emerge from the man's throat, Jer's knuckles collided with the guy's jaw. The *thunk* sliced through the silence.

His pack responded as though he'd set off a warning flare. Before the other human could lift that shiny pistol, Kyle tackled him to the ground. His face morphed into a muzzle, and he shifted mid-leap.

The Coalition members would be packing silver, which meant any shot fired could be fatal.

Gene had turned to his wolf form, along with two other pack members, and they leapt upon the third human in the bunch. Jer couldn't shift. His phone rested like a lead weight in his pocket. He'd told Dax where to find them, but the Silver Springs alpha hadn't arrived yet with the cavalry.

The guy nearest him roused himself from the punch, and Jer caught the glint of a pistol. His fist flew.

He slammed his knuckles into the man's jaw again, hitting the other side this time, and the human staggered back. Another of the wolves pounced on him, knocking the guy down to the ground with a thump. Jer slipped through the opening to close the door that led to a long, darkened corridor. The sounds might've already traveled, but if they had the element of surprise on their side, they stood that much more of a chance at getting Sierra back alive.

By the time he'd turned around, all three humans had been knocked to the floor, and the rest of the pack had shifted into mountain lions and wolves. Jer's heart thundered. As much as his wolf rammed at him, begging him to turn, he didn't. Someone needed to stay in this form to respond if needed, and he was the pack beta. Right now, he led this charge.

"Follow me," he commanded, keeping his voice low as he reached for the door again. The wolves dragged the humans into a pile where they lay slumped over one another. If anyone happened to come down here, their group was screwed. *Time to find our alpha.* Jer listened at the door for a moment, but footsteps didn't pound their way. He opened it a crack, this time peering into the darkened corridor. Amber light filtered in from farther down and around the corner. Somewhere, in this maze of a place, they had to be holding Sierra captive.

He crept forward first, the shadows causing his skin to prickle. In a fight of humans versus shifters, the shifters would win. The Coalition must know that, which meant they had to have some advantage he hadn't discovered to be ballsy enough to kidnap their alpha. His throat tightened while he edged down the corridor one careful step at a time. Sierra needed to be alive. He couldn't fathom the alternative.

As the edge of the corridor neared, all he could remember was the warm crinkle in Sierra's eyes as she'd clapped a hand on his shoulder and offered him the position of beta. His alpha had always treated him like he meant something, even knowing the flawed, broken mess of a person he was. Leaders like her, ones who muddied their hands with the pack as an equal and trusted their people — they were rare.

The Red Rocks wouldn't find another like her in his lifetime.

Behind him, the wolves and mountain lions padded silently across the floor, almost melding with the shadows. Another crash sounded from above, and he winced. If he couldn't comprehend a future without Sierra as their alpha, the idea of anything happening to Raven short-circuited his brain. Total fucking shutdown.

She had to emerge from this safe, whole. *No other option.*

Jer peered around the corner, where the corridor traveled a few paces forward to a short set of steps that emptied into a massive room. It was the size of a warehouse down there. Unfinished cement flooring stretched out across the vast length and joists protruded from the ceiling accompanied by ducts and iron plumbing pipes. Dim bulbs from naked fixtures illuminated the room, casting their amber beams down onto the Coalition's master plan.

He sucked in a sharp breath. At least eight humans milled around the breadth of the place, walking around stacks of pallets and crates prepared to ship. On the far end where the gray bricked wall stretched high, a too-familiar figure sat bound to a chair with her shoulders squared and her dark hair half pulled out of her braid.

Sierra.

Seeing his alpha strapped to the chair like that sent his wolf howling in his chest, frenzying to free her. Even kidnapped, the woman dripped regality. She kept her chin held high and her gaze sharp as a razor. Two guys stood beside her with pistols in hands. After witnessing the sheer disgust and fear rampant among the members of the Coalition, Jer knew they wouldn't hesitate to use them.

Another familiar face strolled into view. Greg Statham, the glorious leader himself. Jer snuck his phone up and snapped a shot. The numbers were evenly matched, but if he and the pack emerged, the Coalition still had the bargaining chip of Sierra. *Fuck.* The bombs, silver traps and kidnapping gave him the feeling that the Coalition wouldn't be amenable to negotiating this peaceably.

Jer clutched the edge, his feet buzzing and his calves tensing to bolt forward. All of a sudden, Greg Statham stopped pacing back and forth and instead started heading for the corridor. Toward them. Three men followed behind him.

Do or die time.

Jer glanced back to the pack and mouthed, "now."

He extended his claws and burst out into the corridor. Nine wolves and mountain lions leapt in close behind. Greg had reached the steps by the time they emerged, and the man froze when he caught sight of them. In an instant, Jer raced across the stretch separating him and the Coalition leader, narrowing the distance.

Greg's pistol whipped out a second later, and he stared them down unflinchingly as he lifted his gun and pulled the trigger. Jer veered to the side before the bullet ever left the chamber. It zipped past him, but a howl sounded from behind, reverberating through the room. His heart leapt into his throat, but he couldn't stop. Not now.

He raced toward them at top speed until he was feet away from the cavernous basement. His gaze locked in on Sierra. Once he got her freed, they could figure out how the hell to get out alive.

That focus caught Greg Statham's attention.

"They're here for their alpha," Greg bellowed, his voice echoing to the rafters as he stopped taking shots and instead bolted for Sierra. At once, every human in the area headed for their alpha as well, rushing in to protect their coveted hostage. Jer let out a low curse. Gene and Kyle loped beside him, soaring faster in their shifted forms. His shins ached as he slammed down the steps then the concrete floor.

He didn't stop, even as the Coalition members raced to surround Sierra. He was so close. Too close.

Greg reached the vicinity first, and he whipped his pistol in her direction. The muzzle bore down on her, but Sierra didn't even blink.

"Stop, or I'll shoot her," he shouted out.

"At least try for some originality," Sierra murmured. "You've been threatening my life from the moment you kidnapped me."

Jer skidded to a halt, and he threw his arms wide to signal a stop to the pack. He couldn't risk it, not with two lives on the line. The rest of the pack followed the cue.

"We planned on waiting until sunrise and sending the video," Greg announced, his charismatic voice echoing to the rafters of this room. "Cut off the head and the rest of the body dies."

Jer's forehead creased. "Is that how you think packs operate?" His palms itched. He needed to move, charge, fight or tear this bastard's throat out. Do *anything*. But the Coalition leader was pointing a muzzle at his alpha's head, loaded with a silver bullet.

"He's not the brightest," Sierra drawled, sounding more and more like her mate.

"Well, we'll have to move up the timeline," Greg barked, drawing the attention back to himself. "Kind of you to show for the execution."

Jer's insides chilled. His pack bristled behind him, growls splitting the air. Insistent glances shot his way as they pulled at their leashes, needing to lunge forward. The other Coalition members stood in a phalanx around Sierra with pistols drawn and dark expressions. Even if he tried to rush in, Sierra would be dead before they could take a step forward. Greg's eyes had a manic light to them that Jer didn't trust, the same undercurrent bubbling beneath the Coalition meeting. They were afraid and angry, the two deadliest combinations.

The stale air charged, as though any moment lightning would strike between them. Jer didn't take his eyes off Greg, whose finger brushed the trigger of his pistol. The man was aiming a silver bullet at his alpha's skull. Jer was paralyzed. Sierra was *pregnant*, and even if he tried to make a move, he couldn't guarantee her safety.

His phone hadn't buzzed. Dax still hadn't arrived.

Every second ticked closer to her execution.

"Bid your pack goodbye, *alpha*," Greg said, his voice dripping with derision.

Jer's gaze landed on Sierra. Her lips pressed together in seriousness, and those intense eyes bored into him like she was trying to communicate.

Her eyes flashed amber.

Instinct took over. "Wait," he shouted out, raising his hands in defense. "Can't we talk this over?" he pleaded, keeping his gaze trained on Greg. Look this way, look this way, look this way.

Greg shook his head. "The Coalition doesn't negotiate with savages."

"You're the ones who threatened children," Jer growled, drawing the attention of a few more members of the Coalition. Greg's expression didn't change in the slightest. However, Jer didn't need him to agree or even understand his perspective.

He needed him distracted.

Sierra's muzzle had already begun to form, her body mutating before the Coalition leader turned toward her. The bonds slipped while she changed before their eyes. The moment she started to shift, he would need to adjust his shot.

They wouldn't give him the chance.

Jer let out a howl, one that ripped through his throat as if carried by his wolf. The pack needed no further encouragement. He led the charge as they raced to free their alpha.

Sierra settled on all four paws right as Greg fired his pistol. Jer surged faster, closing the feet between them. The Coalition members stepped in his way, and he bared his teeth, two seconds from shifting. His heart leapt into his throat.

The bullet burrowed an inch away from Sierra, chipping at the concrete.

Freed from her bonds, his alpha leapt for the leader of the Coalition.

"Let the prisoners loose," Greg screamed, his voice reverberating through the room. He skidded backwards, trying to escape Sierra's snapping jaw. At the command, the guy barring Jer's way darted to the left, along with two of the other armed Coalition members. They bolted toward the shadows on the opposite side of the room, which had been obscured from Jer's former vantage point. Now, with the full breadth of the basement sprawled out before him, he caught sight of what he'd missed before.

Cells lined the far wall, and all it took was a single glance to soak in who the Coalition contained. Shifters — wolves, a bear, and a coyote — all prowled in separate cells, their movements erratic and spittle dripping from their muzzles. When the humans neared, their growls split the air.

Jer didn't need to see their reddened eyes. The Coalition was behind the unleashed berserkers. Greg scrambled away from Sierra as fast as he could, running in the same direction as the others. Of course, the cowards would use whatever weapon they could find. He and the pack were evenly matched in a fight of humans versus shifters, but add berserkers into the mix?

They were screwed.

Jer dropped his phone to the ground, kicking it to the side before he gritted his teeth and shifted. His bones began to move position, fur prickled his arms and his claws and fangs extended. One moment, he stood on two feet, the next, four. From this vantage point, the room appeared different — the ceilings more vaulted, the space more sprawling and the targets even clearer through the eyes of a wolf.

The Coalition guys slammed against the cells they'd trapped the berserkers in and fiddled with the locks. Some of his packmates were already loping after the humans, snapping their jaws, while others tangled with the Coalition members who hadn't rushed off to unleash the berserkers. Sierra surged ahead, making a beeline for Greg Statham.

No, no, no. They hadn't fought the berserkers like he and Rae had. He'd warned them, but they couldn't know, truly know. Jer lifted his muzzle and let out a sharp yowl. They needed to fall back, or they'd be slaughtered.

The cell doors opened and the Coalition members darted out of the way.

His pack bolted straight toward imminent destruction.

The wolves, bear and coyote that had been freed lunged forward. Their eyes were wild and their mouths foamed, their sharp claws glinting in the dim amber lighting. There was nothing for it — he couldn't stand by while his pack was being savaged. Jer launched forward, his padded feet slamming against concrete and the scent of stale earth and terror filling his nose.

Soon, blood would follow.

Gene leapt forward, followed by Mandy as they attacked one of the wolves. Sierra hadn't lost focus of the main target, Greg fucking Statham, and she bolted toward him, even as the bastard lifted his pistol. Jer raced faster, needing time to stop. He needed to be there in the thick of his pack before the slaughter started.

A yip split the air as the bear charged into two of his packmates, sending them tumbling to the ground. That was when the Coalition began firing into the fray, not giving a damn whether berserkers or his packmates died. To them, all shifters were just brutes, beasts meant to be slaughtered.

The coyote veered toward Kyle, who tensed down, ready to spring into the fight. Jer closed the remaining feet before launching himself between them. He slashed down with his claws right as the coyote's muzzle snapped. Spittle flecked against his fur, those dark eyes flashing and the growls growing incessant as they sliced through the air. The bark of pistols followed.

Jer's heart thudded so hard it might burst. A painful howl sounded from the floor above, rending him in two. *Raven.*

Those jaws snapped in front of him, taking a tuft of his fur before he edged away. *No, no, no.* She had to be safe. She needed to survive. All around him, a copper scent bloomed in the air. Growls and barks echoed and the humans stood back, firing indiscriminately. Jer pivoted away. The coyote lunged again while Kyle winged around the other end to sink his teeth into the beast's haunches.

Sierra closed in on Greg, which put her in direct danger. The moment she broke past the rest, she'd mark herself as the clear target. Greg's eyes flashed as he caught sight of the alpha juggernaut of a wolf who loped his way.

No.

A roar sounded loud enough to quake the rafters and the stones themselves.

From the corridor.

Dax and the cavalry had arrived.

C h a p t e r T w e n t y - F i v e

Over Raven's year and a half with the Landsliders, she'd heard enough of Christian's chatter to last a lifetime.

Here and now, the time for talk was over.

She settled on all fours, her wolf surfacing at last, as though stepping out into the morning sun. She should have been terrified, here in this house that had sunk its claws into her all these years and haunted her waking memories. Yet as Christian began to shift, his eyes flashing yellow and the reddish-brown fur emerging across his skin, resolve settled in her gut like concrete.

Raven might not be able to quell the nightmares, the phantom sensations that gripped her, or the terror that descended at the most inconvenient times. However, she could slice Christian's throat open to keep the potential predator off the streets. The small measure of control coursed through her veins.

She bared her teeth and paced back and forth while Christian finished shifting into his coyote form. Years ago, their similar sizes had made them perfect partners to run together. They'd loped through these woods side by side, hitched rides on the back of Lenny's pickup and delivered product for the boss. Everything for their almighty leader.

Now, it meant an even fight. Because as much as Christian might act cocky, the man had always been all talk. While he'd gone off and gotten himself a law degree, she'd been sparring with the best of the best in the Red Rock pack.

They circled each other in the center of the living room they'd spent the majority of their friendship in, back when she'd believed friendship meant someone, anyone, wanting her around. Raven bared her teeth. Christian would never make the first move. He would just pace around her until he found an opening or an avenue of escape. Even in this form, his dark eyes mocked her.

He paced, leaning heavily on his front paws as he traveled around the room. Raven continued her back and forth, not wanting to project her movements. She inched closer and closer with each pass.

Christian's gaze followed her every step of the way with the same desire suspended there, one that made her feel filthy. All those years of having thought they were friends, and he'd always wanted her like Mackey had, as some prized possession.

The coals inside her burned, but the knowledge fed the blaze.

Raven vaulted forward, brandishing her claws. She leapt for his hind legs.

Christian waited, his back legs already tensed to kick. Except at the last moment, Raven whipped around to the front. With his weight pressed down there, his reaction time was slower. She descended, tearing into his flank before he could swerve away.

A copper scent filled the air as she sank the tips of her claws in past fur, piercing through skin. Christian let out a low growl and snapped at her, his fangs clicking together right near her ear. By the time she pulled back a pace, he lunged for her, the gray fangs flashing in front of her throat.

Raven ducked her head at the last minute. He sailed an inch above her, but she pushed forward. Her skull thudded against his throat. The air flew from him in a sharp gasp, but Christian was quick. He tuck-and-rolled to put distance between them, moving with a nimbleness she remembered.

When he rose and their gazes locked, his expression darkened. If he'd been hoping to duck out of this before, now he was delving into this deadly dance for real. *Good.* The Landsliders had always underestimated what she was capable of. She bared her teeth with a low growl that rumbled through the length of her body.

This time, Christian charged for her.

The distance closed between them in a blink. One moment he was pacing before her and the next, he'd bared his fangs and leapt.

Raven tried to veer out of the way, but he was moving too fast. He razed her side with his claws first as they scraped against her skin. He landed on top, his full weight slamming into her. They tumbled around across the wooden floorboards, splintered wood scraping against her back.

This floor. That sensation.

Her entire body locked up as her mind screamed and screamed and screamed.

Christian pinned her down, his jaws snapping for her throat. She thrashed around, for a moment seeing a massive form above her. For a moment, the scent of cloves made her gag.

He sank his teeth into the side of her neck in a vise grip. Pain radiated through her body, enough to snap her out of the cloud of memories. She vaulted to the present, to the musty-smelling beast on top of her, to the teeth digging past skin, and to the fresh scent of her own blood. A ragged breath escaped her throat, and the pain made her blink white.

She howled.

Raven rocked her body in the direction he bit, loosening his grip slightly. Then she kicked hard with her back paw, the blow landing on his side. He dropped his jaw from the hold for a moment. She didn't waste a second. Raven rolled with her weight to knock him off. They tumbled across the floor again, until she leapt away on all fours.

She was sick of freezing up.

Tired of the fear.

No more.

Raven lunged for Christian before he scrambled up. Her shoulder screamed and drops of blood splattered to the ground, but she let the pain turn that blaze into an inferno. He tried to dart back, but she leapt on top of him. She snapped her jaw and sought purchase wherever she could find it. Raven sank her teeth into his flank again and again and again, and each time he thrashed.

He let out a growl that reverberated through his entire body before he bucked forward. Raven wasn't moving. Every time he pushed her off, she returned in a force of fury and fangs. His claws raked into her side and stung like holy hell. It didn't matter.

She wouldn't back down.

Christian swiped for her eyes, but she ducked the swing. It placed her fangs right within reach of his throat.

Raven lunged and she sank her fangs into the soft skin.

Christian let out a strangled howl, the sound burbling from him. Her jaw tightened as she clamped down harder. Hot blood poured into her mouth, but she didn't let go. Raven held on for the life of her, even though her body ached and stung in a thousand places. She held on for the little girl who never could.

Christian's gaze locked with hers, a look of betrayal glossing his expression. Pets weren't supposed to strike back, and that was all she'd ever been to the lot of them.

No more.

Blood flecked against her muzzle, and Christian's thrashes slowed as his body grew weaker, until he stopped moving at all. He hung limp in her grip, but she didn't let go. She couldn't let go. She stood there for what felt like an eternity, her flank heaving in the quiet of the dark room and moonlight carving patterns on the floor.

Finally, her jaw went slack.

Christian tumbled to the ground, lifeless. She wouldn't see the sadistic gleam in his eyes or the sneer on his face any more. She wouldn't hear the mocking way he called her Tigerlily because he knew how much it hurt.

A mournful howl ripped from her throat, one rising to the rafters of this place. Not for him. Never for him. Tonight, she acknowledged her wounds at last. She howled at the way Mackey had violated her mind and spirit over and over during her time with the Landsliders. At the way her so-called friends had watched, had known and never cared.

The sound echoed through the room, reverberating bone-deep. A hollowness spread within her, the hole she'd filled with hurt for so long—the space she'd kept for those wounds. Raven spat the blood onto the ground and padded back and forth along the floorboards as her equilibrium returned.

Clanks and growls came from below, the familiar sounds of a fight. While she'd been facing off against Christian, nothing else had permeated their bubble, but now it all crashed down. Jer and her pack were fighting in the basement below against the threat of the Coalition that the Landsliders had summoned and worked into a frenzy.

A creak sounded from the back door of the house and the slam of paws followed. Raven's heart seized. Not more trouble. She couldn't bear more trouble. She looped through the house she knew from memory and crept around to peer at the intruders.

Except the wolves and mountain lions who poured in through the back door, the ones who hurtled for the basement, were all familiar faces. A large Siberian tiger raced amidst them, who had to be Lucas.

Raven's heart soared. Her paws started moving before she was aware. In seconds, she launched into the fray, running with her pack. Her family.

She surged forward with the others, moving in unison with them. Her shoulder ached and her scratches burned, but she paid them no mind as she sailed down the steps. They raced through the faux basement room and sailed through the door down the corridor. Their footsteps pounded at a marching beat, a thump, thump, thump that echoed to the steady pace of her heart.

She hadn't traveled these corridors in years, but she knew the massive warehouse waiting for them at the end. Drew raced alongside her, followed by Lana, a strange sight given the unforgivable wounds between them. But right now, grievances were suspended in the wake of the most important task—getting their alpha back.

Growls filled the air and gunshots rang out, each noise burrowing through her. Jer had to be safe. He needed to survive. Her paws pounded against the cold concrete as she flew forward, her surroundings blurring around her.

Dax's roar shook the surrounding stones, the primal sound of a lion whose mate and unborn child were in peril.

Their united packs flooded the warehouse like a burst dam. A line of humans wielded pistols against the frenzy of the beasts below, where so many bodies hurtled in motion. Their wolves and mountain lions were fighting bears, coyotes and different wolves, but Raven could barely differentiate. At the sight of their oncoming army, most of the humans lowered their weapons and bolted for the corners of the room—away from the mass of fighting shifters.

A silver wolf with streaks of black closed in on Greg Statham, who hadn't fled. Sierra. The man aimed his pistol and fired.

A shot burrowed into Sierra's flank, but she didn't stop. Her steady amber gaze locked in on her target, and nothing in the world could stop the death on four legs racing his way. His arms trembled and he tried to rush toward the corridor.

Dax was there to greet him, and the Silver Springs alpha wasn't in a forgiving mood.

Raven followed the tide of shifters. They poured into the room, rushing for the massive fight in the center. Crates got smashed, fur flew and pallets careened over as shifters warred against each other. The closer she got, the more she noticed the drooling around the muzzles of the other shifters, and the madness flickering in their eyes.

Berserkers.

No wonder Jer and the others were struggling. However, with the influx of the combined pack, they now outnumbered the berserkers five to one. Raven leapt in with a snarl, searching with every forward step for a flash of russet or those golden eyes—for Jer.

Snap. She dodged around a wolf trying to sink its teeth into her.

Smack. Raven slammed against the bear rearing up against Gene and Mandy.

Crack. The coyote descended from above with a flying leap. She met it headfirst, and her skull was harder.

Jer appeared feet ahead of her. The gorgeous wolf growled as he charged at one of the berserkers. Kyle leapt in on the other side, his claws descending with a blow. The berserk wolf thrashed around in wild, unpredictable swings. However, no matter how much the drugs pushed them to mindlessly fight, one wolf couldn't defend itself against three.

Raven leapt in, baring her fangs.

The wolf whipped around, spittle flying and its movements clunky and erratic. Too slow to catch her. She swerved to the side, nipping it in the flank, enough to distract. Jer's golden gaze met hers from the opposite side. While the wolf snapped at her, Jer launched himself headfirst into the beast's legs.

The berserk wolf swayed with the force of the blow and that was when Kyle struck. He rammed his hard head right into the hollow of the wolf's throat. A crunch echoed through the room and the wolf dropped.

All around the basement warehouse, similar fights ended with echoing snaps, with thuds and with howls. Unlike the Landsliders, her pack knew how to fight together. They understood how every moving part was integral to the whole. Dax and Sierra made quick work of what had once been Greg Statham, leaving a grisly scene of entrails. Their muzzles were coated in blood. Where there had been five berserkers, only the bear remained, and with three other packmates backing up Gene and Mandy, its time was limited.

She rushed up to Jer, sliding her muzzle against his. The warm heat of him and his lupine scent struck deep to the core of her, as though she could take the first real breath since they'd separated. His eyes glowed with something powerful and she couldn't stop herself from brushing against him again and again to convince herself she'd survived the fight with Christian. *That all of this is real.*

Her head shot up as more footsteps pounded down from the corridor. *Who else could be here?* Her heart raced, and not just from the thrill of adrenaline.

Cops in SWAT uniforms burst into the room. "Weapons down," they shouted, their voices reverberating around the room. *Great.* This bloodbath wouldn't look good for shifter and human relations.

Jer began to shift into human form. One moment he was a large wolf hulking at her side, and the next the lithe stunner she'd fallen for. He lifted his hands in the air as he took steps away from her. Since he didn't have a stitch on, it was clear he wasn't hiding any weapons. Still, the cops spread out to start investigating the room with their pistols raised.

"I've got something that'll clear this all up," Jer shouted, his voice ringing through the area. He reached down to swipe his phone from where it had fallen on the ground feet away. Three of the cops edged in his direction, pointing their pistols.

Jer lifted his phone, his eyes twinkling. "I'm pretty sure proof of a kidnapping is enough to exonerate the pack in this situation."

A gasp of relief left Raven's chest. *Thank the Spirits for that brilliant, brilliant man.* Around the room, some of her packmates settled to the ground, while others licked their wounds. She wanted to sag to the floor.

Sierra and Dax both trotted to the cluster of cops and had begun shifting to address the situation with the human authorities. Lucas prowled over, transitioning into his other form as well to bring the Tribe's weight into the equation. While the cops had jurisdiction over the humans involved in this massacre, Lucas was the ruling force on the shifter side. Their Tribe member would be having a long, long chat with the cops about humans kidnapping shifters, and chances were, they'd leave here without a single charge.

Raven's legs almost gave out from under her. Heat stung her eyes as she watched the family she loved take care of one another, a family who always came together when it mattered. She'd spent so long so tethered by the past that she hadn't been able to appreciate her present. However, for the first time in far too long, she allowed herself to dream of the future.

* * * *

Ambulances arrived at the police's behest, and they'd brought plenty of blankets to distribute around. Since the entire pack had shifted, they were all sans clothing, and while none of hers cared, the humans found themselves a little uncomfortable. Over the next couple of hours, most of the pack had filtered out to head home until only Sierra and Dax were talking with the few remaining cops, and Jer pried himself away at last.

Raven sat on his Harley, which she'd driven over, and tugged the blanket tight around her shoulders.

Jer approached with a tired smile on his face and those gorgeous dimples on full display. He'd wrapped a blanket around his shoulders, but that did little to hide his powerful legs. "If this doesn't bury the Coalition, nothing will," he said, taking a seat on his bike beside her.

Raven leaned against him, breathing in his leather-and-vanilla scent, which was still evident even amidst the coppery blood and dirt coating them both. Her heart hurt more than she believed possible from sheer relief.

"You know," she murmured, glancing to him. "I thought all those years of yearning for you because I was trapped by my own bullshit were painful. I think this is worse, in a way."

He wrapped his arm around her shoulders and drew her in, his warmth and presence melting away the ache until she drowned in him. "I'll take any amount of pain if it means another minute with you."

Raven swallowed, her throat tightening at his words. She stared out at the hateful house they'd infiltrated tonight, one where she'd first learned silence. One that had etched itself on her bones. Except, as she opened her mouth, she found the tether loosened. Her voice freed.

"I love you, Jer," she whispered, meeting his gaze.

His jaw dropped and his eyes widened. A moment later, he placed his lips on hers in a kiss so tender it was like the first gasp of a salt breeze after arriving at the ocean. She deepened the kiss, melting into him as his strong body braced her. Raven was grateful she was sitting, because with the way her mind dizzied, drunk on the emotions soaring through her, she would've collapsed. Instead, she dug her heels into the side of his bike and twined her arms around his neck.

When they broke apart for a breath, Jer didn't move back. He just stared at her with a wonder reserved for the clear midnight sky.

"I love you too, Raven Takahashi," he murmured against her mouth, bumping his forehead against hers. "Looks like after all the time we spent avoiding this, we'll have to give it a real try. Think we're up to the challenge?"

A grin stole across her lips. "With you by my side? I'm willing to fight."

Epilogue

Jer leaned against the bar at Beaver Tavern, feeling better than he had in ages. Even though only a couple of weeks had gone by since the final confrontation against the Coalition, his meds had kicked in at long last. Shame nudged at him that he couldn't handle this on his own, but Raven helped him as best she could to keep him on course. He took a sip from his porter.

"You got here before me, Streaky?" Sierra said, an incredulous note in her voice as she approached. She settled on a stool beside him and Kyle swung over moments later with a glass of water. Sierra lifted hers in salute.

"I'm on top of my game, for once," he responded. "I went back on my meds." The explanation tumbled out of him, even though she hadn't asked once.

"I noticed," she responded, crooking one of her sharp eyebrows. The intensity of her Cherokee features remained ever-present. "You're not dipping between swings anymore."

Jer's mouth dropped open. "Why didn't you say anything?" he asked, his grip tightening on his porter. "I was privy to so many important things that rode on me. If I hadn't been so fucked in the head, maybe we could've caught the Coalition before they ever kidnapped you." He couldn't help the heat in his voice, even as he tried to rein it back in.

Sierra gave him a lazy glance. "Stop being an idiot."

"Excuse me?" He placed his pint down. Pregnant or no, his alpha grated at his less-than-stellar patience.

"I have at least a dozen other candidates I could've chosen for beta when Finn left. I chose you, Jer. You ask why I didn't hound you about your meds? Because I trust you. You might have backslides, and you might make mistakes, but your issues are your own. When it matters, you'll handle them to the best of your ability. I need someone loyal and intelligent like you, now more than ever." Her gaze dipped to her stomach.

Jer swallowed hard. He'd expected Sierra to ream him out or tell him to step down. Not this. Instead, she trusted him to step in as needed when she was down for the count with a newborn. The enormity of the trust she placed in him set his feet on solid ground after he'd been floating for far too long.

Sierra fixed him with an arch look. "Now, enough wallowing. I want to know the update on the Coalition."

Jer sucked in a deep breath. "They dropped the petition for Ricketts Glen," he said. "I'm still building the case against them, though, with the evidence we've accumulated. By next month, their organization will have been dealt a sharp blow, if not forced to disband."

"Good," Sierra said, heat flaring in her voice. "They've done enough damage to my pack." Her gaze traveled past him to the door and a grin lifted her lips. "Looks like your mate has arrived. I'll leave you two lovebirds be." At that, his alpha slipped from the stool and slunk off to the back room.

Jer turned to face the door. Raven strode in through the door, moving with effortless grace. Her fingers were stained with blue and purple paint and she wore a beat-up tee and leggings that clung to her long, long legs. With her hair pulled into a messy bun and a warmth in her eyes he'd always longed to see, she'd never been more beautiful.

She swung over to the table where Marcy and Rick sat with their kids and chatted for a second while she leaned down to muss Daria's hair. The relationship between her and the cub sucker-punched him every time. The fond, maternal way Raven looked at her made him dream of things he'd never believed possible.

Then she fixed her gaze on him, and the air evacuated the room.

He still hadn't gotten used to being *seen* by her after years of feeling invisible compared to Finn. However, the incandescent light that flickered between them seemed to grow with the time they spent together into the sort of hearth fire he hoped and prayed would never die. Raven swung by another table on her way over, swapping an exchange with another regular.

Jer leaned back against the bar, watching her approach. He had no problem waiting. After so long searching and so long denying the truth that existed between them, he'd found his mate. He'd been running, running, running, from his problems and even his own mind, but here and now — he wanted to live in this moment for eternity. Because now? Now they had an entire future to explore, together.

Want to see more from Katherine? Here's a taster for you to enjoy!

Tribal Spirits: Forged Futures
Katherine McIntyre

Excerpt

The house never felt as empty as it did in mid-winter.

Lana thought the loneliness would've gripped her by the throat in the early summer nights after Greg died, but those didn't compare to the brittle ache that descended with the new year.

Even though she was standing right beside her microwave, the beep made her jump. She pulled the now-steaming mug of coffee out and took a sip. Since it was nine at night, she needed this to keep from being comatose after the double whammy of a shift on the ambulance followed by three sessions with her massage clients. She might have both bare feet planted on her hardwood floors, but her mountain lion hadn't stopped pacing from the moment she'd returned home.

Her skin prickled. *Something's off.*

She cast a quick glance around her kitchen. The shadows sloped with the dim overhead light splaying across chrome appliances and rustic hickory countertops. Nothing slunk through her kitchen. The heat from the mug of coffee soaked into her palms — the closest she'd come to feeling something all day.

Almost eight months had passed, and still she walked into the house waiting for his deep voice to answer her back. Greg's worn spot on the couch remained empty, almost as empty as the hollow chamber where her heart had once beaten. She headed over toward her living room, winding around a stack of paperbacks that teetered precariously. Her coffee sloshed over the rim, the hot liquid stinging where it splashed her hand. Lana glanced at the windows, waiting for something to pop up, for eyes to be staring back at her.

Great Spirits, I'm going insane. Lana took a seat on the weathered corduroy couch and placed her mug on the scratched and dented coffee table. She needed a roommate, or at least a cat. Maybe a dozen — her local SPCA would be a danger zone for her. She should cave and take Ally up on her offer to move in.

Skritch, skritch, skritch.

Lana sat straight, her mountain lion perking to alertness. That wasn't a squirrel in the bushes. Her heart raced, as it had the night of the bombings. She could still feel the burn of the colloidal silver ropes against her skin. And all she would ever see again on her floorboards was the crimson splatter as her husband slumped to the ground, dead.

Lana's nails turned into claws on instinct, and a low growl built in the back of her throat. The scent wasn't a woodland critter prancing through and didn't belong to her pack.

She crept in the direction of the sound coming from the backyard. Her bare feet jolted with a shock of cold as she stepped onto the cool tile of her screened-in porch. Her heart pounded loudly, becoming almost all she could hear while she crept forward. Any moment, the door would fling open. Any moment, whoever stalked outside would attack.

Night-time breezes swept in through the screen, the chill of winter causing goosebumps to prickle up her arms almost as much as the distant hush that descended. Her throat dried, but she took another step. Even with Marcy and Rick living next door, if someone murdered her here, they wouldn't hear a sound. Who knew if she'd even be found for days? Her eyes throbbed with the familiar pulse of phantom tears — she'd cried so much in the first month that they no longer came.

Her nose twitched from the unfamiliar scent. Where was it coming from? Lana took another tentative step, a heartbeat away from shifting. Her mountain lion paced inside her, begging to break free. Her cheeks iced, but she continued forward, her core temperature rising with the need to shift even as her outside froze. Ever since they had taken down the Coalition of Human Rights in September, quiet had reigned through Ricketts Glen. Too much quiet.

If she hadn't been paying attention, she would've missed the sound — the soft *whump* of padded feet on grass.

Her teeth transitioned to fangs and she stepped closer to the door. *Focus.* Her skin prickled, the fur begging to emerge. She strode up to the handle and rested her palm on the icy knob.

Two sets of eyes glowed on the other side, feet away.

Her gaze landed on the two approaching grizzly bears, and she leaped back, as if the flimsy screen might protect her. With the poised control of their limbs and the menace in their eyes, Lana didn't question for a second that the hulking shifters wanted her dead.

By the time she dived through the door and back inside the house, the bears had begun to charge. Their growls slashed through the air, and her heart leaped into her throat. Lana had made many, many split-second decisions to the point they'd become reflex. She raced through the house, her bare feet burning against the hardwood with the force with which she slammed on the planks. Mesh ripping resounded through her place, and a second later, the heavy pounding of the bears' approach reverberated all the way to her.

She needed to reach her front door. If she got there, she could shift, and in her mountain lion form she stood a chance of outrunning them.

Lana's breath caught in her throat as she crossed the distance from the living room to her front door, running closer and closer. The weight of the bear shifters echoed through the house, their footfalls like tolling bells. She didn't dare look back at the intruders who raced for her, their snarls making their intent clear. They were closing on her, like a noose sliding around her neck and pulling tight.

Her home wasn't safe. Again.

An icy sweat broke out on her palms as she lunged for the handle, scrambling to grab the knob. She fumbled with it, trying to turn it and failing.

The bears crashed through her house, getting closer by the second.

Lana yanked the door open and vaulted out. She shut it behind her, the door slamming so hard she almost took the doorknob off. With all the trouble the Landsliders had caused in the region, she didn't question that they were involved. Roars quaked behind her, muted by the door, and she rushed down her front steps. They'd bash their way through within moments — she needed to take advantage of the seconds while she had them.

The shift overtook her liquid-fast, already brimming on the surface. Her creamy fur pricked across her skin and her nails changed into sharp claws. Lana's surroundings altered with the shift, the crystalline night growing even sharper in her mountain lion eyes, and within seconds she settled her weight onto four paws.

Lana lunged forward, slicing her way through the wilted grass at top speed.

At least, until an unknown wolf stepped between her and the road.

Lana skidded to a halt, churning grass and mud with the force. The inkstain wolf shifter bared her teeth, the golden eyes glowing like lanterns. Quaking came from the house behind her as the bears slammed at the door, straining the timbers. Once they broke through, she was dead. No way could she fight all three at once.

The wolf in front of her growled, the sound reverberating between them in the stark air. Cold filtered through her veins. She needed to escape.

A bang echoed through the air, and her front door burst open. The first of the bears barreled through.

Her world shrank to the wolf before her and the bears behind. She would die. Just like Greg.

Lana lunged to the right, trying to find a way past the wolf who paced in front of her. The moment she moved, the wolf leaped, snapping for her leg.

The ground shook as the bears raced across her front lawn, closing the distance too fast. Dread rushed her in one dizzying sweep, even colder than that winter night. These shifters would kill her, and she'd never know why.

A single roar sliced through the night, loud enough to fracture the sky.

A massive Siberian tiger crashed onto her front lawn, one she recognized from the attack on the Coalition. Lucas, a member of the East Coast Tribe, had arrived.

Those were odds she could work with. Lana whipped around to face the wolf, baring her fangs. Lucas crashed on past her, moving with a grace that defied his size as he charged for the bears. The wolf lunged for her at once, the gray fangs shining in the sparse moonlight. Her paws crushed the withered grass beneath her as she whipped around.

Once the wolf snapped with those lethal jaws, she didn't step back or try to dodge. Lana slammed right in, using the flat of her skull like a battering ram. The collision echoed through the air with a *thump*. The wolf emitted a low, pained sound as she sank onto her paws. As if the Silver Springs pack hadn't spent time sparring with their Red Rock wolf brethren.

Growls lit the air from the two bears, but Lucas raced circles around them, moving with a familiar feline swiftness. The tiger leaped in to scratch one along the muzzle and whipped around to slam into the other before either could react. The way he fought was pure poetry.

This time, she took the offensive. Lana didn't give the shifter a chance to rebound, charging forward with her head down, ready to ram in again. The wolf reared on its haunches. The moment she dove in, the black wolf sprang, sailing overhead.

Lana pivoted around, right when the shifter landed. They both lunged at the same time. The hot breath of the wolf puffed against her fur, and Lana launched in for the kill. The jaws snapped in her face, the fangs scraping against her head, but she'd ducked.

She clamped down on the wolf's throat and tugged. Crimson blood spurted across her cheeks, the heat staining her fur as she refused to let go. Her heart hammered, her adrenaline surged and, like this, the hunt, the chase and the kill commanded her.

The wolf let out a moan before she collapsed to the ground. Lana tried to steady herself. The specks of blood on her face might as well have been acid. A pool of crimson grew around the body, and a violent urge to heave rolled through her. Her mountain lion might've taken the reins in a fight or flight situation, but she should be saving lives, not taking them.

All she could see was Greg's body lying on the floor as they'd done the same to him.

She stepped back one pace, then another, numbness descending. The ground shook when one of the bears dropped, flesh rent as if it had been tossed through a wood chipper. Lucas tackled the other bear, the two locked in their fight, a tangle of limbs and claws.

The moment the bear landed on his back with a crunch, the shifter was sentenced. Lucas tore into him with a similar ferocity, the sort of formidable expected from one of the Tribe. The governing force of the shifters wasn't one to be underestimated — on top of their enhanced skills, they possessed elemental magic and a compulsion they used to force their kind to comply.

Lana prowled, trying to ignore the ache in her heart and the sickness that dizzied her mind like the flu. Blood soaked into her fur, and even her pawprints left smudges on the grass as she stalked forward.

The bear let out one last gasp before Lucas' claws sliced right across his throat. Blood spurted in droplets onto the grass, leaked in pools beneath the massive body and stained the pristine coat of the East Coast Tribe member who for some reason had showed up here at the perfect time. Not like she wasn't grateful — she'd have been dead otherwise.

Lana began to shift, needing some space from what she'd done in this form. Her fur changed to smooth skin and her legs lengthened until she stood back on two feet. Lana's long hair tickled, growing until it brushed her back. She touched the wet spots on her skin, trying to rub away the blood even as she approached.

Lucas prowled over from where he'd left the two bear corpses on her lawn. He'd begun to shift as well, the beautiful orange fur and the white stripes disappearing when he returned to his human form. By the time he stood in front of her, he towered at well over six feet of pure muscle, his tawny, desert-sand skin marred by the blackened flecks of blood across the surface. The Tribe tattoos traveled all the way up his arms and legs, bands of complex linework she couldn't help but stare at.

His dark eyes crinkled with his smile as he came to a stop. "I'm guessing this isn't how you expected to spend your night?"

The sardonic tone drew her out of her shock and she responded on autopilot. "How else do you think I stay in shape? This is my nightly ritual to get to sleep — you might want to try it. Works better than whiskey." She wanted to groan when the words left her lips. She was two steps from vomiting on the lawn, yet here she stood sounding like a homicidal maniac.

A laugh burst from his throat, a rich rumble. The sound calmed her like nothing else and a breath escaped her — the first deep inhalation she'd taken since she got home.

"What are you doing back in the area?" Lana asked, her stomach sinking with the realization. If the Tribe members had returned, so had trouble.

He skimmed a hand through his jet-black hair before glancing at the bloodstains spattered across his chest, his legs and his arms. Lana followed the trail on reflex, but when his eyes met hers, her cheeks flushed. Like she didn't have enough to feel bad about, she might as well add gawking at the hulk of a Tribe member on her lawn.

He lifted his eyebrow and shook out his hands, sending a couple of droplets flying. "Why don't we discuss this inside? If you've got a shower I can co-opt, I'd be in your debt."

Lana nodded before heading toward the door. His dark gaze burned into her, and she should feel unsettled with this big guy she barely knew entering her house. However, her front door hung off the hinges, and she'd been feeling neurotic at every creak and groan for months now. Lucas Diaz was one of the good guys — she'd known within five minutes of meeting him — and he'd saved her from ending up as a body on her lawn.

They stepped to the doorway, and Lana trailed her fingers along the wooden edge as she looked to Lucas. "Just tell me one thing," she said, unable to ignore the gravity settling inside her. "You're here for that reason, aren't you?"

Lucas nodded, the shadows deepening the scar in his cheek, the sharp curve of his nose and the grim line of his lips. "The Landsliders have returned. I'm here to find out why, then I'm going to stop them."

Home of Erotic Romance

Sign up for our newsletter and find out about all our romance book releases, eBook sales and promotions, sneak peeks and FREE romance books!

About the Author

Strong women. Strong words.

Katherine McIntyre is a feisty chick with a big attitude despite her short stature. She writes stories featuring snarky women, ragtag crews, and men with bad attitudes—high chance for a passionate speech thrown into the mix. As an eternal geek and tomboy who's always stepped to her own beat, she's made it her mission to write stories that represent the broad spectrum of people out there, from different cultures and races to all varieties of men and women. Easily distracted by cats and sugar.

Katherine McIntyre loves to hear from readers. You can find her contact information, website and author biography at http://www.totallybound.com.